He lurched to his feet, cudgel pulled back, ready to deliver a blow.

"Lex, Lex, it is I, Anna."

The hissed identification stopped his arm in mid swing.

"Whit? Whit in God's name…?"

"Come along. We're leaving."

As he became able to focus in the midnight darkness, he saw a slim figure in male attire beside him, silhouetted against the open doorway of the hovel. A pistol protruded from her belt, and a dagger scabbard hung at her side. A smaller, slightly stooped figure stood beside her.

"Lady? Mademoiselle?"

"Yes, yes, of course. Who did you think it might be?" The words snapped with impatience. "Don't stand there gaping. We have to be on our way."

"But first…" The Frenchwoman stopped them as she drew something from the sleeve of her gown. "I have a request." In the shadows cast by the moonlight, Lex saw it was a ragged-edged parchment.

"This is a map, the map my uncle Etienne Bouchard entrusted to me many years ago just before he died." She held it out to Anna. "It indicates the location of the treasure I told you about, my dear child. It lies in the bay near where your sister lives. It would delight my heart if you were to find it, to prove its existence and that my beloved uncle was not merely a deranged old man spinning tales."

"Marie, of course!" Anna took the document from the woman. "A quest! Lex, we're to go on a quest as well as an escape." She paused to hug Marie. "I shall guard it with my life."

Praise for Gail MacMillan

Heather, of *HEATHER FOR A HIGHLANDER*, was chosen as Best Heroine by the Trans Canada Romance Writers Maple Leaf Awards. Dr. William MacTavish (same book) placed as second favorite hero. The book's ending also received Honorable Mention.

"I love, love, loved this book [*HEATHER FOR A HIGHLANDER*]! It…begins in England with a murder, and ends with a fiery romance in British North America. And it's all because of a horse bet between brothers. I mean, isn't that how all good stories begin?"

~Romance Novels for the Beach

"Read in one sitting, which hardly ever happens for me. Truly engaging. I would definitely pick up another book by this author."

~a judge at TransCRW competition

"Be prepared to be hooked on the first word of the first page [of *COWBOY COUNTRY CONFESSIONS*] and go on to the next with anticipation."

~Rebecca Melvin, Publisher, Double Edge Press

"Gail MacMillan's stories delight the senses and brighten the dark days of winter like a candle glowing on a windowsill."

~Sue Owens Wright, author, newspaper columnist

"I love this little adventure [*HOLDING OFF FOR A HERO*]!…surprises…one light, wonderful read."

~The Romance Reviews (4 Stars)

"Not sure who I like better, [the] German Shepherd, the Pug, or the sexy next door neighbor."

~Matilda, Coffee Time Romance & More (5 Cups)

"Not your typical romance story [*SHADOWS OF LOVE*], but I couldn't put it down."

~Michelle, Cocktails and Books (4 Cups)

A Trollop's Treasure

by

Gail MacMillan

Riverhaven Rogues, Book 6

This is a work of fiction. Names, characters, places, and incidents are either the product of the author's imagination or are used fictitiously, and any resemblance to actual persons living or dead, business establishments, events, or locales, is entirely coincidental.

A Trollop's Treasure

Contact Information: info@thewildrosepress.com

Cover Art by *RJ Morris*

The Wild Rose Press, Inc.
PO Box 708
Adams Basin, NY 14410-0708
Visit us at www.thewildrosepress.com

Publishing History
First Tea Rose Edition, 2018
Print ISBN 978-1-5092-2308-4
Digital ISBN 978-1-5092-2309-1

Riverhaven Rogues, Book 6
Published in the United States of America

Dedication

To Abba, the dog who saved my spirit.

Also by Gail MacMillan, from The Wild Rose Press

Historical Romance:
Shadows of Love
Caledonian Privateer
Lady and the Beast

~

Other Riverhaven Rogues books:
Privateer's Princess
Heather for a Highlander (winner of "Best Heroine" in the 2014 Canadian Romance Writers Maple Leaf Contest, with the hero taking an award for second best and the ending awarded an honorable mention)
Highland Harry (winner of "Best Opening" in the 2015 Canadian Romance Writers Maple Leaf Contest)
Bandit's Bride
A Baron's Bartered Bride

~

Contemporary Romance:
Phantom and the Fugitive
Rogue's Revenge
Ghost of Winters Past

~

Cowboy Country Connections Series:
Holding Off for a Hero
Counterfeit Cowboy
Cowboy and the Crusader
Cowboy Confessions
Cowboy Country Christmas

~

Non-Fiction:
How My Heart Finds Christmas
To All the Dogs I've Loved Before

Chapter 1

Head bent against the wind, rain, and sleet, he led the stumbling horse through the night. Hunger and exhaustion raked every fiber of his body as he fought to control the cough that would send pain raging in his chest.

"Come on, Gallant," he urged the old gelding.

The animal blew and struggled ahead.

Midnight. It had to be nearing midnight. Darkness had fallen what seemed like hours ago. By his calculation, this journey from hell had to end soon. Narrowing his eyes against the storm, he squinted back at the young man slumped astride the horse.

"Not much farther now, laddie," he tried to reassure him. "You're almost home."

"Home." Clinging to the horse's scraggly mane, the rider breathed the word with the same intonation Lex had heard others use when they spoke of Heaven.

He couldn't blame the lad. All three of them had come through Hades.

A fit of coughing he couldn't suppress overtook him, and he had to pause until it receded. *Bloody hell!* He spit mucus and wiped his mouth with the back of his hand.

"Chust a wee bit farther, old lad." With a gentle tug on the animal's reins, he started forward again.

"Lex?" His companion weaved in the saddle.

"Aye?"

"It would be wise"—he fought to speak—"to disguise your Highland brogue."

"I shall, niver fear, laddie."

He needed no explanation. Even years after open hostilities had ceased, most English had no love for Highlanders. Now Lex was deep into their territory.

Lights. He saw their twinkle ahead. Relieved, he paused to get his bearings. The horse's head touched his shoulder. Lex felt its breath exhaling in long, warm puffs against his wet shirt.

"Almost there," he muttered.

****

"Who are you?" Sir Maxwell Spencer peered out into the storm. "And what do you want?"

"He says he's brought Master Archie home, my lord." The footman stood aside to allow his master access to the doorway of the manor house.

"Your son has come home." Remembering his companion's warning, Lex spoke with the English accent he'd cultivated for use on occasions when he wished to hide his true identity. "He was wounded in France."

"The devil you say!" Lord Dunstan stepped out of the shelter of the doorway into the drenching rain, down the wide stone steps, and around the horse's head to peer up at the young man on its back. "It can't be! I received word of his death."

"Papa"—the young man's words reeked of relief—"you were misinformed."

He toppled from the horse, only his father's arms preventing him falling into the mud.

"Thomas, lend a hand!" his lordship yelled at the

footman gaping from the doorway.

Summoned, the servant rushed to give assistance. Supporting Captain Archibald Spencer between them, they took him into the house. Lex was left standing alone with the exhausted horse in the pouring rain.

Bloody English aristocracy.

"Come along, Gallant," he said to the gelding. "We'll see if we can't find you shelter and a bit of food."

****

"Hie there, who are you…and what do you think you're doing?" A young lad, holding a cudgel, confronted Lex as he led the horse into the stable at the rear of the manor house. "We allow no tramps shelter here."

"I'm not seeking shelter for myself, sir, just for this gallant beast." Lex spoke respectfully. He didn't want any rudeness on his part to cause the exhausted animal to be turned away. "He's been walking for days, with barely enough food to keep him on his feet."

"And why should I be taking in this ragged scrub?" The lad circled the pair, club at the ready, but Lex could see compassion easing into his expression as he perused the old gelding. *A boy with a kind heart.* He pressed home his suit.

"This brave soul has carried the young master of the house, wounded, across the battlefields of France and to the very door of his home. I'm sure Sir Maxwell will sanction the best of care being giving to such a beast."

"Master Archie is home?" The boy's eyes widened. "Saints be praised! We thought him dead. His lordship was fair beside himself with grief." He took the horse's reins from Lex. "This old lad carried him home, you say? Let me see to him." He led the animal into a box stall.

Guid, verrae guid. Lex allowed his natural brogue to speak in his thoughts. He hated hiding his heritage beneath a veneer of smooth English intonation, but he knew, in this country, it was wisest.

He should be on his way before anyone discovered his true identity. Still, the relative warmth of the stable and the shelter it provided from the miserable night held him in thrall. *Just a few more minutes, just a few more...to see how old Gallant fares.*

He knew the last wasn't entirely true. Already he could hear the stable lad talking softly to the horse, telling him he could not have too much hay, else he'd make himself sick, and how he'd have him rubbed dry in no time.

Not overfeeding the beast, and saving the poor bugger from a chill. The old lad is in good hands. I can leave.

Another bout of coughing overcame him. Doubling over, he surrendered to the ragged pain racking through his chest. *Sweet Jesus!* When the spasm ended with a gagging retch, he fell back against the stable wall, drenched with cold sweat.

"Are you all right, sir?" Frowning, the stable lad peered out at him.

"Just a bit of a cough," Lex muttered the reply.

"Rest yourself for a time." His response had softened since his initial address to Lex. "It's a miserable night, and this old animal isn't fit to carry you farther right now."

"Thank you, young sir. I believe I shall." He let

himself slide down into a sitting position, back braced against the wall, and closed his eyes.

Perhaps he dozed. He wasn't sure, but the next sound of which he was aware was the stable door opening. Instantly on his guard, he stumbled to his feet. Two figures in black cloaks entered. Their size suggested women, but he wasn't sure until they threw back their hoods to reveal an elderly one with an age-wrinkled face and another, little more than a girl, behind her. The woman carried a covered basket, the lass a sack.

"You are the gentleman who brought Master Archie home?" The woman spoke with a French accent. "I thought we might find you here. Thomas said your horse appeared in great need of care."

"Yes." He stifled his natural response of "aye."

"We are most grateful for your service." She held out the basket. "Here is a small recompense, a bit of food and drink to warm you after your journey. Violet has a dry shirt and bedding. You must stay the night. I'm sure his lordship will wish to speak to you in the morning…once he's overcome the joyful shock of having his beloved son at home once more. Although you deserve a room in the house, you understand I cannot invite you inside without his permission."

"Thank you, Madame." Gratitude for her kindness welled inside him. Food, dry clothes, and a bit of rest before he resumed his journey to the Highlands appeared a boon from Heaven. He put the back of his hand over his mouth in an effort to stifle another outburst of coughing. The result was a muffled grunt.

"Are you unwell, young man?" Giving him a shrewd look, the Frenchwoman caught his gesture.

"Just a bit of a cough," he again tried to minimize his affliction, but her expression told him she hadn't been deceived.

"Show him into a comfortable place, Bobbie," she called out to the boy involved in caring for the horse. "I take responsibility."

"Yes, ma'am." The boy Bobbie came out of the stall. "There's a clean stall with a gate at the end of the stable…if that would suit you, sir."

"That will be excellent." He took the woman's wrinkled hand and bowed over it. "Your grateful servant, Madame…?"

"*Mademoiselle* Marie Roi," she replied. "And you would be?"

He hesitated. "Lex, Mademoiselle, just Lex." When it had become necessary to hide his true identity, he'd chosen a moniker he believed would be difficult to trace, unlike the name he'd received at the christening font as a babe in the Highlands.

"Ah, a man of mystery as well as charm." Her dark eyes sparkled out at him. "If I were many years younger, you would prove a danger to a woman such as myself."

With a mischievous glance, she turned and headed out of the stable. "Come along, Violet. We must be getting back to the house."

Violet looked at Bobbie, blushed, then lowered her head shyly and hastened to follow the older woman.

When Lex looked at the young stable hand, he saw him staring after the girl, a slight smile curling his lips.

"Your…friend?" He gave special meaning to the last word.

"Oh, no, sir." Bobbie shook his head ruefully. "A

stable lad such as myself can entertain no such hopes." The defeat in his tone touched Lex's heart. "Let me show you where you may sleep."

Lex picked up the basket and sack and followed him down the corridor to a box stall bedded with clean straw at the end.

"You can stay here," Bobbie said, shoving open the gate. "But have a care. Lie low tonight. Mr. Brant, the head groom, is due back from the village. He'll be in a right state, what with the rain and…"

"And drink?" Lex made a knowledgeable guess. Forays into the vicinity of taverns often proved fraught with quite overwhelming temptations for servants temporarily freed from their duties.

"We don't say such things." The young lad turned away and hastened back to his work.

Once alone, Lex closed the stall door and sank down in a corner of the enclosure. He leaned his head back against the board wall and closed his eyes. It was good to be out of the wind and rain, even if only for a night. Maybe it would be enough to cure whatever malady was haunting his chest.

Tempting smells issuing from the basket the Frenchwoman had furnished brought him back to the moment. He opened his eyes and withdrew the cloth that covered it. Inside he found a steaming bowl of broth thick with meat and vegetables, a few slices of bread, a square of cheese, and a flask.

Could it be? God in Heaven, let it be.

He grasped the latter, pulled the cork free, and raised it to his nose. It was.

He swilled the brandy until it made him choke, then let his shoulders sag as he relaxed and allowed the fortified wine to ease its restorative power through his body. Slowly, warmth entered his belly and moved on through his being.

He turned his attention to the food. Bloody hell but he was hungry. He grasped the bowl in both hands and slurped down its contents. Then he turned his attention to the bread and cheese. When he'd finished all he could manage, he remembered the bag the girl had carried.

He opened it to find a shirt, a quilt, and a blanket. All dry, all clean! It had been so long since he'd been dry or clean. He stood—and staggered. *Weariness and too much brandy too fast*. He paused to get his bearings.

As soon as he was sufficiently steady on his feet, he stripped naked, tossed his ragged, wet clothing over the stall gate, and donned the fresh shirt that hung to below his thighs. He took another long drink of brandy before kneeling to spread the blanket over the straw. Moments later he lay curled up on it, the quilt tucked about him, lost in sleep.

Chapter 2

"Stop her! Catch the bitch!"

His shout followed her as she bolted for the brothel door. Clutching her torn bodice, she reached the entrance and had her hand on the latch when she was seized about the waist and yanked back into the hot, smoky room.

"Let me go!" She fought at the brawny arm holding her, lifting her feet off the floor, as its owner dragged her back to face the man who had issued the order to detain her. Bent over, clutching his lower regions, the corpulant man glared at her, his face distorted with pain and outrage.

"Lock the whore somewhere she cannot escape!" he muttered. "In the morning, she'll face a magistrate's court. We'll then see how fine and arrogant you are!" He focused on her, his small, bear-like eyes narrowing. "I doubt you'll enjoy time spent in one of our elegant prisons, you bloody trollop." He swung on the establishment's owner as he sank into a nearby chair. "Get the damned wench out of my sight…now!"

"I have a number of other young ladies who will be only too happy to see to your lordship." The owner of the house rushed to put a solicitous arm about the man's fat shoulders. "I really do not know how this one"—she glared at the young woman still writhing against her constraints—"got in here. She's definitely not one of mine. Take her away, John," she ordered the guard. "Lock her in the garret room."

****

Thrown into the small cell of a room at the top of the house, its only furnishing a three-legged stool, the door barred behind her, Anna paced like a restless lioness. Treat her like a common trollop, would they! Just wait until they experienced the kerfuffle that would occur when she identified herself to the magistrates. A smirk twisting her lips, she paused to reflect on the scenario.

On further consideration, her jubilance faded. What would her father do if he got wind of the incident? Marry her off in a whipstitch to that simpering Duke of Cumberly? Or if His Grace wouldn't have her, maybe ship her off to any convent willing to have such as her…for a price?

Bloody hell, this adventure had turned into more of a fiasco than she'd anticipated. She had to find some means of escape.

Taking a look about the room, she saw a small window at its rear. Her red satin skirts swept the dusty floor as she moved to examine it. A rub removed enough of the grime for her to see what lay outside. Indeed, she was high above the rear of the house, and the window was exceedingly narrow, but several feet below lay the roof of a porch. If she could somehow manage to get through the small opening and, clinging to its sill until she hung by arm's length downward, she might be able to drop to freedom.

Shortly she was struggling out of her gown. There was no way its skirts would fit through the narrow opening. Then, dressed only in her barest of undergarments, she grasped the stool by its legs and lunged to smash the glass from the window. When its shards had ceased to tinkle out onto the roof below, she paused to listen. No sounds of anyone approaching reached her ears, only the continuing cacophony from below. No doubt all were too caught up in their pleasures to give a second thought to the antics of the prisoner above.

With her hand and forearm wrapped in her gown, she set about freeing the sides of the window from shards of glass. Although it slowed her escape, she knew it had to be done, that it would be foolish to find freedom only to bleed to death from a cut.

The frame seemingly cleared, she stuffed the garment outside and watched as it fluttered down through the rain to land on the roof below. She'd need it after she made good her escape. She couldn't go running along London streets in her undergarments on her way back to Lady Balfour's house.

Drawing a deep breath, she leaned out to study her escape route. It appeared a long way down to the porch roof, but there was no choice. She turned and eased herself backward out the window. A sudden, sharp pain in her arm informed her she hadn't gotten all the glass out of the frame, but she couldn't stop. Summoning her courage, she slowly lowered herself downward until she clung by her hands to the wet windowsill.

Her fingers slipped. She dropped to the porch roof with a stifled cry of fright and agony as her left ankle collapsed beneath her with shocking pain.

Huddled on the porch roof, rain drenching her, she gasped for breath.

What have I done? What am I going to do?

Breast heaving, she struggled to take stock of her situation. Blood trickled from a cut on her arm, and she knew she'd done something unpleasant to her ankle, but there was no choice. She had to get off this roof, struggle into her gown, and make her way back to Lady Balfour's before anyone in the brothel decided to check on her presence in the attic room.

Peering over the edge of the roof, she was relieved to see it was only a few feet to the ground. All she had to do was lower herself down, taking her gown with her, and get herself as decently covered as possible. Then, hopefully, she could find a cab to take her back to the manor house on the other side of London.

****

"Hold there!" Drenched and trembling from cold, Anna raised a hand and limped into the darkened street to stop the lone cab travelling along it. "Hold, I say!"

The driver drew rein. Even through the night and bucketing rain, she could see skepticism tainted with annoyance in the man's expression. A woman dressed as a lady of the evening, clutching the torn bodice of her soaked gown to her bosom, didn't represent a profitable fare.

"Take me to Lady Balfour's residence in Belgrave Square." She pulled open the door and stumbled inside before he had time to whip his horse away. "You'll be well compensated."

"Argh!" The man shook his head and spit into the gutter before shaking the reins over the horse's back to set it into motion. "We've nothing better to do, now, have we, Butter?" she heard him remark to the animal.

The moment the cab drew up in front of Lady Balfour's elegant London address, she jumped out, grimacing and all but collapsing as her injured ankle shot pain up her leg.

"Wait here." She hobbled up the steps and raised the ornate door knocker.

Shortly, Gravesfield, the butler, was peering out into the inhospitable night.

"Gravesfield, please see to the cabbie." She pushed past the man into the foyer.

"Yes, my lady." Without comment or question, he pulled a cloak from a rack and headed out to do as he'd been bidden.

Shortly he was back, shaking water from his outerwear and replacing it on its peg.

"A most inhospitable night, my lady," he said.

"Most inhospitable indeed, Gravesfield." In spite of her physical discomfort, she couldn't help marveling at the man's composure and lack of question or comment in view of her condition. Years of service to her mother's friend and her present hostess, the unconventional twice-widowed Lady Balfour, had schooled him in the art of discretion. "I assume my maid is in my rooms?" She hobbled toward the wide, curving staircase.

"I don't believe so, my lady." Gravesfield was standing straight and still as a pillar in the foyer when she turned back at his reply. "I believe…er…she went out."

"Went out? Went out?" Her annoyance boiled over. "Who gave her permission? Certainly not I. Where did she go?" She paused, then continued, suspicion tainting her tone, "And with whom?"

"I cannot say for certain, my lady, but Mitchell, one of the footmen, has had the evening free."

“Bloody hell!” She turned back to continue upstairs. She was wet and cold, her ankle ached like the worst toothache she’d ever had, and the long scratch on her arm needed washing and bandaging.

That girl has been nothing but trouble, not worth my efforts to train her.

“Shall I send Lady Balfour’s maid along to you, my lady? Her ladyship is out for the evening and won’t be requiring Cecile’s services for some hours.”

“Yes, please do, Gravesfield. I admit tonight’s…activities…have left me feeling a bit spent.”

Once in her room, she didn’t wait for Cecile but stripped off her sodden clothing and pulled on a silk robe that had been thrown across the end of the luxurious bed. Sitting down at the dressing table, she noticed a letter addressed to her. It bore the Haven Hall seal.

From her father, no doubt requesting her to return home. With an exasperated sigh, she broke the seal and read, her eyes widening with each line. Her brother Archie had come home, seriously wounded, from France. Her father wanted her to return to be with him.

Archie, alive! She stared at the single sheet of paper. The war office had informed her family he had become missing in action, presumed dead. Now, this.

Joy filled her heart. She loved her brother. But how had this miraculous result been accomplished? How had Archie, wounded, managed to make his way home? Questions flooded her mind as she refolded the missive. There was only one way to have them answered and to be reunited with her beloved brother. She would have to return to Haven Hall as soon as possible.

She surveyed her wet, tangled hair and a bruise,

where she'd struck something on her descent from the attic room, darkening on her left cheek. Shoving up the sleeve of the robe, she examined a long, bloody scratch.

Hell and damnation! I can't go home until I mend. My appearance will raise too many questions. And I certainly can't attend any of Lady Balfour's social functions. I could encounter someone who might recognize me from the brothel. Lord knows, at least half of London's elite gentlemen frequent the place. So I'm housebound here...a prisoner until my appearance is once again presentable.

Frustrated, she began to pull pins from her hair. Her thoughts went back to that disgusting, pot-bellied man in the brothel. He'd called her a trollop. Where had she heard that word before?

Ah ha! The tale of the trollop's treasure. She remembered. Marie, her former lady's maid, had told her a story of a courtesan at the court of Louis the Sixteenth, a trollop in the eyes of those jealous of her success with powerful and wealthy aristocrats, and her cleverness in amassing a personal treasure…a treasure that had later been lost in a shipwreck as she'd fled the horrors of the French Revolution. Was it simply an old folk tale, or was there perhaps some truth in it…maybe the source of another adventure? She'd investigate when she returned home. It would help to relieve some of the ennui she always experienced when held in check by her father's watchful eye.

"Good evening, my lady." Cecile, Lady Balfour's lady's maid, slipped quietly into the room. "May I be of service?"

Another perfect servant, not questioning her appearance, simply ready to be of assistance. She very much doubted she'd ever be able to train Rose to such excellence.

Damn it, where is that girl! Hopefully not getting herself into trouble with a footman named Mitchell.

"Thank you, Cecile. I'm afraid my hair is rather a mess."

"Allow me, my lady." Cecile stepped forward to take over the task.

With a sigh, Anna accepted the maid's assistance. She was weary and longed for her bed.

Chapter 3

Somewhere, in a dream…or nightmare…he was coughing again, his chest aching, his body shaken with chills.

"Lie still, dear boy, lie still." As though through a murky window, he saw the Frenchwoman bending over him, her face wrinkled into a frown. "You're ill. You must rest."

Disjointed impressions tangled in his mind. From time to time he fancied sunlight streaming over him, then darkness…and pain, pain in every inch of his being. Chills attacked his body, making it tremble. A parched mouth added to his misery. And coughing…coughing until his ribs pained, until he gagged up whatever was available to be expelled from his innards. Fantastic nightmares raged through his fevered mind…nightmares in which he'd been captured, tortured, sentenced to hang…

Somewhere, in the midst of the jumble, he thought he remembered the Frenchwoman and a well-dressed older man standing over him. The man who'd welcomed the young captain home. He and the woman were talking, discussing him.

"I've been remiss in my obligations to this man," the man was saying. "He must be moved to the house."

"I would agree, your lordship," she replied. "But

he's ill, and I do not know what malady afflicts him. I think perhaps he should remain here, well tended by myself, until it is determined if whatever sickness from which he suffers is contagious."

"I see the wisdom in your words, Marie. Much as I want to see him more comfortably housed, I cannot risk the health of my entire household."

Lex's grip on reality stumbled at that point, and he fell back into his tortured fantasies.

A bitter argument between another man and the Frenchwoman next invaded his garbled thoughts. Through a haze, he saw them standing beside him and shouting at each other. She was gesticulating at a big, burly, bearded man with a reddened face…

Later he became aware of the woman raising his head, forcing a liquid between his lips. It tasted vile. He struggled to spit it out, but she lowered him so quickly that he choked and swallowed it.

"There. That will help. Rest, rest…"

Her words drifted off as he slipped once more into oblivion, but this time the nightmares turned to dreams…dreams of his Highland home and his family.

The next time he awoke, a sunbeam was hitting him in the face. He put up an arm to block it out and realized it was coming through a window…a window in a horse stall. Memory began to seep back. He'd brought young Archie Spencer home…home from the battlefields of France. A woman, an elderly French woman, had brought him food and a dry shirt and bedding.

Moving out of the sun's beam, he rubbed a hand over his face. Heavy stubble. How long had he been lying here? Sweet Jesus, who knew about him?

He was struggling to a sitting position when the Frenchwoman came into the stall.

"You're better." She smiled at him. "Good. At last."

"How long have I been here?"

"A week. You've been ill. When we found you in the morning after you brought Mr. Archie home, you were raving with sickness. His lordship wanted you to be moved to the house, but I persuaded him against it. I didn't know what type of sickness you carried. It would be unwise to expose the entire household if it could be spread."

"But you came…I remember…I remember you caring for me."

"I'm an old woman. I've been exposed to many maladies and survived."

"Still, you were brave. I thank you. How could you be spared to care for me? Surely you have a position in the house."

"I have occupied many positions over the years. I came here as governess to his lordship's two daughters, Lady Louisa and Lady Anna. When they no longer needed a teacher, I became their lady's maid. Lady Louisa has been gone for several years. Now I simply tend to Lady Anna…and not to any great extent. Lady Anna is a spirited young lady, frequently off on adventures of her own." She sighed. "I have become too old to bear the jolting of the carriage rides her travels involve. She takes a younger woman with her while I stay at home…and worry about her. She is expected from London any day now."

"I have a recollection of your having strong words with a man…a big bearded man with a paunch and red face. Words about me. Was it a product of the illness, or…?"

"It was real enough." Bobbie appeared beside the woman, grinning. "Mad'mo'selle Marie and Mr. Brant had a right battle of words. He wanted to throw you out, report that you may have left the army without…"

The lad stopped, confused.

"Without permission?" Lex looked up into the young man's troubled expression. "That I'm a deserter?"

"Yes, sir." The words came out awkwardly before he hastened on, "But Mad'mo'selle Marie said if Mr. Brant even hinted at such a thing again, she'd tell his lordship of how Mr. Brant had cheated him, had given Sir Maxwell accounts of paying more for harness and saddles and the like than they really cost and pocketing the difference. That shut his mouth." Bobbie grinned proudly until Marie nudged him, her face grave. "Anyhow he had no proof." Bobbie sobered. "You weren't wearing an army uniform when you arrived here."

Definitely not. He'd known he and Archie wouldn't be able to successfully proceed to the coast dressed as British soldiers. Shortly after their journey back to England was begun, he'd managed to steal clothing from a ramshackle tavern for both himself and Archie. One gentleman guest would have awakened in the morning not only with a pounding head and roiling gut, but missing his breeches, shirt, coat, and valise.

"You must not talk of such matters." The French woman was speaking to the lad. "It was not a ladylike thing for me to do. Now, go. I would speak to this man alone."

"You must be careful, my boy." She leaned close after Bobbie had gone. "In your illness, you rambled in Gaelic. I told anyone who overheard that it was only the muddled ravings of your illness. Poor ignorants, they believed me. But I'm not sure Sir Maxwell would have done so, nor would he have taken well to harboring a Highland outlaw…which I'm guessing you are…a rebel pulled from a jail to fight in France, perhaps? I've heard of many such cases."

"I thank you for the warning. I will try to guard my tongue." Lex would admit nothing, not even to this woman who had probably saved his life.

After she'd left, Lex drew a deep breath and looked around. His clothing hung over the door of the stall. And he was half decently clean. Perhaps young Bobbie had had a hand in his care.

He struggled to his feet. Much as he enjoyed the smell of hay and horses, he longed for a breath of fresh air. The garment in which he assumed he'd spent much of his illness hung rumpled and soiled to his thighs.

He wrenched it over his head and reached for his own shirt. It had been dirty, wet, and ripped when last he'd worn it. Now it was clean, dry, and mended. Even his boots, he noticed, as he pulled on his breeches and reached for his coat, had had careful treatment. He guessed he owed Marie Roi a debt beyond that of nursing him back to health.

Opening the stall door, he looked up and down the corridor. It was deserted. From the angle of the sun slanting in at the doorway, he guessed it was near midday. Possibly all the stable lads were enjoying a meal, perhaps in or near the kitchen.

His legs felt tenuous. Relieved there was no one

about to witness his foray back into the real world, he started slowly down the length of the barn. In case his knees decided to buckle, he kept close to one wall.

A soft whicker caused him to look to the right. He turned to see a gray snout thrusting out at him.

"Gallant!" Joy at seeing his faithful old friend flooded through him. "You've survived. And"—he moved closer to look into the stall—"very well, I see. Treated as the hero you are."

The animal puffed and blew softly as Lex laid a hand on his neck. He observed the old gelding had been well groomed and was putting on weight.

"Good lad." Lex gave him a final pat before continuing his careful progress from the stable. Once outside, a spasm of coughing overtook him. *Sweet Jesus!* He bent double and expelled mucus and what he assumed was every bit of what the French woman had recently managed to force into him.

When it was over, sucking in deep breaths, he slumped onto a bench against the stable wall.

Guid God! Can there be anything left in my innards?

It took several minutes, but as stability returned, he discovered the gut-wrenching episode had left him feeling purged and strangely refreshed. Drawing a deep breath of warm spring air, he leaned back, turned his face up into the sunshine, and closed his eyes. Limp as a rag and probably white as paste, he nevertheless was glad to be alive. And he wouldn't have been, he felt certain, if it hadn't been for the kindness and care of a stable lad and a small, elderly Frenchwoman.

A lady's maid, the woman had termed herself, but with no ladies to attend at the moment. One had left home, and the other was off adventuring, but expected to return soon. He wondered about these daughters of Sir Maxwell Spencer, most especially the one due to arrive shortly. The Lady Anna. An adventuress, was she? He'd met adventuring women…a number of them big, buxom creatures who talked like drunken sailors and would as soon backhand a man across the face as speak to him. Was this Lady Anna one of them…six feet tall and so broad of beam it would take a long arm to reach around her? If a man, God help him, was so inclined. He felt a smirk raise a corner of his mouth.

Enough meandering. He opened his eyes to gaze about the stable yard and pulled himself up straight. He couldn't stay here much longer. It was only a matter of time before they'd come looking for him. To test his strength, he attempted a brisk walk about the area…and failed. Slumping against a paddock fence, he realized he wasn't yet ready to run. He'd have to chance a few more days to rest.

The frantic screams of a horse, coming from behind the stable, roused him out of his lethargy. Moving more quickly than he'd done previously, he headed around the building to investigate. In a paddock at the back of the barn, the stable boys stood outside the fence, gaping, as the red-faced man Lex recalled arguing with Marie Roi whipped a terrified carriage horse. The animal was rearing, desperately trying to get away from the brutal beating the man was inflicting on it.

"Hie, there!" Lex stopped only a moment to assess the situation before climbing the fence and dropping down into the enclosure. Anger gave strength to his limbs. "What's going on here?"

"The brute took a kick at me!" Harvey Brant's face had become even more reddened than usual. Even at the distance of a few paces, Lex could smell liquor fumes emanating from the man. "He'll learn who's master or he'll be dog meat! Any road, it's none of your concern, tramp! Get out of here!"

"Whoa, easy, my lad." Ignoring the man's words, Lex moved slowly toward the gray gelding, holding out a hand. "No one wants to hurt you."

"I said get out of here!" Swinging about, Brant raised the whip in the other man's face. "I'm head groom on this estate!"

The next instant his upraised hand was caught in Lex's grip so swiftly it brought a gasp from Bobbie, who stood nearest the pair.

"Enough." Lex bent the man's arm until the whip dropped to the ground and he released the rope holding the horse prisoner.

The two men stood glaring at each other as the horse raced to the far end of the paddock and stopped, trembling and sweating.

"And just who do you think you are to be tellin' me what to do?" Harvey Brant focused his bloodshot eyes on Lex. His fist shot out, leveling a blow at Lex's jaw. It missed, catching him in the mouth instead. Lex tasted blood, and instinct overcame weakness.

He retaliated with a wallop that sent his opponent sprawling into the dust.

"What's going on here?" Sir Maxwell's voice rang out into the paddock as Lex stood over the fallen Harvey Brant. His lordship strode up to the enclosure and, accompanied by two footmen, swung open the gate to come inside. "What do you mean by beating my head groom into the dirt?" He looked down at Harvey Brant struggling up on one elbow. "For God's sake, man, on your feet!" He admonished the groom with a jerk of his head toward the gawking stable boys. "If you want to command any respect, get up! And you—" He swung on the onlookers, his expression so bellicose it brooked no denial. "Back to work. There's nothing more to be seen here."

As the workers dispersed, Sir Maxwell turned his attention to the horse cowering at the far side of the paddock. "And what's wrong with this creature? I paid top dollar for him. Now he appears to be nothing more than a shuddering mound of nerves." He started toward the animal, but it swung away, trembling, sweat darkening its coat.

As Harvey Brant staggered to his feet, nursing his jaw, Lex spoke. "Allow me, my lord."

"Very well." Scowling, Sir Maxwell stepped back. "Since you've seen fit to temporarily disable my groom, let me see what you can do with the creature."

"Easy, my fine lad, easy." Speaking softly, hand outstretched, Lex moved slowly toward the quivering animal. "No one is going to hurt you."

The gelding shuddered, then dropping its head submissively, allowed Lex to take him by the halter.

"That's a good lad." He stroked the animal's neck. "Good lad."

"Are those whip marks I see?" Sir Maxwell had approached and stood back, perusing the fine gray.

"Yes." Lex wasn't about to deny the groom's cruelty.

"Mr. Brant, am I correct in assuming you did this?" Sir Maxwell swung on the groom, who was occupied in brushing dirt from his clothing.

"The brute wouldn't behave, my lord." Harvey Brant's response was a mutter. "You wouldn't want a carriage horse that couldn't be trusted between the shafts."

"No, I wouldn't." Sir Maxwell swung to fully face the man. "Neither do I want any of my animals cowed into submission. Furthermore, being far gone in your cups at this hour of the day is entirely unacceptable. Mr. Brant, you may pick up whatever recompense is presently due to you from my steward and be on your way."

"But, my lord…"

"Go."

Harvey Brant cast Lex a look that if it had carried actual venom would have killed him on the spot before turning to shuffle away.

"As for you, Lex or whatever your name is, I'll see you in my study in a half hour."

Chapter 4

He should have left when he could. Lex stood in Sir Maxwell's study and ran his tongue over his split lip. If he'd taken to his heels as soon as he was on his feet, he wouldn't have gotten into that dust-up with Harvey Brant and wouldn't be standing in this room, awaiting God only knew what fate for assaulting his lordship's head groom.

But he couldn't have stood idly by and watched the brute whip that terrified horse. He could still see the animal's eyes rolling, whites showing, as it fought to escape the whip of the enraged man whose face was red and bloated from drink and anger.

He noticed a chess board set up before the fire, chairs on either side. Curious, he moved to observe the game. One player seemed well on the road to defeat. Quite a conundrum. Lost in contemplation, he began to move the pieces about.

"Mr. Lex." Sir Maxwell's voice snapped him back to the moment. He jerked upright and away from the board to face his lordship as he entered the room.

"Your lordship." Lex acknowledged him with an inclination of his head as the man moved behind his desk and sat down.

"You did well with my carriage horse just now in the paddock." Looking Lex up and down critically, Lord Dunstan leaned back in his chair. "You've got a way with horses."

"Thank you, sir."

"I realize I owe you a great debt for bringing my son safely home." He drew a deep breath. "And I would not have left you ill in my stables had not my trusted servant Marie feared you'd bring contagion into this house." To Lex's astonishment, Lord Dunstan stood and held out his hand. "Will you accept my apologies for your treatment?"

Surprise made Lex hesitate. He rubbed his right hand on the back of his breeches before accepting Sir Maxwell's offered one.

"Good, very good." His lordship returned to his seat behind the desk. "Now to other business. What would you say to taking over my stable…as head groom?"

"Sir?" Lex stared at the man. He'd been prepared for a severe reprimand, but most definitely not this.

"I've had my suspicions of Harvey Brant for some time…drinking to excess, dereliction of his duties. I believe my stable lads were too much in fear of him to lodge a complaint. You, however, took action. Now, what do you say, Lex…if that is your name? I little care. As Shakespeare wrote, 'What's in a name?' Do you accept the position?"

Still digesting what had happened in the past moments, Lex drew a deep breath. As head groom on Lord Dunstan's estate, he'd be safe, at least for a time, at least until he decided his next move. Sir Maxwell apparently wasn't about to turn him in as a deserter, although his lordship could not help but know it to be a fact.

"Yes, sir. Thank you."

"Very good." Sir Maxwell stood and strode around his desk. "There's a small cottage not far from the stables. It's the residence of Haven Hall's head groom. You may move in as soon as Mr. Brant vacates, which will be immediately. I must caution you to keep a close guard on my premises at all times. A pair of highwaymen once hid in my stables, in anticipation of robbing this house. The lads who care for the horses are no match for such villains. You, on the other hand, I suspect will be." His gaze fell on the chess set. "Good God! Just look at that! I thought my position hopeless." He glanced up at Lex, his expression mirroring astonishment. "Did you…?"

"I'm sorry, sir. I shouldn't have touched the game."

"But you did, and brilliantly." Sir Maxwell beamed at him. "I fancy a game with you. From what I see here, you'd be a worthy opponent."

"If you wish it, sir."

"Good. Then shall we say tonight after dinner? I'll send one of the maids to fetch you. Now you may go."

"Yes, sir."

"Oh, and Lex…" Sir Maxwell stopped him as he turned to leave. "My butler Thomas will be in the kitchen. Seek him out there. Tell him I've requested he find you a razor. You're to shed that growth on your face. I prefer my servants clean shaven."

"Yes, sir."

****

"Bloody hell! Not again!" Lord Dunstan squinted down at his companion's last move as he and Lex sat at the chess board. "I swear, Lex, you're a wizard of some sort."

"I enjoyed the game, your lordship." Lex ran a

hand through his unruly thatch of dark red curls and started to rise. It was the fourth evening in two weeks they'd matched wits over the game.

"Hold there a moment." Sir Maxwell stopped him with a raised hand as he himself stood. "A drink to ward off the chill before you go."

He started across the room toward a liquor cabinet. A fit of coughing overtook him, making him pause and press a handkerchief over his mouth. When it finally subsided, he looked back at the younger man, his face registering the ravages of his illness.

"Damn cough!" he muttered. "Serving King and Country can leave a man with all kinds of bloody ailments." He continued on to the display of bottles and glasses, but Lex, not for the first time, noticed the slump in his shoulders, the dragging in his pace. The stable lads had told him Sir Maxwell hadn't been content to sit on his hands and watch as other men died for England in France. He'd chosen to serve, only to arrive back home an unwell man.

Lex watched as his lordship poured generous measures of whisky into a pair of crystal glasses and returned to the chess table to hand one to him.

"Drink up, Lex. It's my finest. Only the best for the man who saved my son from dying on the battlefield in France. Once Archie is recovered from his wounds, he'll be taking over the management of this estate." Sir Maxwell sank into his chair with a heave of breath. "Hopefully I'll be around long enough to teach him the ways of the place, but then I want to sit back and take life easy…watch my grandchildren grow." He looked over at Lex. "My son is engaged to Jane Jonah, the daughter of a wealthy tradesman."

"I congratulate you…and Master Archie, sir."

"I dare say, any talk you may hear of this match around the stables will be of a disapproving tone. My servants are as snobbish as the worst of aristocrats. They think we should marry within our station, and generally I would agree. Nevertheless, while I would have preferred to see Archie espouse one of his own class, this estate is in desperate need of an infusion of wealth."

"'And once they're married, Miss Jonah's money will be your son's." Lex lowered his head to sip the whisky.

"That's the way of it, Lex." Sir Maxwell quaffed his drink and bared his teeth.

"I've been told you also have daughters, sir." Curiosity about the one branded adventurous made him pursue the conversation.

"I have two daughters, Lex, but only one of current consequence. The eldest ran off to America with a Scotsman several years ago." He shook his head sadly. "A waste, indeed a waste."

"Have you not heard from her since?"

"My wife and I had a letter shortly after they arrived in the colony. Said she was well and happily married. She thanked her mother and me for the beautiful cloak we'd given her as a wedding present, even though she knew full well that garment was entirely her mother's doing. My spouse, a beautiful, clever woman, was of a romantic bent. I've no doubt she sanctioned, probably even promoted, this so-called love match."

"Your wife passed over a year ago, I understand. I'm sorry."

"Yes, well, life must go on, but perhaps now you can see how much your saving Archie means to me."

"What of your other daughter? She must be a comfort." Again, that burning curiosity to learn more of the Lady Anna.

"A bit of a handful." Sir Maxwell pulled a wry expression. "I had intended a brilliant marriage for her, to His Grace, the Duke of Cumberly. It would pull the family standing up over Archie's commoner marriage. But the girl has a mind of her own. She's her mother's daughter right down to the ground…independent, proud, and though I'm loath to admit it, with a tendency to be an adventuress." He shook his head. "She's been in London these past months doing God only knows what."

"Perhaps you fear in vain, sir. Perhaps she's been a perfect lady."

"Doubtful in the extreme." He furrowed his brow as he looked over at Lex. "I must warn you to stay away from her. You're not an uncomely man, the kind I've no doubt could draw a woman's attention. Anna has a taste for the forbidden. You, a man of whose past we know little and into which I've advised myself, in deference to your service to my son and consequently to this family, not to delve, might just qualify. I also suspect you're a man who takes life as it's presented to him, not one to shy away from the unconventional…or forbidden. Otherwise you wouldn't have left the army without permission to bring my grievously wounded son home."

Lex appreciated the way his lordship had deftly substituted the words "left the army without permission" in place of the more apt "deserted." He also interpreted Sir Maxwell's warning to include the fact that his lordship would not continue this deference if Lex in any way involved himself with the Lady Anna.

"But enough." His lordship was speaking again. With a dismissive wave of his hand, he shoved the matter aside. "Lady Anna should be home shortly. I've written her concerning her brother's return and his condition. She and Archie were always close. I've no doubt she'll set out for Haven Hall soon. In the meantime, I'm hoping to have shored up marriage arrangements between her and the Duke." He took a drink. "Now to other matters. I've learned you haven't made arrangements to move into Mr. Brant's former cottage. I expected you to do so. It has been the residence of Haven Hall's head groom for many years."

"Begging your pardon, milord, but the man lived as a pig." Lex wet his lips. "I much prefer my accommodation in the stable to trying to clean out his sty." He paused. "And I enjoy being close to the horses."

Carriage wheels crunched in the drive.

"Who can that be, at this hour?" Sir Maxwell heaved an exasperated sigh. "Just when I was about to enjoy a couple of drinks with a most worthy chess opponent."

There was a bustling in the foyer. Then the door opened and a slender figure stood framed on the threshold. Titian curls peeked from beneath an elegant bonnet to frame a face that could make an angel envious. Lex's breath caught in his throat, and he stared.

"Papa!" In a rustle of emerald silk, the vision

rushed across the room, a delighted smile brightening her ethereal face, to bend over the older man and plant a kiss on his cheek. "I've come home."

"My dear." His expression registering his astonishment, Sir Maxwell gazed up at her. "You travelled at night? Alone?"

"Dearest, I had my maid and a couple of stout coachmen accompanying me." The vision turned a radiant smile on Lex. "And who is this, Papa?" She gestured toward the board as she turned toward Lex. "A new chess partner?"

Wide green eyes, alive with curiosity, took in Lex's stableman's clothing, delicate brows arching.

"This, my dear, is Lex, my head groom and quite possibly the finest chess player in England." Sir Maxwell stood, glass in hand. "Lex, this overwhelming creature is my daughter, Lady Anna."

"Lex, is it?" She moved past her father, a sly smile lighting that incredible face. She extended a slender, gloved hand. "My, my, I do admire Papa's taste."

As she approached, a scent so light and exotic wafted from her slender body that, for a moment, it made his senses reel, his body react, and words desert him.

"Lex?" She continued to hold out her hand.

Coming out of his trance, he stumbled to his feet, shoving the chess table aside with such vehemence pieces scattered over the floor.

"My lady." Ignoring the mess, he took her hand, snapped back to the moment, and bowed over it. "Your servant, ma'am."

Offering her hand to a servant. She is an unconventional lass.

"Aha! A stable lad with the manners of a gentleman. Wherever did you find him, Papa?"

She cast an appraising gaze over him. Lex became acutely aware of his scuffed boots, shabby breeches, and mended shirt. And that he was still holding her hand. He jerked away. His action solicited a smirk.

A woman well aware of her effect on men. You must be careful, verrae careful around this lass, my lad.

"It's a complicated tale, daughter, and one better left for a more opportune time." Sir Maxwell was speaking. "At the moment, I think it wisest you take your maid and retire to your rooms. It's late, and the journey from London must have been arduous."

"But first I should like to see my brother."

"As you know from my letter, he was seriously wounded. Each night, Mr. Jones, our apothecary, has ordered a sleeping potion to be administered. This having been done, Archie will, by now, be asleep and beyond his pain. The morning will have to suffice for your visiting him."

"Very well, Papa." She sauntered across the room to the liquor cabinet. "But if I'm to be denied a visit to my brother, I trust you won't prevent my having a small libation." She poured a generous measure into a crystal goblet and quaffed the whisky in a single swallow. "Now"—she replaced the glass and headed for the door—"anon, gentleman. I bid you both good night."

She swept out of the room with all the drama with which she had entered. Lex stared after her.

"Well, Lex, that is my daughter." Sir Maxwell heaved a sigh. "Perhaps now you can see why I have reason for concern."

"I believe every man with a beautiful daughter

shares your anxiety, sir." Lex fought his way back to the moment and framed his reply carefully, although, after meeting the Lady Anna, he believed his employer definitely had reason for concern. The lass was a free spirit if ever he'd encountered one. He bent to begin gathering up the spilled chess pieces.

"You're probably correct, Lex. Still, a man can't help worrying."

"I must be going." Lex placed the last of the pieces back onto the board and straightened up. "If you still want Lancelot bred to Lady Grace in the morning, I'll be needing my rest."

"Of course." Staring down into his glass, Sir Maxwell responded absently, his mind most likely still occupied with his daughter's unexpected return, Lex guessed. Breaking out of his reflections, he looked up at the younger man. "Take care, Lex. Lancelot may be the best stud in the county, but he's one fractious creature. I don't want him to injure Lady Grace. She's a beauty but mild compared to that stallion."

"Yes, sir. I'll do my best to see that you're presented with a warm blood foal." He touched his forehead in salute and headed for the door.

"And, Lex, Jem Davis and his son have finished work on the drainage ditch in the lower field," his lordship called after him. "Make sure they bring back our team of drays in good condition."

"Yes, sir."

"Oh, and one more thing."

He paused, his hand on the latch.

"Sir?"

"Give a care for yourself in that breeding. I'd be at a loss without my best chess opponent."

"Yes, sir."

****

In the quarters he'd fashioned for himself in the vacant box stall at the far end of the stable, Lex drew off his boots and vest and sank down on the straw tick that was his bed. He adjusted a horse blanket he used as a pillow and pulled the quilt up about his shoulders but couldn't seem to settle into a restful position. The spring night was cool, but he'd slept through much colder and in less comfort. Flopping over onto his back, he laced his fingers behind his head and stared up at the raw beams over his head.

The image of a bold, beautiful creature sweeping into the room like a vision out of a man's wildest dream—a woman he'd never be able to enjoy above an occasional glance—cavorted though his thoughts.

With a guffaw, he rolled onto his side and tugged the quilt higher over his body. Tomorrow would be a day to try every ounce of his strength and challenge his ingenuity. He couldn't face it unrested.

But when he finally managed to drift off, she came to him in his dreams…haunting him, mocking him with her unattainability, her utter desirability. The word "succabus" rose to taunt his troubled mind.

Chapter 5

"Rose, please tell Marie I am returned and would like to see her." Lady Anna stepped out of her gown and went to sit at her dressing table.

"She's retired, my lady." Her maid took the garment to a wardrobe to hang it inside. "And…"

"Of course she has, but she won't yet be abed. Fetch her at once." Anna hadn't meant to snap at the young woman, but memories of her incompetence in London still rankled. The night when Anna had returned to her rooms at Lady Balfour's manor, injured and drenched, hadn't been the only occasion on which her maid had seen fit to absent herself from her duties. Rose had disappeared without her permission numerous times. Furthermore, her care of Anna's belongings had left more than one gown in deplorable condition.

"Yes, my lady." With a quick curtsy, Rose turned away, but not before Anna caught the hint of contempt in her expression.

In the mirror, Lady Anna watched her go, then berated herself.

Anna, that was beneath your station to treat that girl so churlishly. Perhaps Marie has spoiled you. Now I must accept that she has become too advanced in years to do for me, that she deserves the retirement Papa has granted her in this house. I will have to make do with Rose…or find someone else.

As she began to remove the pins from her hair, the image of the tall, broad-shouldered man she'd discovered playing chess with her father wafted across her mind. Definitely a face and body to equal that of the statue of Adonis she'd seen on her tour of the continent the previous year. Where had her Papa found him, and when had a man declared to be the estate's head groom become welcome in the Hall to play chess?

Even more puzzling, how had a man in such a position become so proficient at a complicated game? She shook her hair free and decided she'd question her father about this newcomer in the morning.

"My dear child, you have come home." The door of her bedchamber opened to admit Marie Roi. Garbed in nightgown and robe, her feet encased in carpet slippers, wisps of gray curls sticking out from beneath her snowy white cap, she shuffled into the room, a smile brightening her wrinkled countenance.

"Yes, my darling Marie, I've come home." In a gesture distinctly out of keeping with their positions, Anna stood to enfold the elderly woman in a fond embrace. She was startled to discover a remarkable physical change in her former maid's stature. Surely her old servant hadn't been so frail when she'd gone away, her frame so birdlike. "Oh, how I've missed you."

"And I you, dear child. My, my." As Anna released her, Marie stepped back to scrutinize her. "You are pale and thinner. You are in need of the outdoors and some of Mrs. Ginger's good food. And your hair…" She touched the tangle of titian curls spilling over Anna's shoulder and made tsking sounds. "Come, sit at the dressing table and let Marie brush it out."

"I was hoping you would."

Anna reseated herself and heaved a contented sigh as Marie picked up a brush and ran it carefully through her tangled locks.

"Marie, what of this new man in whom Papa has taken such an interest? Lex, or some such, I believe is his name." She feigned only slight interest.

"Ah, Lex, the hero who saved your brother on the battlefields of France and brought him home. A puzzle, that one. He has—what do you call it?—the honor of a gentleman, but at times is severely lacking in the manners of such."

"He saved Archie's life? Papa's letter told me my brother had come home wounded but not how he had been returned. Tell me of it. How? When? And how was this man Lex involved?"

"Several weeks ago, Lex returned Master Archie, grievously wounded, home from the battlefields of France at great personal risk, even though he himself became ill along the way. It was a valiant rescue, one worthy of the hero of a romance."

"How amazing." Causing the woman to pause in her brushing, Anna swung to face her. "Small wonder he's in Papa's good graces. He's also apparently proven a worthy chess opponent. Tell me, Marie, how does this remarkable Lex person live here?"

"He has made himself a home in a vacant stall at the rear of the stables." Marie gently turned Anna's head back to face the mirror and resumed running the brush carefully, lovingly, through the shining locks.

"Interesting, but not exactly the information I was seeking"—she watched her maid's expression in the mirror before them as she continued carefully—"does he have a favorite among the maids?"

"Not that I know of, my lady." Frowning, the Frenchwoman paused in her brushing. "Although even an old woman like myself recognizes he's sinfully handsome, you must not go taking an interest in the man. Remember, you are to the manor born. Your father hopes to arrange a fine marriage for you." She went back to her task and spoke in a tone and manner that would, in other situations, have been out of place. "You mind what I say, child. I'll not have you throwing yourself away on a stable boy."

"He's hardly a stable boy, Marie." Anna drew herself up, squared her shoulders, and decided it was time to change the topic. "Tell me a tale, Marie, one of the stories you used to lull me to sleep when I was a child. The one about the trollop's treasure."

"Very well." The woman heaved an exasperated sigh. "I can see my warning you off that man will do no good. When I finish with this tangle, get into bed, and I'll tell you that old tale."

****

"This is a true story…as I've told you previously, my lady." As Anna snuggled down in her featherbed, Marie, a quilt wrapped about her, settled herself into the comfortable chair by its side, the one she'd used for years when telling her young charge a bedtime tale. She drew a deep breath. "And it is a secret one. I have never told the tale to anyone else but you. It all happened many, many years ago. I believe I am the last survivor to know of it. You may already have cast it aside as the fanciful ramblings of your old nurse, but nevertheless I would not feel comfortable leaving this world without passing the story, now in its truthful entirety, to someone I love and trust."

"Marie, you're not going to..." Horrified, Anna jerked upright in the bed and couldn't finish the sentence. Is that why Rose had been reluctant to fetch the elderly Frenchwoman? Was Marie Roi seriously ill? She stared at the wasted cheeks and the eyes that had once sparkled with life and wit, and she saw them dull and weary.

"Dear child, I am an old woman." She took Anna's hand in her wrinkled one. "The good God has given me more years than those to which I have been entitled. Now I'm tired and ready to join the others of my family. Do not grieve, my sweet. We have had many, many wonderful times together. You, your sister, and your brother have been the children I loved as my very own. Do not begin your grieving for me just yet. First you must hear my story and react to it as you see fit."

She paused, looking around the room. "That girl...Rose...she's gone for the night?"

"Yes, yes." Anticipation beginning to tingle through her body, Anna replied. "Please continue."

"The complete tale is for your ears alone." She settled back into her chair and pulled her robe more securely about her. "I don't trust that one."

****

"The story was told to me many, many years ago." With Anna once more comfortably settled in her bed, the elderly woman began. "I was but a child at the time. Those were dangerous days, when human life counted cheaply." Her eyes took on a dreaming outlook as she cast her thoughts back. "My parents did not survive. I was sent off with a great-aunt to live in the country. She had once been a lady-in-waiting at court, but at the time of the royal family's downfall, there was much chaos, with people trying to flee the guillotine. Wealth was being secreted out of Paris into hiding places where it might be reclaimed when order had been restored."

"Such as my necklace." Remembering the piece of jewelry that had been a gift from an ardent suitor and which had caused so much turmoil in her life, Anna snuggled down among the quilts and pillows. Presently the fabulous piece of jewelry lay ensconced in her father's strongbox.

"Such as your necklace." Marie paused.

"Please continue."

"At the court resided a highly regarded courtesan named Charlotte Dubois. It was reputed she was a favorite of the king. But Charlotte was more than a seductress. She was clever. She realized her days of fame and desirability would not last forever. Therefore, she set about to amass a fortune. By the time the troubles began, she had secretly made herself a wealthy woman.

"The horrors of the guillotine were becoming daily occurrences, but Charlotte Dubois had accumulated a vast fortune. She recognized that she could not safely stay in France. In her position, she would be classed with the aristocrats and quite possibly lose her head. Clandestinely, she prepared her escape."

"An adventuress and a clever one." Anna snuggled deeper into her bed, delighting at the tale.

"She had become acquainted with a sea captain who had come to court on several occasions in attempts to persuade the king to finance his ventures," Marie continued. "She knew Captain Michel Frenette to be a bold and daring man, just the type she needed to promote her plans.

“Shortly, she’d convinced him to take her and her belongings to North America. Captain Frenette, as enamored by the seductive Charlotte as any of her previous admirers, agreed. He would be sailing for Quebec in British North America shortly and would be delighted to take her along. Although Quebec had fallen to the English decades earlier, French ships were once again welcomed at the ports of Montreal and Quebec because of their cargoes of fine wines and brandy.

“So Charlotte, assisted and accompanied by a palace servant, a daring young man named Etienne Bouchard, gathered her treasure hoard and boarded the *Belle Michelle*. Clever Charlotte had enlisted the strong young lad on more than one occasion to assist in her schemes. She knew, besotted with her as he was, she could trust him implicitly.

“She even convinced Etienne her seduction of Captain Frenette was simply to assure his loyalty and their safe arrival in the New World. The chest containing her most valuable possessions she persuaded the captain to keep in his own cabin, knowing it would be safe there. He did so gladly, Charlotte having strongly hinted that he’d be coming in for a share of both it and her once they were safely delivered to Quebec. He hid her spoils, in the chest, beneath the floor boards of his cabin, under his desk. Paramount among her treasures was a magnificent pendant with the letter C as its centerpiece, inlaid with diamonds, rubies, and emeralds rumored to have been a gift from the king himself.”

“Wise woman, keeping Captain Frenette at bay until her purpose was accomplished.” Anna smirked. “All women should be so wise.”

"But then, Charlotte Dubois was not an ordinary trollop," the Frenchwoman continued. "She was clever and manipulative. The British in England had already offered safe haven for French aristocrats, and that gave her reason to believe they'd do the same in America for anyone closely associated with the court of Louis the Sixteenth and his queen. Furthermore, Montreal, the city to which she was destined, was largely a French-speaking city. She'd be able to manage well there."

"Also, taking such wealth that had belonged to European aristocrats to the United States would have been risky since those colonies had just fought a war to end the control of the wealthy upper classes, wouldn't it?" Anna interjected. "The Americans might seize it as fair game."

"Perhaps." Marie shifted on her chair. "As the story goes, the ship set sail, laden to the water line with a cargo of fine wine and brandy. It successfully crossed the Atlantic, but as the *Belle Michelle* neared her destination, a great storm arose, blowing her far off course. The vessel was thrust into the entrance of a bay known as Miramichi. There, driven by the gale, she crashed aground off a place known to the native people as Escuminac, at the very tip of the bay."

"And were all aboard lost?" Anna sat up straight, intrigued, then hastened on, "No, of course not. Someone survived to tell the tale. Now I remember."

"There was only one survivor…Etienne Bouchard, Charlotte's confidant. He was taken in by native people and lived among them for years. Later he managed to return to France. But he soon turned to drink, and his tale of his adventure and the trollop's treasure became a joke as he told and retold it in the taverns for a tankard of ale. His story was regarded as an amusement, nothing more. Now, my child"—lowering her voice, she leaned closer to the bed—"I have a secret I shall entrust to you."

"Marie, what…?"

"I have a map…the map to where the trollop's treasure lies beneath the waters of Miramichi Bay." The words were a hoarse whisper. "Etienne Bouchard entrusted it to me many years ago. I was the only one who listened seriously to his tales, the only one to whom he felt confident to entrust it."

"The map to the treasure?" Anna breathed. "Marie…!"

"I am old, with many more years behind me than ahead." She raised a wrinkled hand as Anna started to protest. "I will never go to America in search of this bounty. Indeed, I've had no need for it. I've had a good life here with my three beautiful children. But I know you're not content, that you have no wish to marry a man of your father's choosing. You are brave and bold. When the time comes for you to go to America, I shall give you the map. You should join your sister, who has married not once but twice to men of her own choosing. Make yourself as free and happy as I wish you to be. The treasure will give you such liberty."

"But, Marie, how did it come about that Etienne Bouchard entrusted it to you?"

"Near the end of his life, he sought shelter with our family. My mother, against my father's wishes, took him in. You see, child, Etienne Bouchard was her brother."

****

"Archie?" Anna poked her head around his half-opened door and smiled. "Are you decent? May I come in?"

"Anna!" The face of the young man ensconced among pillows in the luxurious bed crinkled into a broad grin. He held out a hand. "Anna, come in, come here that I might better see you. This is a delight."

Anna hastened across the room to take his hand and lean forward to kiss his gaunt cheek.

"So you got yourself wounded." She affected a flip attitude in an attempt to hide her shock at his appearance. *Good God, Archie! What has become of you?* The pale, thin man bore scant resemblance to the hearty young red-coated officer to whom she'd waved good-bye several months earlier. In an effort to keep tears and sentiment at bay, she forced her dismay into the background and adopted the teasing attitude they'd shared while children as she drew a chair close to his bed. "That was careless of you."

"Agreed." His expression of pleasure at her arrival remained. "Fortunately I had…have a friend who was able to rescue me from my folly."

"Lex."

"You've met him, then." Archie settled back on his pillows. "He's a fine man, Anna. Brave and honest and caring, but"—he hastened, urgency in his tone—"you must be circumspect about his presence here. Lex may have a past that could make him an object of interest to the British military."

"Archie, are you saying he's a deserter?" Anna stared at her brother.

"How else could he have managed to bring me home instead of leaving me at the mercy of a field surgeon?"

"But then you are a deserter as well."

"It's quite a different matter between being the son of a lord and being a convicted prisoner. Papa has been able to get the powers that be to look the other way in the case of my leaving my regiment without official permission. On the other hand, the unit in which Lex was fighting consisted of men taken from the jails of England to fill the depleted ranks of the British army. They were to fight or be shot. In spite of his gallantry on the battlefield, in spite of having saved the life of the future Lord Dunstan, not even our powerful Papa can have the charges against Lex expunged. He could well face a death sentence if he's discovered. So you see, Anna, it's paramount you keep Lex's presence here a secret."

"Of course. You may depend upon me. I could do no less for the man who saved my beloved brother. Now." She leaned forward to pat his hand. "You must not worry about this man Lex. Your only duty is to get well."

Chapter 6

"You did a fine job, laddie." Lex slapped a hand onto the stable boy's shoulder and grinned down at him. "Breeding can be a hard chore, especially with a stallion such as that great gray."

"Aye, that it can be, sir, but I thank you for trusting me to share it with you." Bobbie looked up at him, admiration in his eyes.

Poor young laddie. Lex saw a large bruise purpling beneath his left eye where the stallion had managed to hit him a blow with his tossing head. *He's got guts and brains, but the best I can do is train him up to take my place when I leave. Not the brightest of futures, but still better than the battlefields of France.*

"I'll be informing Sir Maxwell of your fine work." Lex rubbed his thigh where the stallion had managed to land a glancing blow. "Now you'd best get on with your chores."

"Aye, sir, thank you, sir." Eyes bright with appreciation, Bobbie snatched up a pitchfork and headed into the nearest stall.

"Lex." Sir Maxwell's voice took his attention.

"Yes, my lord." Lex drew a deep breath and tried to stride without limping out of the stable in response to his lordship's call.

In the yard, he found Sir Maxwell with another man dressed in finery Lex considered downright foppish. He was tall and exceedingly thin…scrawny to a point that even his elegant clothing couldn't hide the fact. A long nose seemed to have a constant position in the air as if all under it were either beneath his dignity to acknowledge or smelled exceedingly vile.

"Lex, this is the Duke of Cumberly." Sir Walter made a cursory introduction. "He would like to see Lancelot."

So this pompous, arrogant stick is the person to which Sir Maxwell hopes to marry off the beautiful, vibrant Lady Anna. Bloody hell, could there possibly be a worse match?

Shoving the thoughts aside, Lex replied, "Sir, the stallion is fresh from breeding. Bringing him out on parade at the moment would be…"

"Lex, I said we'd see the animal." Sir Maxwell snapped out the order. "His Grace is of a mind to have his famous mare Lady Duchess covered by him. He's come to make that decision, and he shall be given the opportunity to view the prospect."

"Yes, sir." Recognizing no opportunity for further denial, Lex headed back into the barn.

As he entered the stallion's stall, the big gray snorted and reared.

"Easy, laddie, easy." He chanced lapsing softly into a soothing Highland brogue as he reached to attach a lead to the animal's halter.

"Sir, what are you doing?" Bobbie, wide-eyed, appeared in the doorway. "The stallion is in no mood to be taken out."

"Sir Maxwell has requested he be shown to the Duke of Cumberly…no, demanded." The stallion threw his head sideways, all but knocking Lex off his feet.

"Then let me help you, sir." Bobbie ducked to the far side of the cavorting animal and took a grip on the other side of the halter.

"Have a care, lad." Lex knew denying the younger man's assistance wouldn't deter him. "We've got our hands full, and no mistake."

Struggling, they managed to get the battling stallion out into the paddock beside the stable.

"Lead him about a bit, that I might get a better view." Standing outside the fence with Sir Maxwell, the Duke placed one hand on his hip, snapping the whip he held in the other against the top of his riding boot.

Lex was endeavoring to comply when Lancelot reared. His tossing head hit Bobbie, and the lad was sent sprawling into the dirt at the far side of the enclosure. Against the boards, he lay still, eyes closed.

Lex released the rope and bolted to the stable boy's side.

"Lad." The word came out soft, beneath the hearing of the two men at the fence as he knelt and raised him into his arms. "Laddie."

The young man's eyes fluttered open. Relief flooded though Lex.

"Mr. Lex?" He looked up at the man.

"Aye." Again softly. "Aire ya hurt bad, laddie?"

"No…no." He made an effort to struggle to his feet. "Just winded. Lancelot…?"

"Fit as a damned fiddle." Lex's English accent returned. "Let me help you to your feet."

As Bobbie stumbled to his feet with Lex's assistance, Sir Maxwell's words came across the paddock. "Is he all right?"

"Yes, sir," Bobbie replied before Lex had an

opportunity. "Right as rain, sir. Sorry, sir. We'll be catching up your stallion, sir."

He started, with a stagger, toward the stallion prancing at the far fence, but Lex caught him by an arm.

"I'll do it," he said. "You've had the wind knocked out of you. Go into the stable and rest."

"But, sir, I…"

"Go." Casting the young man a glance that brooked no refusal, Lex pointed toward the barn.

"Yes, sir." Shoulders drooping as he tried to disguise a limp, Bobbie obeyed.

"Good God, man, is that the best you have in the way of stable servants?" The duke smirked at Sir Maxwell. "They cannot even be trusted to handle a viewing of your prized stud."

"It was perhaps an inopportune moment for such an event," Sir Maxwell replied. "Lex, see to the lad. Make certain he isn't seriously injured."

"Yes, sir."

"Come along, Your Grace." Sir Maxwell headed toward the house. "I have some excellent French brandy I think you'll appreciate."

As the pair walked toward the manor, Lex turned his attention to the stallion.

"Now, my fine, fractious laddie, you and I are about to come to an understanding." Blue eyes hard as sapphires, he advanced slowly toward the animal. Their gazes met and locked. For a moment, they stood staring at each other. Finally, as if recognizing a strength and determination not readily denied, Lancelot blew, pawed the earth a few more times, shook his head, and then allowed Lex to take up the lead rope. Walking as quietly as the best trained carriage horse, he followed the head groom back into the stable.

What an arrogant ass. Lex's thoughts went back to the duke as he secured Lancelot in his stall. *What woman could want to marry such a self-centered fop as that, never mind the Lady Anna.*

Well, it was none of his concern. The ways of the English aristocracy had always seemed stupid and inane to him.

Suddenly he felt a pair of eyes on him. Turning, he saw Lady Anna watching him. She tilted her head to one side and gave him a smug smile of approval, one that gave him a gush of pleasure.

"Good morning, Lex." She stood silhouetted against the sunlight flooding in through the stable's open doorway. "I trust you've completed the breeding my father requested?"

"Yes, Lady." He granted her a nod, instantly aware of the filth of his person, of his sweat-soaked shirt and grubby breeches. The duke's visit and ensuing events hadn't allowed him time to clean away evidence of his morning's work. A need to avoid this hauntingly beautiful woman overwhelmed him. Touching his forelock, he turned away.

"A moment, Lex."

Bloody hell, she was approaching him. Dressed in a dark green riding habit, a small matching hat perched jauntily on her shining curls, she was as beautiful as she'd been in his tormented dreams. He paused.

"I should like to go riding this fine morning." She rounded so that she stood close in front of him. Again that soft, overwhelming scent, again the prickling sensation it evoked in body and soul. The woman was no less alluring, no less ethereal than she'd been by candlelight the previous evening.

Leave me be, woman, leave me be.

"I'll have one of the lads saddle Nellie." Chafed by his inner reaction, he forced himself to meet her bold gaze.

"Nellie! That poor old hack!" She struck the riding quirt she carried across her gloved hand. "What do you take me for! I'll be riding Silverbell."

"Silverbell hasn't been ridden of late, Lady. She's full of…"

"Piss and vinegar?" She smirked out the response before he could finish the sentence.

"Energy, Lady. Silverbell is full of energy." A small sense of satisfaction settled over him as he checkmated her bold comment.

"Ah, a man of words as well as action. I've learned of how you rescued my brother in France and managed to get him back to England." She paused to let her green eyes gaze into his. "Now"—she stepped away to clear a path for him to the gray mare's stall—"I'd be most grateful if you'd get on with saddling my mount and whatever animal you choose for yourself."

"I'm not riding, Lady. I have work here."

"You'd not have me going out alone, now, would you, Lex?" She cast him a sly, sideways glance. "Papa would be most distressed if you allowed such a thing."

"I'll have one of the lads accompany you. Bobbie is dependable and a fine rider."

"No, no, no! Not a stable boy. I have decided you will accompany me, Lex." Hard and unyielding, she faced him. "Although you're here because of your rescue of my dear brother, I also know that you survive at my father's pleasure." Her eyes narrowed. "I'm not sure how long that would continue if I were to tell him you refused to do my bidding."

He stared at her, feeling his jaw twitch. The woman might look and smell like heaven's gift, but inside she was as brazen and notorious as the boldest trollop he'd ever met.

"Well?" She crossed her arms and began to tap the toe of her boot. "What is your decision, Lex?"

His name came out harder than the first part of her sentence, daring contempt in her tone.

"Very well, Lady. But"—realizing they were alone in the stable, he decided to match her audaciousness—"I'll not be responsible if the mare throws you onto your arse."

"My, my, I wonder what Papa would say if he heard you using such language in my presence?" She feigned shock.

"I think your Papa would believe you quite up to lying your way out of any situation." He went into the mare's stall and caught her by her halter.

"Oh, and you two have become such boon companions he'd take your word over mine?"

"He might." Lex led the prancing animal out into the walkway and secured her in crossties. "He knows *I* don't lie."

"An honest rogue." A corner of her mouth curled. "How unique."

"Rogue?" He stopped to shoot her a cutting glance.

"Oh, don't look shocked, dear boy. You left the army without permission to bring my brother home. Although both my father and I will be eternally grateful, the situation brands you a deserter. I think it's absolutely delicious that we have an outlaw hiding out under our bounty here at Haven Hall. This old place is finally living up to its name."

"And would it also be delicious to inform the authorities and to watch while I was dragged away to prison?" He went to fetch a saddle and cloth.

"No, it wouldn't." She swished her riding crop petulantly against her skirts. "You need not worry that I'll betray you. I've had a few minor skirmishes with the law myself and have no love for authority."

"Have you now?" Although curious, he managed to feign indifference as he swung the cloth into place and placed the saddle over it.

"Just to put you at your ease, it was nothing too terrible, neither theft nor murder…nor dereliction of duty." She added the last with a sly glance in his direction. "My latest adventure simply involved my deciding to delve into the mysteries of a brothel."

Astonished, he stopped and turned to her, letting the girth dangle.

"You're gaping, Lex. I did nothing so awful. I didn't allow myself to be compromised…in any way. I was thoroughly enjoying tempting and teasing several of the clientele until one of them became a bit too aggressive."

"What did you do?"

"I hit him with my knee…in a vulnerable area." She sashayed back and forth beside the horse. "The scoundrel was so enraged, he demanded the madam to imprison me in a garret room until morning, when he planned to bring me before a magistrate. Now enough of my adventures. Saddle your horse. Sunlight is being wasted."

****

Bloody woman.

Lex followed Lady Anna down a bridle trail that wound through the estate. His mount, Storm, was a well-trained hunter with a smooth gait. Still, his hip ached where Lancelot had managed to land that kick. He would have preferred working about the stable until it had time to supple out.

At least she's keeping to a decent pace. And managing that fractious mare well.

In spite of his discomfort and annoyance, he couldn't help admiring the way she kept the big gray to a modest trot. A beauty with her dappled body, dark mane and tail, and arched neck, one of Lancelot's first batch of foals, Silverbell was a magnificent, hot-blooded creature.

"Come on, Lex!" she cried, suddenly kicking her mount into a full gallop. "I'll race you across the meadow!"

"Bollocks!" He slapped his heels to his mount's sides, gritted his teeth, and took off after her.

For a time they kept to the bridle trail, then abruptly she swerved to the right and took a low stone wall in a soaring leap. Lex swore and urged Storm in pursuit. When his mount hit the ground on the far side of the barrier, he grunted as pain rushed through his hip.

"Hie, there! Hold up!" he yelled. *Damned woman! I won't have her torturing me further.*

She glanced back over her shoulder, laughing.

"Hold up, I say!" Anger turned to fear as he realized she was heading for the drainage ditch recently dug by tenant farmer Jem Davis and his son. "Hold up!"

His warning came too late. With a shriek, Silverbell catapulted into the depression. Her rider flew over her head.

As Lex drew to a sliding halt at the rim of the excavation, he saw the mare, dripping slime, struggling to her hooves. Lying beside her, so coated in mud she appeared a lump of wet earth, was Lady Anna.

"Lady!" He leaped to the ground and skidded down the slope to join her. "Lady!" He knelt to raise her into his arms. "Aire ya all right, lass?"

"Silverbell…?" She looked up at him, eyes wide.

He glanced over his shoulder to where the mare had bolted upright. "She's back on her hooves."

"Thank heavens." She drew a deep breath. "I couldn't face Papa if she'd been injured." She paused, then continued, an impish expression breaking though the dirt, "And I'm also fair ta middlin', my fine Highland laddie."

Son of a bitch! In his concern for her, he'd lapsed into his native inflection. *Now she's got me over a barrel and no mistake.*

Fighting to hide his anger at himself, he pulled out his shirttail, the only bit of his clothing he deemed decently clean, and began to wipe her face.

Fool! Ya bloody great lout!

"Aren't you going to beg me to keep your secret?" she asked as she allowed his ministrations.

"What secret?" He feigned innocence. *Convince her she's been in shock, not hearing right.*

"Do you think I'm so stupid as not to recognize a Highland accent when it bursts through, even for a moment?"

"Scottish." He made an effort to mitigate the

validity of her idea as he continued to remove filth from her forehead and cheeks.

"Highland, I'll wager, not because I'm so clever as to be able to recognize Highland from Lowland accents, but simply because I've had a suspicion about you since we first met. An English soldier having deserted his post wouldn't have chanced bringing a lord's son home. No, only an outlaw with a fearless heart…a Highland rebel pulled from an English prison and forced to fight for his nemesis in France…"

"You talk too much." He finished wiping her countenance as clean as he could manage, stood, and held down a hand. "Get up."

"Aren't you going to sweep me into your arms?" Ignoring his offer, she remained seated in the mud.

"No. Come along. Sitting in a puddle will do you no good."

"Argh!" Scowling, she grasped his hand and stumbled to her feet. As she tried to steady herself in the slime underfoot, he released her and headed toward Silverbell. It was his duty to see to the mare…and his need to get away from the woman provoking him.

He slogged through the mire to the mare's side.

"Easy, easy, girl." He caught the shuddering animal's reins and ran a hand gently down her neck. Kneeling, he began to check her forelegs.

"Has she been injured?" Slipping and sliding through the mire, Anna came to his side.

With a grunt, he straightened. Silverbell's left foreleg was skinned and bleeding, but Lex's knowledgeable fingers told him it wasn't broken, nor was the damage serious.

"She'll survive." His anger receding somewhat, he

asked, "Yourself?"

"I'm perfectly all right. Did you think I couldn't weather a small toss? I assure you, I've taken far worse during a hunt and lived to enjoy dancing at the ball that evening."

"Then I imagine you can ride home."

"Of course." She patted the mare's neck. "I'm sorry, my girl," she continued to the horse, her tone softening. "I didn't take proper care." She swung back on her companion, her words returning a mocking tone. "My, my, Lex, it looks as if you and your lads will have a sizeable task getting my darling clean again."

"Your maid as well, Lady. Now we'd best be getting home. I want to tend the mare's leg properly." Gently urging, leading carefully, he got the animal out of the ditch. Anna followed, her elegant riding habit dragging up the muddy bank.

"I thought you might be a romantic," she said when they paused at the top. "After such a dramatic incident, I expected a Highland outlaw to sweep me up into his arms and carry me up out of that ditch."

"Don't be daft." Her taunting brought annoyance seething back. "Since your tongue tells me you're fit as a fiddle, I see no need to provide such a service."

Sweep you into my arms, indeed! He guffawed as he went to catch up Storm. *You might have haunted my nights at first, but now that I know what a deceptive, wily creature you are…*

"You'll be riding Storm." He led his mount over to her. "I'll hoist you aboard."

"Hoist me aboard? How prosaic! Lex, Highlander or not, you're no silver-tongued devil!"

"Chust give me your foot." He cupped his hands

into a stirrup as he stood beside the black gelding. "And swing your right leg over his rump when you get up there. You'll be riding astride."

"Very well." The two words came out as a sigh.

Once in place, a leg on either side of the horse, she kicked her foot free of the left stirrup and held down a hand. "And you, my fine laddie, will be riding pillion. Walking is out of the question. I've noticed that for some reason you're limping. Get aboard."

He hesitated. Much as the thought of riding pressed against her back, her titian hair, even now dirty and disheveled against his chest, galled him, he could see little choice. His injured hip was aching like a fury after that wild ride and trundling down into that irrigation ditch to rescue her and her mare. Thoroughly disgusted with himself for giving in to physical weakness, he gathered Silverbell's reins in a more secure grip, put his foot into the proffered stirrup, ignored her hand, and vaulted up behind her. He didn't manage to suppress the grunt the pain caused him.

"What's wrong?" She apparently caught the sound, and the awkwardness he tried to suppress as he mounted. "Lex, are you in pain? Do you have an injury?" Her tone surprised him with a concern that sounded entirely sincere.

"Your father's stud clipped me," he muttered. "Nothing a bit of liniment and a good night's sleep won't fix." He reached around her to take command of Storm's reins and shuddered inwardly as her body pressed against his, as her intoxicating scent, even after a dipping in mire, still prevailed.

"I'm sorry. I didn't know. If I had, I certainly wouldn't have forced you to go riding with me."

Her words sounded truly contrite.

"Nothing to concern yourself about, Lady." He nudged the gelding into a walk. "I'm tough as boot leather."

Sweet Jesus! Every fiber in my body is urging me to put my lips to her neck, to take her from this horse and make love to her. And wouldn't that place the noose about my neck, sure and certain.

****

They rode back to the stable in silence. In the yard, Lex dismounted, struggling to suppress the grimace that his aching hip was causing.

Bloody hell, what a day! The further I can stay away from this woman the better.

"Good God, Anna, what happened?" As Lex helped her to dismount, Sir Maxwell emerged from the stable to stare at his mud-caked daughter. "Lex…?" He glowered at the groom.

"I wasn't aware of that new drainage ditch you've constructed, Papa." On the ground, she turned to her father. "Lex tried to warn me, but I was being reckless."

"Damnation, Anna, when will you ever learn!" Sir Maxwell scowled down at her. "As if it isn't enough your sister has run off to America and your brother lies seriously ill…"

"I'm sorry, Papa." She took his arm and smiled up at him through the grime on her face.

"Water under the bridge now, I suppose." Lex saw the Lady Anna's charm working its magic on her father as Lord Dunstan replied with a heaved sigh.

"Or in the ditch." Her eyes twinkled at she snuggled up to his side. "Come along, my dear. I'm cold and wet and hungry…and we must let Lex get on with his work."

"Minx!" Her father shook his head in a resigned fashion. "Well, come along and let Rose clean you up. Lex"—scowling, he glanced back at the groom as he steered his daughter toward the house—"see to those horses. Make bloody sure Silverbell hasn't been injured."

"Yes, sir." He gathered up the horses' reins and, leading them, limped into the stable.

Chapter 7

"Pardon, Mr. Lex, sir." The shy little scullery maid stopped him as he came out of the stable after putting the horses up.

"Yes, Violet." Recovering from his recent annoyance with Lady Anna, he forced a smile down at the girl. "What can I do for you?"

"It's Mr. Archie, sir. He's sent word down to the kitchen that he wishes to see you."

"Much as I'm obliged to you for bringing me the message, and much as I'd like to do Mr. Archie's bidding, I don't think my presence would be welcome in the manor at the moment." He looked down at his clothes, still bearing the signs of his recent adventure in the mud. He'd tried to brush them clean, but stains remained. He'd have to wash them in a horse trough that evening and let them dry overnight.

"Oh, please, sir!" She looked up at him, eyes wide. "Mrs. Ginger said I wasn't to return without you. She'll be right put out if I fail to bring you back. And"—she held out a paper—"Mr. Archie sent this."

He hesitated, then took it. Unfolding it, he read, "My friend, I must see you. It is a matter of urgency. Please come at once."

"Very well." He thrust the message into a pocket. "Lead the way, my lady." Blushing, Violet headed for the house, Lex behind her.

****

"Lex." Archie Spencer's greeting held all the warmth of being reunited with an old friend. "Thank you for coming."

"You said the matter was urgent, sir." Lex paused inside the door of the luxurious room as he looked at the young man propped up among pillows in the wide bed. The younger man was still pale, with dark shadows under his eyes, but he was home, cared for and, hopefully, recovering.

"Come closer and take a seat." Archie indicated a chair beside the bed. "And for God's sake, don't call me 'sir.' It's I who should be calling you such, after all you've done for me. And"—he continued as Lex did as he'd been bidden—"now I'm about to ask yet more of you."

"At your service." Puzzled, Lex inclined his head in acquiescence as he took the proffered seat.

"This is a task I fear may prove nearly as daunting as rescuing me from France…and you're the only man I would trust with such a mission." He paused, a hint of a twinkle coming into his eyes.

"Yes?" Suspicion rising, Lex waited for him to continue.

"I want you to look out for my sister Anna." He raised a hand as Lex made a move to protest. "Please hear me out before you decline. You've met her and, according to household gossip, have already had an adventure with her. Therefore, you've some idea of how she behaves. Now she's confided in me that, if Papa continues to press for her marriage to the Duke of Cumberly, she will run away to join our sister in America. Lex, I know our father plans to push such an arrangement forward. I also know Anna was sincere in her threat. In my present condition, I can do little to stop these events. Therefore, I'm appealing to you, the man who saved my life, a man of courage and strength, a man of good character…"

"Good character?" Lex shook his head. "I'm an army deserter, a man who was forced to sign up to fight against his will. You know nothing of my past before…"

"You risked your life to save mine." The green eyes of the young man in the bed took on a pleading expression. "You have a brave heart. Lex, I love my sister. She needs a protector. Please do not deny me this further service."

"I cannot agree to such a commission." Lex bent forward, clasped his hands between his spread knees and focused on them.

"If my sister does run away to America"—Archie Spencer paused to revise his words—"when my sister does run away to America, if you go with her, you'll be free to start a new life. Your past will be expunged. Think of it, Lex. And"—he continued when the man beside the bed didn't reply—"when I become in a position to do so, I'll see you're repaid handsomely…financially."

He made another effort to deflect Archie Spencer's request. "How do you know I'll not take advantage of your sister on such an escapade?" he asked.

"I may not have proven an outstanding soldier, but I do believe myself a decent judge of men." The younger man drew himself up on his pillows and assumed what he apparently believed a commanding stance. "You are not such a man. Furthermore"—again that burgeoning twinkle—"you are not the type of man who has to force himself on women. I'm sure more than a few ladies have found you attractive, Lex." He paused before renewing his request. "Please."

The last word came doused in such appeal that Lex, meeting Archie's gaze, felt trapped.

"If the need arises, if your sister decides to make for America, I will accompany her." He stood with a sigh of exasperation. "But then, and only then, will I become her companion."

"Thank you, Lex." Sincere gratitude emanating from his expression, Archie Spencer leaned forward, grimacing with the effort, holding out his right hand. "As I'm already deeply in your debt, this will only serve to make me forever at your service. Your hand on our agreement."

Lex hesitated before accepting the young man's gesture of a seal on a covenant he felt could well cast him into the vortex of any number of dangerous adventures. When he did, the confidence in the younger man's grasp made the agreement final.

****

Lex left the manor with only one plea in his heart. *Please don't let that headstrong minx decide to bolt to America.*

As he headed to the paddock beyond the stables, he saw the old gelding standing near the gate, head drooping.

"Gallant," he called as he approached. "How are you faring, my fine laddie?"

In answer, the horse raised its head. Gray trimmed its once-chestnut hair. With a gentle whicker, he walked stiffly toward Lex. A blue ribbon adorned his forelock.

"You're looking right fine, my friend." Lex reached to rub the animal's neck as the old animal paused at the fence. "Good food and rest are working wonders. And you'll have them for the rest of your life, if Sir Maxwell has anything to say about it. It also appears"—he continued touching the bow—"as if someone has been giving you a right serving of special care. Where did you get this fancy trimming? And your hooves." He looked down at them. "They've been brightened up with gloss…gloss reserved for the carriage horses. I'll speak to Bobbie about using such products on you. He can brush you to his heart's content, but dressing you up with costly shine is not acceptable."

Lingering to enjoy the old horse's company, he recalled how the emaciated animal had borne the wounded Archie Spencer through the battle-torn fields of France as he led the half-starved animal to the coast. Stumbling, sometimes going to its knees in exhaustion, the gelding Lex had found roaming, wounded and disoriented after a battle, had persevered until they'd reached a seaport.

When he'd secured passage for himself and Archie aboard a smuggling vessel, Lex had had to give most of what coin he'd managed to purloin during their journey across France to the captain to convince him to take the winded horse aboard. In England, the horse that Lex had by then named Gallant had taken up the task of bearing Archibald Spencer the final miles to his home.

Lex doubted if the formerly abused animal would ever be entirely sound again, but Gallant would live out his days in luxury and the best care one of England's finest stables could offer.

"He's recovering well?" The Frenchwoman's voice made him turn. Marie Roi stood leaning on a cane, smiling at the pair.

"Aye, doing as well as can be expected." He was always pleased to see Marie, the woman he credited with saving his own life.

"You and he have done Sir Maxwell a great service in bringing Master Archie home." She came to stand at his side and reach out a wrinkled hand to caress the old gelding's nose. "I cannot but think his lordship might have done better by you than making you his groom."

"He hardly could do more." Lex rubbed Gallant's neck. "My past would make anything else look suspicious."

"I doubt you've done anything so terrible, my boy." She smiled up at him. "You have a good heart. Otherwise I wouldn't have come down here to entrust my darling girl to you."

"What?" Lex jerked as if pinched. "Your darling girl?"

Good God! Not this woman to whom I owe my life. Surely she, as well as Archie, won't ask me to take on that notorious creature.

"The Lady Anna needs a caretaker." Marie looked up him, eyes wide with anxiety. "I'm growing old. I am not well. Until now, I have in some small way managed to keep her decently safe from her wayward tendencies, but now she's told me of her recent adventures in London. Her stories prove she's now, more than ever, in need of supervision I can no longer provide. Presently she talks of going to be with her sister in North America. She must not travel alone. Lex, I want you to go with her, take care of her."

"Mademoiselle…"

"I've come to know you in the time you've spent on the estate. I've watched you not only with animals in need of care but with people as well. The stable boys trust and admire you. You've a kind, good heart. Moreover"—she paused and looked up at him with what he could only term a roguish gleam in her dark eyes—"you're strong and brave, a warrior. You will be an excellent protector. Do not be hasty in your decision!" Marie caught him by a sleeve as he made to protest. "She's determined to go. I cannot bear to think of what might become of her alone on such a trek. Lex, she's a good girl at heart, a caring child. Once you come to know her…"

"I'll do my best…but only if she decides to run away to America. I will not chase after her all over England."

"Thank you, my boy. I can ask no more of you."

Leaving the old woman with the old gelding, Lex headed into the stable. He had a pair of carriage horses to train, and they were proving a handful. Their antics would soon rub the memory of Marie Roi and her proposal from his mind.

"Lex, she needs a champion," she called after him. "She's like a daughter to me. She deserves to be protected by someone like you. Who do you think spent the whole of an afternoon caring for your old war horse while you were off with Sir Maxwell purchasing new carriage harness? Who do you think tied her best ribbon in his mane?"

He stopped. Turning back to her, he saw her nodding her head gravely.

Chapter 8

Lex woke to the sound of someone moving about in the stable and the muted snuffling of a horse. Remembering Sir Maxwell's telling him that a pair of notorious highwaymen had once hidden in the stables while planning to rob the house, he grasped the cudgel he kept by his bed and got stealthily to his feet.

Easing out of the stall, he squinted down the length of the corridor and saw a hooded figure in a floor-length cloak outlined in the light of a single candle burning inside the lantern the intruder held. The trespasser was paused outside Silverbell's stall.

"Hie, there!" Lex strode forward, weapon raised.

"Lex?" The familiar female voice shocked him as Lady Anna, bringing the lantern to shoulder level, swung to face him. The green cape whirled open to reveal a filmy white garment of some sort. A nightgown? "My, my, you are an excellent guard. I will inform Papa." In the dim light, he caught that all-too-familiar smirk curling her lips.

"What are you doing here?"

"I came to see how Silverbell is faring after our adventure." She rubbed the mare's nose and avoided his glowering. "This is my father's stable. I need no special pass to be allowed to visit my mare."

"Aye, but perhaps midnight is not the most auspicious time. I might have floored you." He let the cudgel drop to his side.

"Sir…Mr. Lex…is all well?" Pulling a coat over his bare chest, his hair standing on end from sleep, Bobbie appeared half way down the stairs leading to the stable boys' quarters above.

"All is well." Lex was quick to reassure him. "Lady Anna has come to check on Silverbell, that's all. Go back to bed, lad."

"Oh, excuse me, my lady." Bobbie touched his forelock as he recognized her. "I didn't recognize you."

"Perfectly understandable, Bobbie." In the flickering light, Lex saw her cast a kindly smile at the young man. "It's not an hour at which you would expect me to pay a visit."

"Silverbell's fine, my lady. Mr. Lex has taken good care of her."

"I'm sure he has. Now, please, return to your bed. I apologize for interrupting your rest."

"No trouble, my lady, I'm sure." With another touch to his forehead, Bobbie glanced at Lex, who gave him an acquiescent nod. Stifling a yawn, the stable boy made his way back up the stairs.

"I'm delighted you didn't see the need to use that thing." After Bobbie had disappeared from view, she indicated the cudgel and cast him a taunting glance. "Papa would have been far from pleased."

"Well, now that you've seen that your mare is fit as a fiddle, you can take yourself back to the house. I'll walk you to the door."

"I got here safely on my own, sir. I'm perfectly capable of returning in a similar fashion. Furthermore, I would not want any of the servants seeing you accompanying me, attired as you are." Green eyes raked up and down his length.

For the first time he became aware that he wore only the shirt Marie had brought him on his first night in the stable. While it hung to his knees, his legs and feet were bare. A hotness spread up his neck and over his face.

"My clothes were a mite soiled after our incident in the ditch today. I saw fit to give them a scrub in the trough and hang them to dry before I retired."

"Ah. And have you no other apparel besides this…this…?" She indicated the dangling shirt.

"Only this, courtesy of Mademoiselle Marie."

"Ah. So you arrived with only the clothes on your back?" She stepped close and looked up into his eyes.

"That's right, Lady. Now, I suggest you return to the manor."

Sweet Jesus! Don't stand so near! Don't look at me like that! Why did you have to come out here with only that cloak over your nightshift? Leave me, just leave me in peace!

"I'll follow at a discreet distance." He forced out the words.

"Very well." She heaved a sigh, gave the mare's nose another affectionate rub, and turned to leave. "What is that awful stench?" Stopping short, she swung on him, holding up the lantern to better see his face.

"Manure."

"I'm quite familiar with the smell of manure. This is much worse." She stepped closer to him and sniffed. "It's emanating from you. Good God, Lex, what is it? No human being can stink so terribly on their own."

"Liniment." He was glad for the shadowy darkness that would prevent her from seeing an ever-deepening blush suffuse his countenance.

"Of what variety?" She stepped back, placing a hand over her nose and mouth.

"Horse."

"Horse liniment? You've slathered yourself with horse liniment? Why, in God's name?"

"I've told you. Lancelot managed to land a kick during this morning's breeding." Embarrassment made him snap at her. "This mixture works a treat on the beasts."

"And so you thought it might work a miracle on a human." She faced him squarely.

"Yes."

"You must be in considerable pain to slather yourself with such vile-smelling stuff. You must have been suffering when I forced you to go riding with me this morning. Why did you not speak up?"

"You may recall you threatened me."

"Yes, I did, but I should have noticed you were favoring your leg. Good God! Sometimes I think I'm the most selfish creature in the world. Lex, I'm truly sorry." Her words softened with sincerity as she looked up at him in the shadowy lantern light.

"You were keen on going riding and using your own mare. Your thoughts were elsewhere." Astonished by her apology, he mumbled his reply.

"Still, I acted like a spoiled child." She turned and headed out of the stable. "You may escort me back to the house, Lex. Only please keep a respectable distance. That smell has quite set my stomach on edge."

He followed her to the stable door, then paused to watch her make her way toward the house. In the starlight, she appeared an ethereal figure, her cloaked figure moving softly through the star-lighted night.

Once she was what he judged to be a discreet distance ahead, he moved outside and followed. Stepping in a pile of horse manure, he jerked up his foot and cursed. As he endeavored to rub himself clean on a plot of grass, she vanished inside.

The image he must have presented to her came gushing back to shame him. He'd stood before her, barefoot, hairy legs protruding from beneath his shirt, stinking to high heaven, admitting he had but one outfit of clothing to his name.

And had she, through that worn shirt, been able to perceive his carnal interest? Heat flooded through his entire body.

Bloody hell! He kicked at a hummock, then suppressed a yowl as his great toe hit a rock.

****

Inside the manor, Anna scurried to her room and scrambled into her bed, unnoticed. Snuggling down beneath its satin quilts, she curled up into a delighted ball, a smile curling her lips.

That man Lex interested her…no, excited her…even in his smelly, half-dressed state. Incredibly handsome and virile, with his dark red curls tousled from sleep, and near naked, he pleased her no end. She wanted to spend more time with him, to explore where a closer association would take them.

She grinned. Whatever would Papa think if he became privy to her thoughts? Her lips still curled in pleasurable thoughts, she snuggled deeper into the sensuous warmth of her bed and fell asleep, visions of an earthy stableman filling her thoughts.

****

"Damn and blast!" Scowling, Sir Maxwell threw the paper onto the breakfast table. "Wouldn't you know!"

"What is it, Papa?" Anna looked up from her plate.

"Only rebellion and war could be worse." He shoved aside his plate. "I've been summoned to London on the eighth. Some sort of emergency meeting of Parliament. I'm getting thoroughly annoyed by these demands, most of which do not warrant the importance these messages imply. Perhaps the prime minister has become bored, or his gout is kicking up, or…"

"Darling Papa." Anna cast her most endearing smile down the table toward her disgruntled parent. "A few days in London would do you a world of good. You've been stuck to this estate too long. A breath of fresh air is just what you need."

"I'd hardly call breathing London fog exactly that." He leaned back in his chair, frowning. "Still, when I took on representing this region in government, I knew…or thought I knew…the obligations it entailed. But"—he came back forward toward his daughter—"this time it's more than damned inconvenient. The tenth is the day of the duke's fancy dress ball. I was hoping…"

"To escort me and dangle my charms under His Grace's nose?" Anna cut him short, taunting him with a roguish grin. "Really, Papa, do you imagine you can pawn me off so easily…and advantageously?"

"No, I suppose not." He stood, a resigned sigh drawing back his shoulders. "But I had hoped to at least try. After all, fancy dress is one of your favorite entertainments. I thought you might thrust yourself wholeheartedly into it."

"Have no fear." She got to her feet and rounded the table to take his arm, rise on tiptoes, and plant a kiss on his cheek. "I shall attend the ball and do my very best to make an impression on the duke."

"But how?" He drew back from his daughter's impulsive gesture. "Surely you're not considering going alone?"

"Of course not." She gave him a final impish look before swinging away toward the door. "I have a plan."

"That is exactly what does give me trepidations." Her father's words reached her just before she was out of hearing. She chuckled.

****

"This is one daft plan if ever there was one." Lex stood in a guest bedroom at the far end of the second floor and fidgeted as Anna adjusted the plaid over his shoulder.

"There." Tilting her head to one side, she stepped back to gaze at the tall, broad-shouldered man standing before her in full Highland kit. "My, my, you do look handsome. What do you think, Marie?" She turned to the elderly woman seated by the bed.

"He is very handsome, indeed, child, but…"

"And chust how handsome will I be, hangin' from a gallows?" Exasperated, he let his Highland brogue surface.

"Dunnae greet." Smirking, she aped his inflection. "No one will expect an actual Highlander ta come ta the ball flauntin' his lineage."

"No one in his right mind, for sure and certain. And ya can also be sure and certain this one wouldn't if ya hadn't threatened him." He scowled down at her.

"Threatened you!" She stepped back from him,

tilting her head flirtatiously. "A wee bit of a thing like me? Lex, surely you jest."

"Aye, well, a wee bit of a thing like ya, Lady, can wield more than a weak clout when ya threaten ta tell yer father that the reason ya rode full tilt into the irrigation ditch was ta escape my unwanted advances."

"Oh, Lex, do stop whining. You'll enjoy the ball. Your costume at least allows for freedom of movement." She patted her breasts. "With the depth of this décolletage, I dare not bend forward in the least."

"Then why did ya choose ta go as the French queen? She's been dead for years. Her brazen styles are long out of fashion."

"Ah, but she was a fascinating creature." Anna sauntered over to a jewel case on her dressing table and extracted a necklace. The diamonds, emeralds, and rubies that came into view sparkled in the candlelight with such vehemence that Lex's sudden intake of air made him choke. "And I have this bauble reputed to have belonged to her. I had Papa's steward fetch it up here from his strongbox this afternoon explicitly to complement my costume."

"Where did ya get it?" Lex couldn't take his eyes off its entrancing glitter.

"From a former suitor desperate to impress me." She put it about her neck. "Come, Lex. Fasten it for me."

He hesitated. Surely this was the duty of the lady's maid, but Marie looked so weary as she sat in the chair… Slowly he moved to take the ends of the fabulous adornment that Anna held up on either side of her slender white neck. *Bloody hell, did she have to be wearing that fragrance that made his senses tingle?* As his fingers touched the softness of her skin and the necklace's clasp snapped shut, he fought the urge to slip his arms about her slender waist and bury his face against her neck, below the shining ringlets she'd had fashioned in keeping with her costume.

"There." His voice was gruff as he stepped back. "Aire ya satisfied?"

"Reasonably." She preened before the mirror, her hand on the necklace. "Oh, do stop grousing, Lex." She swung on him. "It will be much better than spending another night in that stall in the stable. And you do look fine." She reached to adjust his sporran, but he shoved her hand away.

"Afraid I'll seduce you, my fine laddie?" Stepping back, she chuckled.

"I'll chust be gettin' the carriage." He started to leave, but she stopped him long enough to swing a long, hooded cloak over his outfit.

"Even though Papa is in London, I will not risk some of his loyal servants seeing you thusly attired and sending word of our little adventure to him. By the time he returns, I'll have devised a plan on how to deal with any small annoyance he might feel."

"Small annoyance! With all yer skill with fine words, can ya no' find any ones stronger?" Jaw tightening with anger, hot outrage flooding through every inch of his body, Lex glared at her from beneath the hood as she stood on tiptoe to pull it over the bonnet covering his dark red curls.

Marie broke into a fit of coughing.

"Bollocks!" Lex swung away from Anna. In two long strides he was in front of Marie and kneeling before her.

"Lass, lass, ya should be abed." He took her wrinkled hand in his. "Ya've no' been well, and now our squabblin' has upset ya."

"I do enjoy when you call me 'lass.' " With her free hand, she touched his cheek affectionately and smiled into his eyes. "You're a charming one, and that is a fact."

"Go!" Lady Anna pointed him toward the door. "I won't have you seducing my lady's maid. I'll meet you at the carriage shortly."

"Have a care, my boy, have a care." Marie issued the warning as she gazed fondly into his eyes.

"Niver fear, lass." He kissed her hand and stood, the fondness he felt for her in his outlook. "I will manage. Chust take care of yerself. I'll be fine."

In spite of his words of reassurance, he left the room feeling as if he had already set foot on the first step to the scaffold.

****

"It's fortunate it's fancy dress." Lady Anna smiled at him from behind the mask that covered the upper half of her face as he handed her down from the carriage. "No one will be announcing guests. We're only required to show our invitation to a servant at the entrance. Take off that cloak and stow it in the carriage. From the forbidding appearance of the weather, you'll need it on the drive back to the manor. By the bye…" She paused to look up at him. "Why do you call me 'Lady'? I'm sure you know the proper form of address is 'my lady.' "

"Ya might be a lady to a manor born, but yer no' my lady."

"Ah, a sly hint of disrespect." She favored him

with a taunting smirk.

"I feel the right fool, comin' here, makin' a mockery of Highland dress and hidin' my face like a blessed footpad," he muttered, pulling off his cloak.

"Do stop complaining. You'll enjoy yourself… once you get into the spirit of the evening."

"Aye, aye." His muttered assent gave no hint that he would. He stuffed the cloak inside their conveyance. "Bobbie, drive on. I'll send for you when we're ready to leave."

"Yes, sir." Bobbie, proud in his newly acquired coachman's attire, clucked to the team and urged them forward to allow room for the arrival of the next party of ball invitees.

"Stop scowling." She reached up to adjust his headgear. "And do try to keep your cap in place. You've got it all askew, perched on the side of your head."

"It's called a bonnet, and that's the way it's meant to be worn." He jerked back from her ministering hands.

"Is it? Oh, well, I suppose you'd know. Come along. Give me your arm. We've a ball to attend."

The servant who stood at the door to check invitations gave Lex an astonished look as Lady Anna held out the embossed paper. Seeing it quite in order, he moved aside with a bow to admit them.

"So far, so good," she murmured as they advanced into the candlelight of the over-warm ballroom.

"Whit?" He stopped short. "I thought this was a lark, no trouble expected."

"It will be…is. Come along."

Feeling as if his heart was dropping like a stone

into his tongueless shoes, he advanced into the ballroom.

As they entered, Lex immediately became the object of murmurs and glances. Fortunately, the notice was brief and the attention of the assemblage soon returned to music, drink, and dancing. He was just another costumed guest, albeit a rather inappropriately attired one. Culloden Moor had been over fifty years previous. The rebels had been soundly trounced. No one cared about those long ago, barbarian upstarts. He and Lady Anna were absorbed into the crowd. His gut relaxed from some of the knotted tightness that had inflicted it since she'd first shown him his outfit and announced its purpose. Maybe, just maybe, he would survive this night.

Chapter 9

"We'll be going." Lady Anna caught his arm as the dance ended and he bowed to his partner.

"Why?" He swung on her. "The champagne is flowing and the ladies are right beautiful and charming. I'm fair enjoying myself."

"I can see that you are." A whiff of satisfaction wafted over him as he looked down at her pursed lips below the mask. "But the unmasking will be in a few minutes. I doubt you want to be revealed."

"My, my." He let a taunting grin curl his lips. "I do believe you're upset by my success with the ladies."

"Don't be daft!" Her use of one of his favorite words amused him further as she caught at his arm and began to draw him toward the door. "We simply cannot be revealed."

"And here I thought that was the whole point of this adventure." He stopped and refused to move another step.

"Meaning?"

"To give this crowd a shock, to provide them with tales to tell for months to come of how the infamous Lady Anna Spencer came to the ball with her family's groom."

"You thought wrong." She gave him another tug. "If my father finds out, he will not be amused. He'll be completely adamant in enforcing his plans for my future."

"Lady Anna, I believe." The duke himself was suddenly blocking their retreat. He bowed to her, and she, after a slight hesitation, bobbed a curtsey.

"Your Grace?" Her words reeked of innocence.

Lex smirked. *Feigning uncertainty as to his identity.*

"I'm delighted you arrived back from London in time to attend this little soiree." His mouth, smiling beneath his mask, was as stiff as a January frost.

Trouble. Here is trouble. Bloody hell. Lex steeled himself.

"I would not have missed it for the world, Your Grace." She fluttered her fan, her mouth beneath the mask curling into a simpering smile.

"And who is your mysterious companion? In spite of disguises, I believe I've been able to recognize most of my guests. This gentleman, however, evades my recollection."

"A friend from London."

"Sir, may I have the pleasure of meeting you face to face?" His Grace removed his mask and stood squarely in front of Lex.

Lex could see no alternative. He slid away his mask and bowed. "Your Grace."

"Well, well, as I live and breathe! Dunstan's groom, if I'm not very much mistaken. I believe I saw you, sir, on a recent visit to Spencer's stables to meet that fractious stallion of which he's so proud. Lady Anna, whatever have you been up to? I had no idea you could fancy such an…earthy creature." He circled Lex, eyes contemptuously raking over him from head to toe. "Do you know, my dear, I was on the verge of speaking to your father." When he came to stand once more in front of the couple, he continued, "I actually believed you might make a decent duchess, even if you have been a bit nefarious over the years…I do like a bit of spirit in my ladies. But I have to say, one who cavorts with stable lads is a bit too much. Good evening, Lady Anna. I trust your carriage is not far off."

Replacing his mask, he swung away and minced back to his guests.

****

Inside the carriage, they sat in silence as the vehicle, under Bobbie's control, jolted out of the courtyard and headed down the road to Haven Hall.

"That was a lark, was it not?" Looking across at Lex, Anna was the first to speak.

"A lark, indeed." A chuckle rumbled in his throat. "If this is to be my last 'lark' on this earth, it was a right decent one. Fine wine, excellent food…"

"Hoards of ladies simpering to share your company?" she interrupted,

"Not jealous, aire ya, Lady?" In a taunting tone, he let loose his Highland brogue in all its soft, sensuous intensity.

"Of course not!" she snapped. "You're a servant, my father's head groom."

"Oh, aye, of course. However could I forget?"

Again there was silence for a few moments before he continued.

"Is yer father seriously plannin' ta marry ya off to that stick that calls himself a duke?"

"Yes." The word came out in a heaved sigh. "Papa sees it as an excellent match, one that could have the power to settle me down."

"And would it?"

"Hardly." She scoffed. "Did you see the way he strutted off? I could barely contain my mirth."

And suddenly they were chuckling, then outright laughing together.

"I'm thinking it would be a disappointed lass on her wedding night, with the likes of him," he chortled.

"And you would not cause a lady such distress?" She became serious, a taunt in her tone.

"Definitely not…not if I loved the lass and she felt the same about me. For certain sure I would not be marrying her unless such was the case."

For a short time there was silence except for the squeaking, bumping, and groaning of the carriage and Bobbie's voice advising the horses.

Gave her something to think about, I did. He leaned back against the cushions and closed his eyes. Finally, curious, he cautiously raised one lid.

She was adjusting her shawl, fussing with it, ignoring him.

A smirk curled his lips. *She's not the only one who can scuttle a person with words.*

****

"And then he said, 'I trust your carriage is not far off,' and pranced away." In her chemise, giving her best imitation of the duke's mincing steps, Anna crossed her bedchamber to collapse into a gale of laughter on the chair before her mirror.

"Oh, my dear, perhaps this time you've gone too far." Marie sat in her comfortable seat by the bed, a worried frown wrinkling her brow. "You must know your father has plans for you and His Grace. Now…"

"Now I'm out from under that dark cloud, and my

future is once more my own. Oh, Rose, do have a care!" She broke off as her maid began to remove the pins from her coiffure. "I won't have a hair on my head if you continue in this manner."

"I'm sorry, my lady." Rose's words were submissive, but looking into the mirror, Anna saw belligerence in the expression of the young woman standing behind her. London hadn't mellowed her new lady's maid. In fact, it had made her more difficult.

I really must see about replacing her.

"Allow me." Marie got to her feet and hobbled across the room to take the brush from the younger woman. "Rose, see to putting away Lady Anna's gown."

Casting the French woman a contemptuous glance, Rose relinquished her task and swung aside to begin putting Anna's clothing away.

"At any rate," Anna continued, "perhaps Papa will never hear about it. Quite possibly he'll think His Grace has simply changed his mind about asking for my hand."

"Tsk, tsk!" Marie made clucking sounds of dismay as she set about removing the remaining pins from her charge's hair. "You are dreaming, child. Your father and the duke share a deep interest in fine horses. There is no way they will never again be in company, no way your dear Papa will not learn of this night's infamy."

"Marie, Marie, you worry too much. All will be well. But first thing tomorrow morning, Rose, go down to the stable with the clothing Lex left in the guest bedroom. I doubt he has many changes of garments, and he can't go to work in full Highland kit."

An image of the groom, his legs and feet bare,

chest and shoulders broad and hard beneath that worn shirt that dangled to his knees, dashed across her mind. My, my, he was, as the duke had said, an earthy creature.

"As you wish, milady." The words flat, empty of any willingness to comply, brought Anna back to the moment.

Damned girl! I'll be glad to see the back of her!

A fit of coughing interrupted her thoughts. Marie had doubled over. Anna jumped to her feet, put an arm around her, and helped her to the chair by the bed. The woman's pallor had turned gray, nearly green in distress.

"Dear, dear Marie!" She knelt beside her, heart pounding with fear. "You are unwell. I'll send one of the stable lads to fetch the doctor. I'll…"

"No, no, child." Marie caught Anna's hand as she made to rise to carry out her words. "A doctor cannot be of any assistance. Get the bottle from my bedside. That is all that can help…now."

"Yes, yes, of course. Rose"—Anna turned to her maid, who'd paused in her chores and was staring at the pair—"run to Mademoiselle Marie's room and bring back whatever medicines you can find. Hurry!" she snapped when the young woman hesitated.

By the time Rose had returned, flask in hand, the old woman lay back in the chair, breathing heavily.

"Drink this, dear Marie." Anna opened the bottle and held it to the woman's lips.

She sipped, then leaned back once more, her distress seemingly eased.

"Rest." Anna leaned forward to plant a kiss on the wrinkled cheek.

"Yes, rest…a little rest is all I need." Her eyes closed, and she appeared to be drifting off to sleep.

Anna placed the medicine on a table, took a quilt from her bed, and gently covered the elderly woman. She was relieved to see that her color was returning to normal. Perhaps all would be well. It had to be. She couldn't imagine what she would do without her beloved Marie.

"We shan't disturb her," she whispered to Rose. "You may go. I'll watch over her."

"As you wish, my lady." Again that same annoying, condescending tone.

****

"What were you thinking?" Sir Maxwell's face glared at her, distorted with outrage. "Taking Lex to the ball…and dressed as a Highlander? And you, Marie, facilitating this madness! I expected better of you!"

"I'm sorry, my lord." The Frenchwoman dropped her gaze to her clasped hands.

She and Anna stood before the outraged aristocrat in the dining room. Her father, newly returned from London, was red-faced and breathing hard.

"You certainly should be!"

"Papa, please," Anna interceded. "Marie is not to blame. It was entirely my idea. She was only following my instructions."

"Well, she should have known better." He swung back on his daughter. "Good God! You couldn't have more effectively ruined your chances with His Grace if you'd run him down with a carriage!"

"What an absolutely delicious idea!"

"Is that your response? An absolutely delicious idea? In an earlier age, you'd be confined to your room until you came to your senses and agreed to marry the man!"

"Oh, dearest Papa, do calm down. His Grace simply recognized Lex as your groom. That was quite enough to outrage him."

"Are you so naive as not to realize that Lex is a deserter from His Majesty's army? How else could he have been free to bring Archie home? And just what do you think might be the penalty for him—never mind for me, a former army officer, if it's discovered I'm harboring such a fugitive?"

He turned and crossed the room to the liquor cabinet.

"I can see there's no reasoning with you this morning." She headed for the door. "Come, Marie. I bid you good day, Papa."

Chapter 10

In her room, Anna began to pull clothing from drawers and wardrobe.

"What are you doing, child?" Marie watched her, fear in her voice.

"I'm going to America." She continued to strew personal items across the wide bed. "Fetch a pair of bags that may be tied to my saddle. Oh, and don't let Rose see you. The less that one knows, the better."

"Child, you cannot attempt such a journey alone! It would be madness!"

"What would be madness, my dear Marie, would be to stay here and have my father force me into a marriage with His Grace. No, I must go. I'll leave tonight, under cover of darkness."

As she returned to her task of sorting through her clothing, Marie shook her head ruefully and turned away.

****

"You must go with her." In the stable, Marie confronted Lex. "Please. I'm begging you!"

"To America? Mademoiselle, you must be daft. Do you know what the penalty would be for running off with a woman such as Lady Anna? The charge would be abducting if not kidnapping. If caught, I'd be hung!"

Remembrance of his promise to Archie snagged in his mind. Still, when he'd made it, he'd never thought she'd actually do anything so mad.

"But not in America. In America, you'd be free. You'd no longer be a servant, or a fugitive. Think of it."

"No. If Lady is daft enough to run away, let her do so. Alone, she won't get far. Her father has more than enough resources to run her to ground before she leaves the county."

He turned back to his chore of trimming the hooves of one of the carriage horses.

"Very well." The elderly Frenchwoman turned slowly away. "I thought you were a man of honor, a man who would protect the weak…and the sometimes feckless. I was wrong."

Lex paused in his task to watch her go, her shoulders slumping under the black gown. He owed her, he realized. She'd saved his life. But not that headstrong siren who would only further endanger him if he cast his lot in with hers. He went back to trimming the hoof.

****

"They've come!" An hour later Marie, her face taut with fear, stumped back into the stable as fast as her legs, supported by a cane, could carry her. "You must go at once! There's a deserted hovel a half mile along the bridle trail that runs to the left of the stable. It's hidden in the trees. Go there and wait! I'll bring a horse and provisions after dark."

"What?" Lex stared at her. "What are you talking about, Mademoiselle? Who has come?"

"The redcoat soldiers! Even now, their officer is conferring with Sir Maxwell. They've heard rumors of a man who brought Master Archie home. You must go, and quickly!"

"God Almighty!"

"This is no time for blasphemy! Go! Run!"

"Thank you, lass." He paused only long enough to plant a kiss on Marie's cheek before bolting out of the stable and starting across the pasture land in the long, loping strides that had taken him away from capture many times in the Highlands. In his hand he gripped the cudgel, the only weapon available.

****

He jerked alert to a hand on his shoulder. Reflexively he lurched to his feet, cudgel pulled back, ready to deliver a blow.

"Lex, Lex, it is I, Anna."

The hissed identification stopped his arm in mid swing.

"Whit? Whit in God's name…?"

"Come along. We're leaving."

As he became able to focus in the midnight darkness, he saw a slim figure in male attire beside him, silhouetted against the open doorway of the hovel. A pistol protruded from her belt, and a dagger scabbard hung at her side. A smaller, slightly stooped figure stood beside her.

"Lady? Mademoiselle?"

"Yes, yes, of course. Who did you think it might be?" The words snapped with impatience. "Don't stand there gaping. We have to be on our way."

"But first…" The Frenchwoman stopped them as she drew something from the sleeve of her gown. "I have a request."

In the shadows cast by the moonlight, Lex saw it was a ragged-edged parchment.

"This is a map, the map my uncle Etienne

Bouchard entrusted to me many years ago just before he died." She held it out to Anna. "It indicates the location of the treasure I told you about, my dear child. It lies in the bay near where your sister lives. It would delight my heart if you were to find it, to prove its existence and that my beloved uncle was not merely a deranged old man spinning tales."

"Marie, of course!" Anna took the document from the woman. "A quest! Lex, we're to go on a quest as well as an escape." She paused to hug Marie. "I shall guard it with my life, and once in America we will find this treasure and send you proof of its existence." She tucked it into the top of her shirt. "It will be safe there…won't it, Lex?"

In the shadowy light, he saw her cock her head in his direction. He made a derisive snort.

"Do not forget the pendant," the woman continued urgently. "If you rescue nothing more than the jeweled C-shaped pendant, it will be enough. It will prove that the treasure exists and belonged to the trollop Charlotte."

"I will remember, my dearest Marie." Anna hugged her. "You shall have your pendant."

"Treasure, what treasure?" Lex wasn't following the topic of their conversation.

"Nothing you have to be concerned with at the moment." Lady Anna brushed their remarks aside. "I'll tell you about it later. For now, we must concentrate on our escape."

"Woman, yer daft!" Lex felt a whirling sense of unreality. "This whole idea is insane. Passage across the Atlantic costs dear, even in steerage. Where do ya expect to get the means?"

"This will assure us both a comfortable voyage." From an inside pocket of her jerkin, she pulled something that glittered in the moonlight. "Remember this bauble?" She waved it before his astounded eyes. "Its stones should fetch a pretty penny."

"You've no' stolen it from your father?" Appalled, he recognized the necklace she'd worn to the ball. Infamies were piling on infamies. From what he so far knew of this woman, he wouldn't put purloining jewels beyond her.

"Of course not." Casting him a smug glance, she replaced it in her pocket. "I told you about it on the night of the ball. It's mine, given to me by a persistent suitor who thought he could buy himself a bride, a lady, no less. Men who've become rich in trade are often eager to join the aristocracy no matter what the cost. Today I convinced Papa's steward to fetch it from my father's strongbox on the pretext that I wanted to see if it would set off a new gown I'd recently purchased."

"The pillock who gave it to you must have thought you a right prize."

"And you don't."

"I think you a great pain in the arse."

"That being said, I think it's best you take the pistol." She pulled it free and handed it to him. "I'm not quite certain how to fire it. I assume you do?"

He hesitated, then, with a guffaw, took it and shoved it into his belt. *So my role as protector starts now.*

"We must go." She turned to give Marie a final hug before she swung on Lex. "I have horses and provisions outside. Now, are you coming, or would you rather stay here and face a bunch of soldiers ready to drag you kicking and screaming back to prison?"

"Hardly kicking and screaming," he muttered, but he followed her outside to where a pair of horses bearing packed bags waited, both fitted with similar saddles.

"Ya'll be ridin' astride?"

"Dressed as I am and hoping to pass for a young man, I could hardly do otherwise. Take this." She took a sword in its scabbard with a belt from one of the horse's saddles and moved close to hand it to him. "I've no doubt you know how to use it, as well."

He hesitated as an inane thought struck him. Where was that exotic scent he'd come to associate with her? God almighty! Did it matter? All that should concern him at the moment was getting away.

Slinging the belt over his shoulder and across his chest, he felt the familiar heft. Familiar and disconcerting. He didn't want to fight any more. He was weary of fighting. Maybe in America…

"Come on, come on!" She swung onto the mare he recognized as Silverbell and jerked her hand toward the other horse, which he saw was Storm. "We've not got all night to dally! Farewell, Marie. Rest assured we'll find that trollop's treasure and send you back that pendant as proof."

****

As they rode through the night, Lex damned himself for a fool. He'd allowed himself to be coerced into this mad caper. Still, he couldn't think of any viable alternative. The only other destination to which he might run was the Highlands of Scotland, but he'd be endangering family and friends if the redcoats tracked him and sought to extract knowledge of his whereabouts from them.

As his anger and frustration cooled in the night air, he began to have other thoughts. She had the means of financing a voyage to America, and there he'd be free, truly free after months, even years of running, of being a fugitive. He could start a new life. Putting his heels to Storm's sides, he urged the horse abreast of her mare.

But I'm not about to let this brazen creature run my life any further. No, indeed. Or entice me into some mad quest to find a mythical treasure. Once we're aboard that ship, I'll be in charge of this undertaking.

"Which way now, Lex?" She reined to a halt. They'd come to a fork in the road. No road sign indicated direction.

"Aire ya not knowin', ya who was so clever as ta seduce a man out of a king's ransom in jewels, so clever as ta draw another man away from a secure home and inta a mad adventure that may well cost him his life?" Annoyance urged him to speak in his native dialect.

"Oh, stop it, Lex! A secure home indeed! A horse stall in a stable with every day the possibility of a visit from soldiers? Do stop complaining and point us toward Portsmouth. And drop that Highland brogue. I don't want you arrested as a rebel the moment we arrive in the town."

"Portsmouth?"

"Of course. Where did you think we were bound? I've been told there are any number of ships leaving the town almost daily for America. That's where we're to book our passage. That's where you'll sell a few stones from my necklace to finance our endeavor."

"Sell yer necklace? Sweet Jesus, woman, yer ideas

become more daft with each passing hour. Do ya think anyone will buy such a piece without askin' any number of unanswerable questions?"

"Don't be ridiculous. Weren't you listening? Of course you won't sell the necklace as it is. Once we get to Portsmouth, we'll find an inn, take rooms, and you'll pry out some of the stones. Then you can sell them individually about the town. And buy yourself some decent clothing. I won't have you accompanying me to America dressed in those rags. Now, which way?" She returned to her original subject. "I have a feeling that, come morning, when I'm not down to breakfast, Papa will begin to search. I'm hoping that by midday we'll be safely aboard a ship and well out over the Atlantic."

"Chust how far do you think it is to Portsmouth?" Her lack of knowledge surprised him.

"A few more miles."

"Woman, it's a good deal more than a single night's journey. Even if we could ride these beasts without stopping—which I will not allow—it would take us until Thursday to reach the town."

"Damn!" In the moonlight, he saw annoyance in her expression. "Well, let's get on with it. Again, which way?"

****

"We'll rest here." As dawn brightened the sky, Lex turned Storm off the trail and down into a stand of trees. Once they were hidden from the road, he dismounted and led his horse to a stream that burbled through the forest. He didn't turn back to assist Anna. She'd pushed herself into this escape. Now she would be treated as an equal partner.

Walking, she joined him, leading Silverbell to the

water. The mare lowered her head to drink.

"How much farther?" she asked, watching her mount enjoy the fresh water.

"We made good time last night. We'll rest here until darkness, then take to the trail once more. If we keep up a steady pace, I'm thinking we'll make Portsmouth by the following dawn." He sniffed as she came near to him. "You smell right different."

"What?" She swung on him, astonishment in her expression.

"I chust said you smell different." Sorry he'd spoken reflexively, he mumbled the statement a second time.

"Ah, my perfume." She cast him a coquettish glance. "You liked it, did you?"

"That hardly matters." He turned his attention to Storm.

"Well, dressed as I am, I can hardly go about with that kind of scent wafting from me, can I?"

"I suppose not."

"I must say, I'm delighted you haven't retained your former odor. That horse liniment was more than a bit off-putting."

"At least it served a decent purpose." Her taunting suddenly chafed him to the bone. "I wasn't using it to enhance my charms."

"Enhance your charms! Are you implying I was wearing that scent simply to attract the likes of you? Well, let me tell you…"

"We've no time for bickering. See ta your mare. I trust you've brought food?"

"Enough for a meal." She heaved a sigh. "I had no idea we'd have more than one night's travel ahead of us. I thought if we rode hard…"

"And winded these fine beasts," he scoffed.

"Very well, be sarcastic." She turned to lead Silverbell away from the stream. "Even with only a single repast available, I'm sure you'd agree it's better than being in the hands of redcoats."

****

Later, as they sat in the growing dawn sharing bread, cheese, and, from a pair of flasks, some of the finest French wine Lex had ever tasted, while the horses grazed on a small bit of grass nearby, he drew a deep breath of the cool spring air and thought this was what freedom, true freedom might feel like. In spite of his misgivings about his companion, the prospect of America had begun to tantalize him. A new life, a new identity, peace…

"Who are you, Lex?" she asked suddenly.

"What do you mean? I'm Lex. I was your father's head groom." He turned what he hoped was an indignant gaze on her.

"No, I mean really. Surely Lex isn't your actual name. Sometimes you act like a barbarian, yet you play chess and can behave like a gentleman when the need arises. You must have family somewhere, a family that taught you how to conduct yourself in polite company, who gave you an education."

"You know all you need to know about me." The words came out gruff, and he took another quaff of wine before continuing, "This is fine stuff."

"Ah, there! You know good wine when you taste it. It's some of the best from Papa's cellar. More evidence that you weren't born to be a servant…or a footpad forced to be a soldier."

"I only know it pleases my palate. And it doesn't taste like any of the local piss. Ya were wise ta put it into flasks. Bottles wouldn't have lasted, the way we've been riding."

"I do have some good ideas. Now, come, Lex. Tell me at least a bit of your past. We're about to embark on the adventure of a lifetime. You know about me and my past. Surely I have a right to know something of yours."

"Verrae well." He quaffed another mouthful of wine and began, "I grew up in the Highlands. I had good parents. They sent me to be educated in France. Perhaps I learned more than I should have during my years there. By the time I returned home at age sixteen, I wasn't interested in becoming a farmer like my father. I fell in with a group of young lads bent on raising hell."

He paused.

"Go on." Her expression was bright with interest, eagerness.

"At first, our escapades consisted mostly of pilfering a few bottles from local taverns, getting drunk, and generally acting like idiots." He paused to look up into the trees. A slight smile quirked his lips as he remembered those days. Finally, he sobered and continued. "Over time, it got more serious. We started stealing cattle, and then horses. Mounted, we were no longer regarded as footpads but had become full blown highwaymen, with prices on our heads."

"But you didn't get caught." Her words reflected her excitement at the tale.

"My companions did. I managed to escape into the hills." He frowned as he looked over at her. "Ya seem to be enjoying the tale, but let me tell ya, Lady, it's no a pleasant life, living like a hunted animal, cold and wet and more than often near starving, not yer idea of a nice little adventure."

"No, no, it wouldn't be." Her compassionate words surprised him as did her change in expression. She'd suddenly become grave. "It must have been lonely, having lost your companions and not being able to return to your family. I assume you were eventually caught. That is how you ended up being taken out of prison and forced into the army?"

"Aye." He heaved an exasperated sigh. "Now if ya know enough ta satisfy yer raging curiosity, perhaps ya'll oblige by telling me about this treasure Mademoiselle Marie is so dead set on us findin'?"

"Very well." She settled back. "Here is the story as she told it to me."

When she'd finished, he gave a derisive snort. "Trollop's treasure, indeed. An old wives' tale if ever I heard one. I'll no' go chasin' after such a fantasy."

"Not even to give dear Marie's hopes vindication?" She looked at him, green eyes wide with appeal.

"Ya brought victuals for more than one meal…or several." An appropriate reply eluding him, he looked down at what remained of their food. "Did ya also see fit to pack blankets, even though ya weren't expectin' to be sleepin' in the forest?"

"I brought several." She gave an annoyed toss of her head. "I've heard there are few such comforts available for passengers aboard ships."

"Well, then, wrap yourself up in one and get some rest. We'll continue our journey as soon as darkness falls."

"You'll be needing one as well. You have only

your clothing…and they're worn thin."

"I'm accustomed to sleeping rough." He handed her the flask, rolled a saddle cloth into a semblance of a pillow, and turned his back to her to lie down and stretch out, hopefully to sleep.

He heard her exasperated sigh, then sounds of her preparing to do his bidding. He started abruptly as he felt the sensation of a blanket being dropped over him.

Chapter 11

"Argh!" He awoke to her half cry, half scream and bolted to his feet, hand grasping the pistol that had lain close beside him.

"Whit…?" He scanned the sunny surroundings as she flung herself against him, her arms grasping his neck.

"Over there!" She pointed to the place where she'd made her bed. "Oh, God, Lex, it was awful!"

"It? It? Whit…?" Not catching a glimpse of anything to cause her outburst, he looked down at her as she huddled against his chest.

"Something…small and warm and squirming…I think it might have been a mouse."

"A mouse!" Relief flooded through him. "A bloody mouse! God almighty, woman!"

"Lex, you have no idea how awful it is to wake up to find something like that against you." She looked up at him, green eyes wide and, for the first time since he'd known her, frightened.

Resistance left him, and he gathered her into his arms, the pistol in his hand behind her back. And suddenly he was kissing her, kissing her with all the pent-up passion he'd been feeling since she'd entered her father's study that spring evening, since he'd first caught sight of her. He desired her in every particle of his being, and now, here, starting out on a wild adventure, she'd thrown herself into his arms…

And she, after an initial moment of surprise, was returning his ardor but with a naiveté he hadn't expected…as if it were the first time she'd been truly kissed by a man, as if she was discovering a new territory, a new region she was far from disdaining but actually eager to explore.

"No." With an emotional wrenching that had it been physical would have left him bruised and bloody, he released her and moved her out and away from him.

"No?" Her response was a startled gasp.

"No." He dropped back down onto his improvised bed. "Get some rest. It's noon already, and we ride again at dusk."

"Lex…"

"Go."

With a huff, she swung away. A moment later he heard her rustling about as she settled back into her sleeping area.

Damn it! All but undone by a bloody mouse!

****

"Robert Burns called a mouse a wee cowerin' beastie." His equilibrium returned as they rode through the early evening darkness. "Nothing to get afeared of."

"I don't care what a drunken Scottish poet called the creatures." He glanced over to see her square her shoulders. "They're nasty things that slither over one."

"Not slither, Lady. That would be a snake. A wee mousie can only scamper…like a kitten or puppy."

"At any rate, I don't like them and never will." She tossed her head, golden-red curls once again concealed under her cap. "But at least it gave you an opportunity to take advantage me, didn't it?"

"Whit?" They'd been riding abreast. Now he urged Storm ahead that he might grab Silverbell's bridle and halt both horses. "Take advantage of you? Lady, I've had a bit of experience with lasses, enough to recognize a willing one when I encounter such."

"Are you saying I welcomed your advances, that I would have gone even further?" Her anger blazed out at him. "Are you saying I'm as common as a trollop?"

"I'm sayin' "—his tone took on a soft Highland lilt—"that I believe you're as attracted ta me as I am ta you."

"Really, sir, you flatter yourself," she scoffed. "Release my mare at once."

"Very well." He did as she commanded, but as she put her heels to its sides and headed off up the road, he called after her, "I'm chust sayin', we must not let this go any further. It won't bode well for either of us."

He clucked to Storm and sent the gelding in pursuit.

****

"Hie, there! Hold up!" In the star-lighted darkness, two figures, their faces hidden behind crude burlap masks, leaped onto the trail in front of them. Startled, the horses snorted and pranced as they drew rein. Anna saw one brandished a sword and the other had a bow, an arrow in its taut string aimed in their direction. Her hand went to the dagger at her belt.

"Your money or your life!" the second robber ordered.

"Good evenin' ta ya, lads." Lex's response astonished her. "A right fine night, is it not?"

"A right fine night for killing you both," the one holding the sword replied.

"Easy now, easy," Lex continued in his calm Highland brogue. "We've nothin' worth takin'. We're just a couple of poor folk on our way ta America with only the clothes on our backs."

"You've more than your rags," the second brigand, holding the bow, said, taking a step closer. "That's a pair of fine horses you're riding. They'll fetch a decent price."

"Aw, ya dunnae want this one." Anna saw Lex's heels sliding into position along Storm's sides, his hands tightening on the reins. "He's a right fractious beastie. There's nary another besides myself that can handle him. Only last week he kicked a stable lad near ta death."

"None of your tales. Get down!" The sword holder stepped up to take Storm's bridle. Lex's heels hit Storm's sides. The gelding snorted, rearing up and into the robber. The bandit, his mask knocked off, tumbled to the ground. An arrow flashed through the air, ripping the arm of Lex's shirt.

Anna, taking her cue from her companion, leaped Silverbell into this second robber before he could pull another arrow from his quiver. He, too, was sent sprawling, losing his mask in the process.

Why, they're nothing but boys. Anna could barely believe her eyes as she brought Silverbell to a prancing halt. *A pair of boys, surely no more than sixteen at the most, gaunt and scrawny.*

With a swift, lithe movement, Lex leaped to the ground and confiscated the sword that had been thrown from the bandit's hand when Storm hit him.

"Now, my fine laddie." Lex towered over him, holding the weapon. "Let us be civil. And you there"—

he addressed the second robber as he sat in the dust, cradling his arm where Silverbell had struck him—"don't even think of taking up that bow again. I can remove your friend's head with a single blow." He paused, looking the pair over before continuing in such a consolatory tone it astonished Anna. "Aire ya hungry? We have a wee bit of cheese and bread that might fit right good into yer gut."

"We're not beggars!" the one who had held the sword snapped.

"I niver said ya were, but I've done without sustenance myself for longer than it felt comfortable." He held down a hand to help the lad to his feet. "Come now. A meal will do ya the world of good."

The lad ignored Lex's offer of help and stumbled to his feet. He was not yet about to trust this big man with the Highland accent.

"Archie," Lex turned to Anna, who was still garbed in her male attire, hair concealed under her cap. "Give these brave lads what food we have left. We'll be in town by mornin' and able to get more. Meanwhile"—he stepped over to the fallen archer and picked up the bow—"I'll chust be confiscatin' these weapons. I'll leave them for ya up the road a bit after we're once more on our way."

Following Lex's instructions, Anna dismounted and opened the saddlebags carrying the remains of their last meal. A quantity of bread and cheese had been left over. She held these out to the boys and was appalled as she had a chance to closer scrutinize their thin, ragged figures. *Poor boys! Driven to crime by hunger!*

"We aren't beggars," the one who'd held the sword repeated.

"Of course you're not." She made her voice as gruff as she could. "And my friend here isn't a Highlander with redcoats hot on his trail," she continued sarcastically in an effort to gain their confidence. Lex had made his heritage no secret in speaking to them. "Have you ever heard of Highland Harry?"

"Highland Harry? That be you, sir?" The archer had come to his feet and now stood staring at Lex, awe in his tone.

"I was a bit of a lad back home." Lex's tone was light. "Now take the food. Archie and I have ta be on our way."

"Before those bleedin' bastards catch up with you." The archer took the sacks from Anna. "Thank you, sir. We're obliged…Harry."

"Chust keep this encounter ta yourselves, and I'll consider the favor returned. And here"—he pulled a few coins from a pocket in his breeches—"buy some provisions for yer family. I reckon as how ya look enough alike to deem ya brothers."

Lex caught up Storm's reins and, with the boys' weapons still in hand, swung into the saddle. "Pull your arse onta yer beast, Archie. We have to get the hell out of here."

"Thank you, sir. Many thanks," the archer called after them as they rode off. A few yards down the trail, Lex dropped the sword and bow to one side before urging Storm into a spritely trot.

"You got us out of that problem rather smoothly." Anna rode up to keep abreast of him. "However, I'm not sure that rewarding their criminal venture was the proper thing to do."

"Did ya not see how scrawny they were?" he snapped. "Mere lads, so hungry they were willin' ta try anything to survive. I've no doubt there's a passel of young brothers and sisters at home, and probably a ne'er-do-well father given to the drink or scrambling to make a living out of a poor bit of a tenant farm. They were desperate."

"Perhaps you're right." For a few moments she rode in silence before continuing. "But where did you get those coins you gave them? I thought you were a pauper."

"Dunnae forget I was gainfully employed on your father's estate. He paid me."

"But not all that well, I'll wager. I'm thinking you gave your entire earnings to those boys."

"So whit if I did?" He paused Storm, slanting the gelding across the mare's path to bring her to a halt as well. He glared at her. "Ya've got that suitor's fancy necklace, haven't ya? What need do we have of my few paltry coins? And by the bye, what gave ya the idea of introducing me ta those lads as Highland Harry?"

"I've heard he was once the scourge of the Highlands." She shrugged. "And with that accent you were displaying, I thought those young lads might be impressed by the idea that they'd met the rogue himself."

"An outlaw who hasn't been heard of in this country nor Scotland for several years, who's quite possibly dead and buried…"

With a jerk on the reins, he turned Storm away and urged him into a gallop.

Anna hesitated a moment, then clucked Silverbell into pursuit. She'd injured his male ego by inferring he was a pauper. She wouldn't do it again.

Their encounter with the young footpads had given even further knowledge of this man to whom she'd entrusted her future safety. He was as clever as he was physically strong. He could rightly judge a situation and use his brain to plot a way out of it. Although she felt confident he was perfectly capable of violence, he'd proven it wasn't his first line of defense.

****

"We'll have a pair of your best rooms, landlord." Anna pulled her cap from her head, letting free a flood of golden-red hair as she dropped a pair of coins on the counter. They'd arrived in Portsmouth shortly after dawn after a long night's ride.

Behind her, their saddlebags slung over his shoulders, Lex stared. He'd had no idea she had any financial means aside from the necklace and its gems that had yet to be sold. Now here they stood in one of the best inns the port town had to offer while she demanded fine accommodation with more than generous compensation. The lass was full of surprises.

The landlord had been staring at her unusual attire, but with the dropping of the coins on his counter, his attention fell on them.

"Of course, mistress." He looked up at her and favored her with a cordial smile. "There is a pair at the top of the stairs."

"We've left our horses with your hostler," she continued with all the arrogance of her class. "I trust you'll see to it they are well tended?"

"Of course, mistress, of course, only the best of care."

"Thank you. Come along, Lex. I'm weary and

dusty from our journey. Landlord, please see that hot water is sent to both of our rooms."

"At once, mistress. This way, mistress." The landlord was leading the way toward the stairs, half bowing as he sidled across the room.

With a sardonic grin, Lex adjusted their saddlebags on his shoulder and followed. Money definitely did hold sway.

****

"You may put my belongings in here, Lex." After perusing the two rooms, she indicated the larger and better furnished one. "Landlord, I trust that hot water won't be long in coming and that you have decent fare to offer in the way of a repast once we've refreshed ourselves? We've traveled far and are dusty and hungry."

"Of course, mistress. At once, mistress." The rotund man turned and hurried back down the stairs.

Anna sauntered into the room she'd chosen and gave the bed a pat.

"Decent," she said.

"Where did you get those coins?" He strode inside to throw the saddlebags on the bed.

"My father has always seen to it I have sufficient finances to handle an emergency." She sauntered to the window and shoved aside the curtains, letting in a flood of early morning sunlight. "Did you think I stole them?" She stood watching the traffic below in the busy street.

"Any woman who'd venture into a brothel on the vague excuse of curiosity…" He planted his feet shoulder-width apart and crossed his arms. "You never did tell me the rest of that story."

"Nothing much more to the tale." She shrugged. "I've already told you the man I subdued ordered me detained in an attic room until he could bring me before a magistrate in the morning."

"Did he…bring you before a magistrate in the morning?"

"Of course not!" She swung to face him, a wicked twinkle in her eyes. "My stay in that prison was brief. I escaped through a window and made my way back to the house where I was a guest of a friend of my mother's…who, by the way, is also a woman not averse to adventures."

"It appears you don't have a great deal of common sense." He cast her a disgusted look before turning toward the door. "I can only hope you'll show more restraint on the voyage. Otherwise, the captain of whatever vessel on which we manage to book passage may feel justified in throwing you overboard."

"Wait!" She stopped him. "You can't go yet." She reached inside her shirt and removed the necklace. "First, we must pry out whatever jewels you think necessary to provide for our voyage. Then you will go out to sell them…and purchase decent clothing for yourself. I won't have my companion looking like a vagabond."

"Vagabond!" He swung on her. "Might I say you hardly look a lady, at the moment."

"I admit, I do miss the services of a lady's maid"—she sighed—"although the last woman to fill that position left much to be desired. Do you know, when I was in London, she spent every moment she could manage to sneak away from her duties with a footman named Mitchell?"

"She's a young woman, no doubt with the desires of most young women. You can understand." He couldn't resist making the comment flavored with innuendo, not after how she'd behaved in the forest, not after she'd brought him near the breaking point.

"Don't defend her." He was pleased to see a blush spreading up her cheeks as she tossed the necklace to him. He caught it in a hand long trained to lightning swiftness. "Be a good laddie and get to the task at hand. I want to have the financial means to tempt a ship's captain to take us aboard by evening…if not sooner."

"Your servant, Lady." With a bow, he stuffed the jewelry inside his shirt. "I'll find an instrument, go to my room, and set to the task. I'll not have you badgering me over it."

"But don't forget"—she stopped him as he once more made to leave—"wash and make yourself as presentable as possible. You'll find your bargaining will be much more productive if you look at least halfway civilized."

"Is there anything else, Lady?" He put mockery into his words.

"No, that will be all." She sank down on the bed and looked at her soiled hands. "My, my, I can do with cleaning myself. I'm as filthy as the lowest street trollop."

"A trollop wouldn't be so demanding." He couldn't resist the comeback as he turned to leave the room. "Is there anything else?"

"Please tell the landlord to send food to my room. I have no desire to eat downstairs among the common rabble."

Chapter 12

Once the water arrived, Anna barred the door and stripped herself of her dusty traveling apparel. Naked, she washed herself from head to toe, then donned the one nightshift she'd packed. With a contented sigh, she sank down on the bed to free her hair from its pins and began to brush it about her shoulders. It wasn't an easy task.

With a sigh, she had to admit she missed the services of a lady's maid, at least one like Marie. Rose she could do without. When a servant tapped on her door to inform her of the arrival of her meal, she instructed her to leave it outside, saying she would fetch it herself. She wasn't about to dress again simply to admit a servant.

After she'd eaten, she stretched out on the bed. She hadn't meant to sleep, but after the long ride and now clean, fed, and refreshed, she drifted off.

She woke to a knocking on the door.

"It's Lex. Let me in."

How long have I been sleeping? How has he fared? From the length of the shadows spreading across the room, she assumed evening was approaching.

She scrambled from the bed and across the room to disbar the door. Opening it, she received a surprise that, for a moment, left her speechless.

Lex, clean and garbed in new, well-fitted breeches,

shirt, vest, and coat, looked a proper English gentleman. Freshly barbered and clean shaven, he was a man who would easily capture any woman's eye.

As she came out of her initial shock, she realized he was staring back at her. And small wonder. There she stood before him in her nightshift. In an attempt at modesty, she wrapped her arms about her.

"Come in." She stepped back to allow his entry and managed to regain her self control. "I assume from your attire that you had success in selling at least a few of the stones."

"That I did." He accepted her invitation, closed the door after him, and took a moment to run his gaze over her before he went to the bureau. There he pulled a small bag from inside his waistcoat pocket and dumped out a heap of gold coins on its surface. "I also managed to find a tailor who had two suits of clothing that fit me right down to the ground. He'd made it for a gentleman who failed to come back to claim his purchases…taken off to prison for stealing, the tradesman later learned." He looked down at the coins. "I believe this will more than suffice to pay our passage and any other needs we might have."

"Oh, Lex, this is wonderful." She went to stand beside him and stare down at the largess. "We can begin searching for a ship as soon as we've had our supper! We may even be able to sail this evening!"

"I doubt it, Lady. Tomorrow at the earliest, if I know anything of tides." His tone was gruff as he turned to look at her with those amazing blue eyes.

"Have you eaten?" In an effort to defuse the situation, she asked the mundane question.

"Aye, in the common room below."

"And enjoyed more than a few ales?" Her first remarks hadn't taken away the effect of his virile appearance, of those penetrating sapphire eyes. She struggled to make this second query sound sarcastic.

"Aye, and more than a few ales." That sensuous Highland lilt colored his words.

Her heart began to thunder at her ribs as she looked up at him. If she'd thought him appealing previously, now she found him nearly irresistible. She remembered how the ladies at the duke's fancy dress ball had flocked to dance with him. But most of all she recalled that kiss in the forest…a kiss the utter sensuousness of which she could never have imagined, a kiss that was forever imprinted in her mind…

"Whit?" He continued in the Highland inflection that made butterflies flutter in her innards. "You're staring, Lady."

"You've made a remarkable transformation." With an effort, she turned away in pretended indifference. "Now, off with you. We are both in need of a decent night's rest. And I"—she picked up the brush she'd left on the bureau—"I must try to bring order to this mass."

With an exasperated sigh, she sat down on the single chair the room had to offer and set to work. "Damn!"

"Allow me." He took the brush from her hands. His fingers skimming her skin, he drew her hair back over her shoulders and began to draw the brush through her tangled curls. His big hands, hands she'd seen grip a sword with threatening intent and handle a fractious stallion with expert ability, now moved as tenderly, as skillfully, as those of a lady's well-trained maid in restoring order to her hair. His actions tempted her, brought back memories of their previous intimate encounters, and left her longing for more.

"It appears you've had practice at this chore." She squared her shoulders as she fought to contain the flutter of pure, erotic pleasure his ministrations were sending charging through her. She had to struggle to speak normally.

"Aye." He continued to ease the brush through her hair. The word came out with the soft inflection she found totally arousing.

"So there have been ladies in your life who required such…services?" She put emphasis on the final word.

"At times." The brush slid through the curls, down her back.

"Many?" The question was out before she could stop it.

"That's no' yer business, Lady." He stroked again.

"Isn't it?" She came to her feet, whirling on him. "I should like to know exactly what type of roué I'm travelling with!"

"I think we both know all we need to know about each other." Still holding the brush, he stood looking down at her, his gaze so intense she found herself drowning in it, not caring how many women had been in his past, interested only in the moment and to what it might lead.

"Lex." Her arms went up and about his neck, her lips parted in invitation. He accepted, drawing her to him, opening his mouth in a reply she willingly accepted.

His hands slid down her back to encompass her bottom, to press her against him so intimately she could feel his desire rising against her belly. Her senses swirled—she was floating, whisked away into an erotic world where there was only this magnificent, mysterious warrior and herself.

"Lady." He breathed the name he'd chosen to call her against her hair as he released her lips and moved his mouth to her neck. "God almighty, Lady!" The last words were a near moan. The next moment she was standing alone, a cold draft washing between them as he stepped back, out of her arms, to stare down at her, a scowl disfiguring his handsome features.

"Lex, what…?" Staggered by the sudden change, she stared up at him.

"This will no' happen again." His jaw worked in a tick, his features becoming rock hard. "Yer no' the kind of woman a man tarries with. I've promised the old Frenchwoman I'll care for ya, and I will. I owe her a great debt. Takin' ya ta bed would be a betrayal of that vow. So good night ta ya, Lady. We must be ready ta sail in the mornin'." He turned toward the door. "I'll be seeing ya at daybreak." He threw the brush on the bed and strode out.

****

"Captain Marston?" Lex stood back as Anna stepped up to the gray-haired man seated at a table in the tavern. "The barkeep pointed you out."

Surprise registering on his weathered face, the man looked up at the young woman in breeches, shirt, jerkin, and riding boots. Her left hand held a riding quirt, while her right she extended to him.

"You *are* Captain Edgar Marston?" Giving him a perusing scrutiny, she cocked her head to one side.

"Aye, aye." He scrambled to his feet to accept her

introduction. "And you would be?"

"Anna…Smith." Lex, decked out in his new clothing, stifled a smirk at her stumble over her last name. *Almost tripped yourself up there, didn't you, Lady?*

"Your servant, ma'am. How may I help you?" Captain Marston recovered from his surprise to regain his manners.

"I wish to book passage for myself and my servant on your ship. I've been told you're bound for Riverhaven, New Brunswick." She sat down at the table. "Please be seated, Captain. I cannot abide straining my neck to look up."

An aristocrat to the bone. I doubt that will serve her well in the colony. Keeping to his role as servant, Lex remained standing but moved behind her chair in a protective stance.

"I wish to book two cabins on your vessel for the voyage. I'm prepared to pay in advance," she continued as the captain reseated himself.

"One cabin, if you please, Lady." Lex was quick to intervene. "I'll be swinging a hammock with the crew, the captain permitting."

She glanced up at him. He gave her a look that warned her to accept his suggestion.

"Very well, one cabin and space for my servant to…swing his hammock."

"Well…"

"You do take passengers, do you not? I was told by the barkeep that last year you took a pair of young ladies and their servant to the same destination."

"Aye, that I did, but that was my niece and her lady's maid. My niece was going out to be married and had promised to reach her intended as soon as possible. The man went along to tend the horse they were taking with them. My vessel is a merchantman, ill equipped for passengers. I've but one decent cabin and another only fit for sleeping."

"Well, then, I see no problem. I'll be taking a pair of horses. Lex here is their groom."

"Miss…Smith, I don't think…" The captain was reduced to stammering. He'd looked Lex up and down. Dressed as he was, Lex hardly resembled a groom. The thought that the captain might assume he was her paramour gushed over Lex, filling him with a dash of guilty pleasure.

"You've just admitted you have at least one private passenger cabin." Anna took him up quickly. "You'll find I can accustom myself to whatever fare your ship and crew have to offer." She drew the sack of coins from inside her vest and threw them on the table in front of the captain. "I believe you'll find more than enough to cover our passage in it." She stood. "One of your crewmen has told me you sail on the next tide. We'll be aboard."

She swung around and strode arrogantly toward the door. Lex gave the stunned captain a resigned shrug before he followed her.

"Now what was that nonsense about not wanting a cabin for the voyage? Surely 'swinging a hammock with the crew,' as you described your wishes, won't be nearly as comfortable as a private accommodation." As they walked away from the tavern, she looked up at him.

"I'll not have the captain and his men thinking I'm your fancy man." He squared his shoulders, head held high.

"Bloody hell!" She stopped, grabbed his arm, and turned him to face her. "You're protecting *your* reputation!"

"Aye."

"Lex, you are a puzzle." Chuckling, she released him and continued on down the crowded street.

****

Anna awoke to a rolling toss. *Where in the devil am I?* Sitting up, she bumped her head on a beam and remembered. Yesterday she and Lex had boarded Captain Marston's ship bound for America. Swinging her feet onto the floor, she rubbed the spot she'd hit and looked around. What a rabbit hole! The captain hadn't been exaggerating when he'd said he was ill equipped to handle passengers. And this was supposed to be the best of the pair of cabins he had to offer.

With a sigh, she reached for her clothing and began to dress. *At least supper last evening was palatable. Perhaps breakfast will be as well.*

She was eating in the small dining room that served the captain and his officers when the master himself joined her. After pouring himself a cup of coffee, he sat down opposite her and smiled.

"How did you pass the night, Miss Smith?" he asked. "As comfortable as possible, I hope."

"Quite comfortable, sir." She'd finished her meal and moved the plate aside. "I'm hoping my servant did as well. He's not come to breakfast."

"Since he chose to share quarters with the crew, he'll be eating with them."

"Ah. I hope your men get decent meals. Lex is accustomed to good food."

"More than acceptable, mistress. One big reason I have no trouble recruiting sailors is the fact that I'm well known for providing the best victuals possible. I'll get no work out of a man with an empty or ill-satisfied belly."

"An admirable premise, Captain. Now, if you'll excuse me, I'll take some air. It appears a fine morning, even if a bit windy."

****

"Have you seen my servant this morning?" Anna stopped a sailor as she stood by the rail on the rolling deck. She'd discovered that, under gray skies, the North Atlantic was serving up a taste of what it could deliver. "Has he come on deck yet this morning?"

"Hardly, miss." The sailor smirked at her. "He's not taken to sailin'. He's still in his hammock, spewin' up his guts."

"Sick? Lex is seasick?"

"Aye, miss, as sick as can be."

"But surely it will pass...once he becomes accustomed to the movement of the ship?"

"Some does overcome it, miss, but for most they spends the whole of the voyage retchin' over the rail or a bucket."

"Mr. Murray, get on with your duties!" Captain Marston's mate bellowed, and the sailor, with a touch of his forelock, moved away.

Anna drew a deep breath. There were two horses to be cared for, and Captain Marston had made it abundantly clear that he and his crew did not tend passengers' livestock. Glad she'd dressed in her riding outfit of breeches, shirt, and boots, she looked around for another sailor who could direct her to the hold where Silverbell and Storm were stabled.

****

"How are you, laddie?" The big Scottish sailor paused by Lex's hammock.

"Near death and wishin' it will come soon." Lex tried to wet dry lips with an equally dry tongue. "Sweet Jesus, how much longer to America?"

"Four weeks or thereabouts." With a grin, the man started to move off, but Lex struggled up on elbow to catch him by a sleeve.

"My…mistress and I brought a pair of horses aboard. I'm to care for them. Sweet Jesus, they must be starvin' and up to their knees in shit."

"Never fear, they're doing well. Your mistress is a dab hand at mucking out and feeding them."

"My mistress?"

"Aye. Your beasts will survive the voyage under her care, I've no doubt."

The sailor walked away, and Lex dropped back into his hammock.

Lady looking after the horses, shoveling manure. I'd never have thought…

Another bout of nausea welled. Thoughts of Lady Anna vanished as he retched over the bucket by his hammock.

****

"Miss Smith." Captain Marston stopped her as she came up from the hold where she'd been tending the horses.

"Yes?" She walked to the rail and dumped a bucketful of manure overboard before turning to the captain. The word came out more harshly than she'd intended, but she was tired and dirty. Caring for the horses wasn't a chore for which she'd expected to be responsible.

Bloody hell, when will that man I brought along to care for the animals get back on his feet and start measuring up to his chores?

"A word, if you please." The captain drew himself up before her. His expression told her he was about to embark on a grave subject.

What now? Isn't this voyage turning out bad enough without adding more troubles?

"It's concerning your servant, Miss Smith. One of my sailors informs me he's in a bad way, in danger of becoming severely dehydrated. He's holding nothing in his stomach and vomiting constantly. We're sailing short-handed on this voyage…no surgeon, no one who can be spared to give him care."

"Are you telling me Lex…my groom…is in danger of losing his life?"

"I'd stop short of giving such a dire pronouncement…seasickness alone has never been responsible for any death that I know of…but he is very ill."

"Good God!" She drew herself up and paused for a moment, reeking bucket in hand.

"You said you have another small cabin for passengers, Captain." She looked up at the tall, gray-haired man. "I'm willing to pay the cost of it for the remainder of the voyage. I'd be much obliged if you'd spare a couple of your seamen long enough to assist my servant into it. With him in the cabin next to mine, I'll be able to undertake his care."

"Are you sure you can manage such a task?" Captain Marston's expression was grave. "Miss Smith, forgive me if I speak out of turn, but I've a notion that even though you've managed the care of those horses amazingly well, you've been to a manor born."

"What are you saying, Captain?" She narrowed her eyes as she squinted up at him in the sun.

"I'm saying that the care of a sick man may be...more than a bit unseemly...for a lady."

"Perhaps it shall be, but Lex is my servant. I've a responsibility to him. Please have him moved to the vacant cabin at once."

****

"No!" The word flew from Anna's mouth as two sailors assisted Lex from the bowels of the ship. She couldn't believe what she was seeing.

His complexion had a hue beyond gray, more nearly green, and his eyes were dark holes sunk in a face with a skeletal appearance. His boots dragged as the men struggled to hold him upright.

"Lex." She swallowed hard before striding across the deck to confront him. The stench emanating from him made the memory of the odor of the horse liniment pale by comparison. "You've been unwell, I've been told." As soon as she'd uttered the sentence, she flinched inwardly at its inanity.

He stared at her, and she saw undeniable contempt registered in his bloodshot blue eyes.

"Just a tad," he muttered. "Bloody hell, get me to the rail!"

The two sailors half dragged him to the bulwarks and managed to arrive at it before another bout of vomiting overtook him. When he signaled they might bring him back, Anna took charge. *A lady never reveals she is out of command of a situation.* Marie Roi's words echoed in her mind even as a roil of unsettledness resonated in her own gut.

"Thank you, gentlemen." She squared her shoulders and spoke imperiously. "Now, if you will please take my servant to the cabin next to mine and settle him into the bed, I shall be greatly obliged. Captain"—she turned to Edgar Marston—"I'll be needing two empty buckets and another with clean, warm water, and a length of toweling linen. I shall also require a teapot filled with hot water, a measure of ginger, and a tankard."

Chapter 13

"Hold there, lass." Weak as he was, Lex found the strength to protest as she rubbed a washing cloth down over his naked chest to the belt at his waist. "That's quite far enough." He caught her hand.

"Oh, for heaven's sake!" She shrugged off his restraint and drew back to glare down at him. "Do you think I'm such a voyeur as to want to see your lower regions?"

"Ya did frequent a brothel." He squinted up at her, struggling to quell the turmoil in his belly.

"I was simply curious about the activities." With a haughty squaring of her shoulders, she dipped the cloth into the bucket of clear water and began to rinse it. "I can assure you, I had no desire to see men in a state of dishabille."

"Chust a pretty word for neck-ed." His Highland accent colored the annoyance in the words.

"Well, whatever you choose to call it, that wasn't my intent." She let the washcloth fall into the water, stood, and picked up one of the other buckets. "I'm going on deck to empty the contents. Shortly we'll know if that ginger tea is having any effect on your malady."

"Vile stuff." He grimaced as he recalled the strong, biting taste. "If it doesn't cure me, it sure as hell will kill me. Where did ya ever hear of such a hellish remedy?"

"My sister is a healer. She was married to a doctor. She told me of it in one of her letters. She suggested I take ginger along if I ever took a sea voyage. I'm sure it's not so bad as what some of the sailors suggested."

"Which was?"

"Salt meat and onions. Now rest."

She went out, shutting the pocket door behind her.

Pulling the blankets about his bare shoulders, Lex rolled to face the wall. He groaned. Salt meat and onions, indeed. At least she hadn't forced that disgusting mixture on him…yet. He wasn't sure but what it might have been better to risk being captured by redcoats than living like this. He burrowed down into the bedcovers as other thoughts came into play. He had to admit he felt slightly better for being at least half clean, and he wasn't sure that miserable mixture she'd fed him hadn't minimally quelled his roiling gut.

He acknowledged that she was proving tough and adaptable beyond his previous imaginings. The tables were turned, with her having to take charge of the horses, never mind his own self, and Lady Anna Spencer was taking the situation in hand and dealing with it well. But, damn it, once he was back on his feet…

"Now." The sound of her voice made him roll back to face the door. She had come back inside, carrying a bowl of steaming water. A length of toweling linen hung over her arm, a piece of metal he recognized as a razor clutched in her hand.

"No, no, no, a thousand times no!" He struggled back in the bed away from her as she placed the items on the floor. "I'll not have ya shavin' me! You'll cut my throat, you'll…"

"A beard is most inconvenient when one is constantly vomiting." Casting him a roguish look, she took up the square of soap she'd used to wash him, dipped it into the warm water, and lathered her hands. "I'm sure I can master such a simple chore."

"Whit? You mean you've never shaved a man before?" He stared at her. "Yet now yer about to try…on a rolling ship?"

"If you stay perfectly still, quite possibly no harm will come to you." She placed her soapy hands on either side of his face and began to rub lather gently over his cheeks, chin, and jaws. With no alternative, he lay still and was startled to find the tender massage startlingly stimulating. *Sweet Jesus! This is all I need!*

As she leaned over him, their gazes met, and she paused in her ministrations. The moment froze.

"Well." She came back to animation and reached for the razor. "Let us get to it."

"Lass, why are you doin' this?"

"Doing what?"

"Carin' for me. You could have left me in the bow with the sailors."

"I urged you to come on this voyage. And while I may have abandoned my title on the shores of England, I have not abandoned my duties. You are my liege man, and as such I am responsible for you."

"Whit? Liege man?" He felt his breath catch as the razor slid smoothly down his face. "Surely there's no such title these days, surely…"

"Perhaps no title as such, but the responsibilities remain. Now, relax your jaw. Your muscles are bulging."

****

"We're almost there!" Lady's enthusiasm greeted him as he came up on deck to join her. Although his innards still felt queasy, he'd managed to subdue them sufficiently to wash, shave, and dress in clean clothing when she'd announced they were nearing their destination. The ship, on entering the river that would lead to their goal of Riverhaven, had found smoother sailing, and Lex had been able, with the added incentive of being near the end of this voyage from hell, to make himself decently presentable.

"You look much better." She smiled at him as he joined her at the rail.

"The prospect of getting off this rolling pile of planks has done wonders," he muttered. He looked off across the water to the verdant countryside along the river.

"Isn't it lovely!" she enthused. "So fresh and green."

"And nary a shelter in sight." Still not feeling back to his former self, Lex wasn't about to become ecstatic about this wild, new country. "I'm hoping your sister has some sort of roof to put over your head."

"Over *my* head? And what about you, Lex? Are you saying you're willing to live like a savage?" She shot him a taunting glance.

"I'd prefer not, but I could manage." He scowled. "I've not been born with the silver spoon in my mouth."

"Ah, so you're saying I might not be able to manage, to live a bit rough?"

"I'm chust sayin'." His words thickened with the Highland accent annoyance brought to the fore. "I'm chust sayin' this new land might not be all ya thought it would be. I doubt it's quite the place of sunshine and honey you imagined."

"But it is the land of sunshine…at least." She favored him with a saucy smirk. "Just look at these blue skies. And, you must admit, the sun is warm on your face."

"Argh!" He turned and, steadying himself on the rail, headed for the bow.

****

"Anna!" The woman waiting on the dock, her golden-red hair vivid in the sunshine, cried out to his companion as the sailors lowered the gangplank. A face that would have done an angel proud looked up at Anna and Lex, bright with delight.

"Louisa!" Replying with equal enthusiasm, Lady Anna rushed down the lowered board to meet her sister, arms outstretched. "How did you know I was coming?"

As they embraced, Lex wet his lips, thanked the Good Lord they'd found dry land, and followed her slowly. A month of seasickness had left his gut raw, his head light, and his knees in an uncertain state.

Once on land, he paused to take in the community into which they'd arrived. The village consisted of log and plank structures along the river bank, crude by most British standards, but he'd seen worse in the Highlands and among the hostelries of the poor. Their surroundings, however, pleased him. In the warm spring sunshine, tall trees, green fields, fresh air, and a sense of freedom surrounded him. He just might take well to this place, this Riverhaven.

But what of Lady? What did she think of it? He looked over at her to get her reaction, but she seemed too absorbed in the delight of her reunion with her sister to be paying much attention to her new environment.

As the fresh air and sunshine of a fine spring day revived him, he noticed a man, tall and broad-shouldered as himself, standing by a cargo wagon to which a snow-white horse was harnessed. Arms crossed on his chest, he was watching the women, a satisfied smile on a face Lex had no doubt many a lass had found handsome.

Is this the husband? Looks a right fit lad. But he's got a pistol stuck in his belt and a sword at his side. Is this such a place that a man is required to go about armed to the teeth?

"How did you know to meet this ship?" Anna was staring at the other woman. "I had no time to send you word."

"Since I got your letter a week ago, announcing your intention to join me, I've been watching and waiting. Although I couldn't meet every ship that arrived from England, I did come to the dock as often as possible. Still, being here to greet you today was largely serendipitous. We had to come in for supplies. When I saw a ship heading toward the wharf, something told me you were aboard. Aside from being sisters, we've always had a special connection, you'll recall. Anna"—the woman took her sister by an arm and was drawing her toward the man bearing pistol and sword—"this is my husband, Brodie. Brodie, this is my darling sister, Anna."

"Your servant, ma'am." Instantly the man in rough homespun became a gentleman, snatching off his cap to reveal a thatch of sandy curls and taking her hand to bend over it.

"Oh, my, you didn't tell me you'd married a

gallant." Lady Anna accepted his greeting. "Louisa, you've been keeping secrets."

"Purely by accident, I assure you." Lex saw Louisa was casting the man she'd identified as her husband the same sly, teasing glance he'd seen more often than he could count on Lady's countenance.

Aye, it's for certain sure those two are sisters.

As if suddenly remembering him, Anna turned back to the man standing several feet behind her and held out an indicating hand. "This is Lex, my manservant."

"Manservant?" The man identified as Brodie squinted over at him. "Don't ladies usually travel with maid servants?"

"I've brought two horses with us." She sidestepped further, more accurate explanations. "He's very good with the creatures. My lady's maid would have been useless."

"Well, then, laddie, welcome." Brodie's face crinkled into a grin. "Ya look as if ye've not enjoyed the voyage overmuch. Lex, is it?" He held out a hand. "Nothin' more, nothin' less?"

Lex drew a deep breath as he accepted the greeting, willing his rubbery legs to keep him upright.

"Aye, Lex it is." He accepted the welcome and felt his innards begin to settle now that his boots were on dry land.

"Scot?" Brodie met his gaze squarely.

"Aye."

"Highlander?"

Lex hesitated.

"Ye've nothin' ta fear here, laddie." Brodie stood back, hands on his hips. "We're most of us a community of refugees from Scotland's north. Ye can feel safe and at home among us."

"Thank you, Mr. MacMillan." Anna had told him her sister's married name. "Then it's a Highlander I am."

"Brodie, if you please. Now let's you and me see to those horses you brought, while the ladies natter away. If you think you're up to ridin' a beast that has been cooped up for over a month, you and I can ride back to the homestead. I came mounted. I enjoy ridin'."

"I'd fair enjoy it."

"Come along, then." Louisa MacMillan took her sister's arm and urged her toward the cargo wagon. "We'll leave the horses to the men. Our transport awaits. I hope you weren't expecting a carriage, or even a barouche. Such fancy vehicles wouldn't last long on the trails and roads in this country."

Lex glanced at Lady as her sister propelled her toward the wagon. He caught only the slightest of hesitation before she accompanied her sister to it. He and the husband followed. He waited until Brodie MacMillan had hoisted his wife aboard before catching Lady about the waist and lifting her up to join her sister.

"Your servant, ma'am." He bowed his head in mock submission as he backed away.

Catching the whiff of sarcasm in his actions, she made a derisive sound as she settled on the board seat.

****

"Care for a wee dram?" As they rode behind the wagon carrying the two women, what baggage they had from the ship, and the supplies Louisa had mentioned, Brodie reached inside his coat and pulled out a flask. "Ya look as if ya could use it."

"Aye." Lex managed to hold Storm to a prancing walk and accepted the offer, pulled out the stopper, and took a swallow. He handed it back to his companion. "Right fine. Thank you."

"Sometimes a man…or a woman…needs a swallow ta keep goin'." Brodie MacMillan indicated Silverbell tied to the back of the wagon. "That's one fine mare if ever I saw one. Belongs ta your lady, right?"

He hesitated.

"Ah, perhaps not exactly?" Brodie broke into a sly grin. "Perhaps neither does that fine black you're ridin'? You needn't be afraid ta admit the pair weren't exactly sold to either of ya."

"That's a right fine animal you're riding." Instead of replying with an answer, Lex jerked a thumb at the charcoal mare Brodie MacMillan rode.

"Aye, that she is." Pride filled his tone. "She carries the proud name of Scotia. I borrowed her from my partner. My filly is but a yearling, too young ta break or ride, but she promises well. I owned her father. He was a wonderful beast. Died saving my life." His voice cracked ever so slightly. "But before he was killed"—his tone picked up—"he sired a filly. His name was Fox. Hers is Vixen."

"Fittin'."

"Aye."

For a few moments they rode in silence, Lex enjoying the freedom from the ship's tossing and the beauty of the spring day in this new country. Revived by the whisky, he took stock of his surroundings and continued to like what he saw. The trail they followed led through a veritable tunnel of fresh greenery that in places formed a roof over the narrow lane. Birds twittered in the trees, and all seemed unspoiled and new.

"You're likin' the place?" Brodie MacMillan broke in on his thoughts.

"Aye."

"It's a great country, free as the breezes that blow over it. Have ya got any experience in the lumber business or millin'?"

"None."

"Aye, well, we'll soon teach ya. My partner, his family, and I run a fair ta middlin' operation in such…also grindin' grain. We're in need of more hands. Of late, the business has prospered ta such an extent we've had ta take on Irish workers and build accommodation for them near the mill. In winter, they'll head off into the bush ta get more fodder for our operation. Would ya be interested in such work?"

"Paid work?"

"Aye, well paid by today's standards."

"I'm interested, but it depends on Lady. I am her servant."

"Not in this country ye aren't, laddie. My partner, Harry Wallace, and I don't stand for indentures and the like."

"Wallace?" Lex started so abruptly Storm snorted at the unexpected tug on his reins.

"Aye." Brodie's eyes narrowed at he looked over at his companion. "Would ye be knowin' him?"

"Hardly." He avoided the man's penetrating stare.

"Listen, laddie." Brodie stopped his mare and reached to halt Lex's horse with a hand on Storm's bridle. "Ye'll find ya have no reason in Riverhaven ta hide whatever happened in the Old Country. We're a community of folk many of whom have left troublin' matters back across the sea. We're content to live and let live. There'll be no need ta hide that Highland brogue. We're not considered rebels or barbarians in Riverhaven." The grin returned slowly to his face. "Understood?"

Lex hesitated, then let the corners of his mouth curl upward.

"Guid, verrae guid," he replied.

Laughing, Brodie released Storm, and they headed off again behind the wagon.

"Fancy a wee race ta our settlement?" Brodie winked at Lex. "It's a mile ahead. I'm reckonin' that fine geldin' of yours would like ta stretch his legs after being cramped up in that ship."

"Aye, that he would."

A moment later he and Brodie dashed past the wagon, leaving Louisa to calm the startled white mare pulling it and Anna to soothe the gray one at the back, rearing to join in the race.

****

As the two men galloped past the wagon, the white horse harnessed to it jerked and shook her head.

"Easy, girl." Louisa at the reins calmed her while Anna turned on the seat to face the gray wrenching at her rope at the back of the wagon. The men's behavior had promoted the competitive spirit in both animals.

"Silverbell, whoa, whoa. That's a good girl." Anna turned back to her sister as the mare calmed to a slow prance. "It seems as if our fine lads have hit it off." She grinned.

"And you're thinking that's a good thing?" Louisa

urged the white mare onward with a flap of the reins. "Anna, Brodie can be a bit of a handful. From what I've just witnessed, he and Lex might be birds of a feather. Together…"

"Don't worry, sister dear." Anna settled back onto the seat and cast her companion a coy look. "I hold the reins where Lex is concerned, and I can assure I've got an excellent grip."

"Some men can't be entirely held to a stance." Louisa met her sister's glance. "You have to let them run and hope they bring themselves back under control."

"Is that what you've been doing with Mr. MacMillan? Louisa, I cannot believe you've let any man, even one as handsome and seemingly affable as your husband, take command of your life."

"I haven't. I simply managed to settle on a way of life that allows Brodie to believe himself free as the wind. When it's necessary, trust me, I can crack a whip hand over him."

"That's more what I expected." Anna smiled.

"Now, I must remind you—as I did in my last letter—you're not to reveal the fact that we're both ladies…Lady Louisa and Lady Anna, I mean. Brodie doesn't know, and I'm sure that if he found out, he'd be more than slightly perturbed. Have you warned your manservant of this condition as well?"

"I've told him our titles no longer apply in this country…even though he insists on calling me 'Lady.' Do you think I want to leave a glowing trail of my whereabouts for Papa to follow? I left a note telling him I'd run off to the continent with Lex. Archie is in on my plans and will back up that story"—she paused, then continued—"although I doubt he wants to run me to ground and take me back…now that I'm supposedly damaged goods."

"And are you? Anna"—Louisa turned on her sister, astonished—"I wouldn't have believed it of you."

"No, no, of course not. Lex is simply what he appears—my servant—but Papa will never believe it. I have established a reputation of being a bit notorious."

"From what you've written in your letters, you certainly have. But then, both of the Spencer ladies are regarded as such, are they not?"

They grinned at each other before Louisa flapped the reins over Snow's back again to send her forward at a brisker trot.

Chapter 14

At the Wallace-Fowler-MacMillan settlement, Louisa stopped Snow on the hill above a valley that contained a wide pond filled with logs and a long wooden structure, one end of which was tall, the remainder stretching out from it. Men were working busily about the latter, in the yard of which tall stacks of freshly sawn lumber stood in piles beyond hills of sawdust. She could hear saws whining and men shouting. To Anna's eyes, the place seemed a veritable swarm of alien activity.

On the opposite hill stood a rambling log house, visible through the trees. Beyond it, Anna could see various outbuildings, which included a large barn.

"My goodness, Louisa, this is an entire community." She gazed about. "As we were driving through the forest, I must admit I was having apprehensions as to what type of place you were taking me. Now…"

"Our families have been decently successful. Especially since Brodie joined the group. He's a millwright by profession, and an excellent one. Now"—she turned the horse toward a lane to their left along the top of the rise on which they'd paused—"to our homestead. I hope you won't find it too rustic. Brodie hastily added a room, a separate cabin of sorts, at the end of our veranda when we learned you were coming.

We had no idea you were bringing a manservant." She glanced at her sister. "Perhaps Lex wouldn't mind sleeping in the barn or with the workmen in their accommodations down by the mill?"

"At the estate, Lex had made himself quite comfortable in an empty stall in the stable. No need for concern as to his sleeping arrangements."

"Good. Well, here we are, the manor house of Lady Louisa Spencer-MacMillan." They'd reached the end of the lane, and she drew rein before a modest log house, a barn of similar construction a distance beyond it. On the veranda, one of the largest dogs Anna had ever seen rose from where he'd been lying, chained beside the door.

"Meet Jasper." Louisa jumped to the ground. "I've never been quite sure if he's a dog or a wolf or a cross between the two. We refer to him as a dog to keep people from being too fearful. Rest assured, however, that once I introduce you, you'll have a friend for life."

"I'm glad you told me." Not accustomed to the wagon's height, Anna got down more carefully than her sister. "He does have the appearance of a creature nasty parents might use to give their children night terrors."

"Jasper, this is Anna." Louisa was releasing the creature. "She's very dear to me."

The dog approached Anna cautiously, neck extended. She felt a thrill of fear but trusted her sister's judgment too much to give in to any sign of discomfiture.

"Hello, Jasper." She stretched out a hand. "Shall we be friends?"

The dog sniffed the offer, and then slowly his tail began to sway.

"You've been accepted." Louisa laughed as she fastened her mare to the veranda railing.

"And who is that?" Anna turned to indicate a sorrel horse dancing and whinnying in a paddock beside the barn.

"That's Brodie's filly Vixen. She's too young to be broken or ridden yet, but I foresee doing such will prove a challenge even for my husband, who has a way with horses. This"—she indicated a washstand with a basin, a square of soap, and a length of toweling linen beside it, a bucket of fresh water beneath it, as she stepped up to the veranda—"is where I encourage Brodie to clean up after a day at the mill or working on the farm."

"A fine idea, I've no doubt." Anna looked at the setup, remembering how sweating and dirty workers on her father's tenant farms had often appeared.

"I hope you won't be too disappointed," Louisa continued, glancing at Anna as she pushed open the door to reveal the home inside. "It's a long way from Haven Hall."

"I am not expecting it to be anything like Haven Hall," she replied as her sister held out a hand to indicate she was to precede her inside.

And it certainly wasn't. She gazed about, taking in the wide fieldstone hearth, the board dining table with chairs at both ends, plank benches along either side, a pair of rocking chairs on either side of the fire. A bowl of lovely flowers (wild ones, she assumed, since she'd seen no cultivated beds around the cabin) graced the center of the table's snowy white cloth, while colorful quilts softened the backs and seats of the fireside chairs.

The board floor was swept clean, and counters and

shelves built against one wall held a neat assortment of dishes, while a hand pump sat on the lip of a metal sink. The log walls and glassed windows that let in bright spring sunshine suggested security, a place of comfortable safety. Beyond, a curtain covered a doorway she assumed led to a bedroom. All in all, the room gave off a homely ambience she was far from disliking.

"It's quite lovely…charmingly bucolic." She turned to smile at her sister.

"I see all those years of Marie Roi's training weren't entirely wasted." Louisa chuckled. "Always the polite response, never offensive."

"No, really, Louisa, I find it all quite delightful."

"Hie, you there, lasses!" Grinning, Brodie strode into the cabin, followed by Lex. "What kept ya? Lex and I have been here for a dog's age."

"Perhaps we simply had more common sense than to go hurtling at full gallop over rough terrain," Louisa replied.

"Saucy wench." In long strides, Brodie was with his wife, catching her up in his arms to kiss her lips quickly and soundly.

"You'll have to forgive my husband, Anna," Louisa said, once he'd released her. "He's an impulsive lad."

"Aye, and ya wouldn't have it any other way." Brodie turned to the man who'd followed him. "Lex, would ya oblige by finishin' rubbin' down our horses while I unload the wagon and get the ladies set up in here?"

"Aye."

"Lex, wait." As he turned to leave, Anna indicated

the dog sitting by Louisa's side and stopped him. "You'd best let Louisa introduce you to Jasper. He mightn't take well to strangers moving about the homestead."

"We've already met, Lady…before you arrived," Lex called back. "Come along, Jasper."

Leaving his mistress to trot obediently behind the newcomer, the dog headed off to do Lex's bidding.

"He spoke ta the beast in Gaelic when first we arrived," Brodie explained. "It only took a few words for Jasper ta be eatin' out of his hand, so ta speak."

"Lex has a way with animals," Anna said.

"Aye, well, maybe he can lend a hand with my filly," Brodie said. "She's a right saucy wench." He turned to Anna. "Stay well back from her, lass. She's got her sire's spirit and her dam's cunning. Now"—he squared his shoulders—"I'd best get ta the task of seein' ya settled into your new home."

After giving his wife a peck on the cheek, he turned and strode outside.

****

"We've invited the Wallaces to supper." Louisa bustled about, checking a pot that hung over the fire on the hearth. "I hope you don't mind, but I do want them to meet you as soon as possible. They're our best friends. Just Harry and Margaret, mind. Since there are so many children, we thought it best not to overwhelm you with them this first day."

The sounds of Brodie and Lex washing up at the stand on the veranda interrupted their conversation for a moment.

"You said they had nine. My, what a formidable group! They must have been married for some years to have produced such a number."

"Seven are stepchildren. When their birth mother died, Margaret married their father out of the goodness of her heart in order to help care for them. Then he was killed, murdered some believe, and Margaret was left alone—at a little over twenty years of age—to care for them, the farm, and the mills. When Harry arrived on a ship from the Old Country, she learned of his prowess in fighting off privateers while on the voyage and decided he was exactly the man she needed. She asked him to marry her."

"A bold move, to say the least." Anna was astonished.

"Yes, but it's worked out well…for both of them. Now they have twin boys of their own and are very much in love."

"Horses all safely put up for the night." Brodie entered, followed by Lex. "I won't trouble ta return Harry's mare just now. He can take her home tonight when he leaves."

"Brodie, I *will* trouble you to put on a clean shirt." Louisa stepped back, hands on hips. "I can see you and Lex have washed up, but your clothing still bears the marks of that mad race today, and we are having guests to supper. I sent a note over as soon as we got home, just as you suggested."

"Only Margaret and Harry, darlin', but if 'twill please you, I'll find something better." He turned to the man standing silently just inside the door. "I reckon ye'd be included in my wife's admonitions if she weren't too much of a lady ta say so." He grinned as he caught Louisa's startled glance at her sister. "Since ya haven't had time ta unpack your gear, I'll lend ya something clean. Come along."

As the two men vanished into the first bedroom, Louisa looked at Anna, shaking her head. "Perhaps too much alike?"

****

"Fancy a wee dram before we eat?" Brodie took a bottle from a shelf in the cupboard and looked the question at both Lex and Anna. The men, clad in fresh shirts, had returned to the kitchen.

"I'd be delighted," Anna replied quickly.

"Well, then, good." After a quick glance at his wife to which he received a nod of assent, he reached for glasses. "Louisa, you as well, darlin'?"

"I think not. I'll be content with tea."

Shortly they were seated around the plank table with their chosen drinks. Glancing from one to the other, Lex saw the delight the sisters were sharing in their reunion.

"Tell me everything." Louisa cradled her teacup in both hands as she looked over at her sister. "How is Archie? What made you decide to come to Riverhaven now? What…?"

"Enough." Anna laughed. "You're overwhelming me, sister." She took a sip of her whisky before continuing. "First of all, Archie is recovering nicely. As I told you in my letter, Lex rescued him from the battlefield. As to why we chose to come to Riverhaven at this time"—she drew a deep breath—"I'm escaping marriage to the Duke of Cumberly. Marie enlisted Lex to come along as my companion and protector. And there's another reason, as well." Again she paused to savor her drink.

A gob of apprehension rose in Lex. Was she about

to reveal him as a deserter, a man plucked from prison to serve in the army? He quaffed a mouthful and waited.

"And that would be? You said nothing of it in your letter." Louisa leaned forward. "Anna, I know that twinkle in your eyes. There's something more…a lot more."

"We're on a quest…a quest to find a sunken treasure. We have a map."

The sound that escaped Lex's lips was a wheeze of half relief, half disgust.

"Treasure?" Brodie came alert, leaning across the table toward Anna. "Here, in Riverhaven? Ya say ya have a map?"

"Brodie, you look like a bird dog on the point," his wife admonished. "Your days of seeking wealth to support the Scottish cause are behind you, remember."

"Oh, aye." He relaxed back in his chair, but as Lex looked at Brodie MacMillan, he recognized that the man's interest in the map and treasure were far from quenched.

This could be trouble.

A knock sounded at the door.

"Ah, that will be Margaret and Harry." Brodie moved across the room to answer it. "We'll speak more of this matter later. Welcome, welcome!" He swung open the door to admit the couple.

Anna choked on the whisky she'd just taken into her mouth and stared, aghast. The dark, handsome man standing beside the chestnut-haired woman on the threshold looked equally flummoxed. For a moment there was absolute silence.

"Whit…?" Brodie glanced from one to the other.

"Well, well." Harry Wallace was the first to come out of the trance. "Lady Annabelle Spencer, as I live and breathe. We meet again."

Chapter 15

"Highland Harry, as *I* live and breathe." Anna managed the recognition.

"Aye." Crossing his arms on his broad chest, he stood beside his wife, shoulders back, seemingly conquering the shock of suddenly coming upon the woman who'd deceived him, who'd sought to imprison him and perhaps see him hung. A slow, sardonic grin began to curl the corners of his mouth. "I trust you've come with this gentleman"—he gestured toward Lex—"bearing a warrant for my arrest."

"You're quite wrong, sir." She drew herself up and stuck out her chin. "I'm simply visiting my sister."

"Bloody hell, if she's Lady Annabelle, then you must be…" Brodie stared at his wife.

"Was." Louisa faced him. "*Was* Lady Louisa Spencer."

"Sweet Jesus!" Brodie upped his mug and gulped down his whisky. "Sweet Jesus!" he repeated when he'd finished. "Lady Louisa Spencer! Sister ta the woman who near brought Harry and me ta the gallows! And a blessed lady, ta boot! When were ya thinkin' ya might enlighten me as ta these intriguin' facts?"

"Brodie, I'm equally confused. What do you mean nearly brought you and Harry to the gallows?" Louisa was staring at her husband. "What are you talking about?"

"This woman"—Brodie pointed a trembling finger at Anna—"laid a plot ta capture us when we were workin' back in the Old Country. She lured Harry into her bedroom at the manor house with a promise ta show him a magnificent necklace…one supposed ta have belonged ta the late French queen. Harry planned ta snatch it and run. I hid in the stables with our horses, ready ta make a quick escape."

Lex, watching the drama, recalled the reason the stable had to be carefully guarded was because two highwaymen had once hidden out there. Brodie MacMillan and this man Harry Wallace? His mind searched quickly. Brazen Brodie and Highland Harry? That's what the stable lads had told him. He'd heard of that notorious pair. Were these the two men standing before him?

"Brodie, calm down." Louisa tried to place a placating hand on his arm, but he shrugged away. "We agreed to leave your past behind. I thought it only fair the agreement extended to mine, as well."

"Oh, aye, ya did, did ya?" The words barked out. "Ya never once thought to tell me that before ya were Louisa Abbot, wife of Dr. Neil Abbot, ya were Lady Louisa Spencer? The daftness of a Highland rebel bein' married to an English aristocrat never once crossed your mind, never mind the fact that her sister tried ta have Harry and me hung?"

He strode to the hearth to put one booted foot on the fender, his right hand grasping the stones above his head in a knuckle-whitening grip.

"Consider yourself fortunate, Brodie." The chestnut-haired woman who was Harry Wallace's companion spoke for the first time as she stared at

Anna, green eyes flashing outrage. “At least Louisa is guilty only of being this woman’s sister. Harry apparently was her lover!”

She whirled and strode out of the cabin.

“Margaret…!” Harry headed after her. At the door, he paused to swing back on Anna, countenance registering exasperation. “I almost wish you had come with a warrant. It would have been easier to deal with than what I must face at home now!”

Slamming the door behind him, he went out. Brodie snatched up the whisky bottle and, after a final bitter glance at Louisa, followed him, equally abusing the door. Lex hesitated a moment, then went after the other two men, but he closed the panel with more respect.

For a few moments, silence reigned in the cabin. Finally Louisa put her hands on her hips and drew a deep breath.

“Well,” she said, looking over at her sister, a rueful expression encompassing her countenance. “It appears that, as always, sister, you’ve stirred up a hornet’s nest.”

“Louisa, I’m so very sorry for the trouble I’ve caused.” Anna faced her. “As for meeting Highland Harry, well, I can honestly tell you, I was as shocked as he. I never expected to see that man again.”

“What exactly was your relationship with Harry?” Louisa moved to the dresser by the window and took down a second bottle of whisky.

“I tried to trap him, to capture him for the Crown.” She watched as her sister replenished her mug and splashed a small measure into her teacup. “I lured him to my bedroom with a fabulous necklace given to me by a wealthy merchant who hoped to win my hand. Harry caught on to my plan and fled before I could see it to completion."

"Were you his lover?" Louisa paused, bottle in hand, to look her squarely in the eyes.

"Definitely not! Louisa, how could you…?"

"We've been apart for years, sister." Louisa shrugged. "And you always were more than a bit notorious. Our mother's blood shining through, no doubt. What of this man Lex? Is he exactly as you've described…a servant?"

"Exactly. Louisa, I've not become a wanton. I'm…" She paused.

"What?"

"Still a virgin." The three words came out barely above a whisper.

"Well, then, good. Keep it that way until you find the right man." Louisa replaced the bottle on the shelf and indicated chairs by the hearth. "Sit. We have much to talk about."

"Yes." The word was a breathed sigh as she accepted her sister's offer. "Louisa, I'm sorry for all the trouble I've caused today. It appears as if I may have destroyed or at least seriously damaged two marriages."

"Don't worry about Brodie." Louisa settled with her drink into the seat opposite her sister. "He's fiery and impulsive, but he loves me absolutely. He'll be back once he's had time to think, once he's had time to"—she cast Anna a sly wink and a grin—"truly miss me."

"If you're certain." Anna looked down at the whisky in her mug and swirled it about.

"As Brodie himself would say, certain sure."

"But what of the other couple?" She raised her gaze to her sister once more. "Should I go to see Harry's wife and try to explain?"

"Not just yet. Let the dust settle a bit. Give Harry a chance to work his charm on her first. You must realize he has a way with women."

"Yes, he certainly does. In fact, given a bit longer with the rogue, I might have given in to his charms…that is, if he truly planned to seduce me."

****

Lex followed Brodie back behind the barn and down the hill into the trees beyond the millyard. He strode fast to keep up with the other man's anger-lengthened strides. He had to talk to him. Letting Lady Anna's arrival ruin a marriage wasn't something he was about to allow, not if he could prevent it.

When Brodie reached a place where the stream that provided power for the mill once more settled into its quiet journey to the bay, he paused, hands on his hips and threw back his head to emit a half-moan, half yowl. It sent birds fluttering out of the branches overhead.

Lex stopped behind him and stood silently. For a few moments the only sound was that of brook water bubbling over rocks.

"Well, say something!" Brodie snapped, swinging on the other man. His countenance puckered into a scowl of outrage that wasn't inviting to a conversation. "But don't ya dare try ta convince me that my wife bein' a lady makes no difference…because it sure as hell does!"

"I was chust goin' ta say, it appears Lady and myself have upset the apple cart with our arrival." In an effort to soothe the man, Lex deliberately lapsed into his Highland brogue. "It must have come as a great shock ta ya, a Highlander, learnin' ye're married ta an English aristocrat." His tone softened. "Maybe yer someone like myself and ya lost family at Culloden. If so, yer not about ta forgive the English easily."

"Culloden." Brodie's tone broke, and he looked down at his boots. "It may ha' been over fifty years ago, but 'twill never be forgotten by our people. Their blood soaked the moor that day."

"Six men from my family died there. Three more were captured and shot." Lex's words held the emotion he felt. "They went into that battle cold and exhausted and half-starved, with axes and pikes against muskets and cannon. They didn't have a chance, and yet they fought ta the bitter end. They didn't give up in the face of bein' outnumbered by the English."

"And yer point would be?" Brodie narrowed his eyes as he looked at Lex.

"My point would be that they didn't give in ta the English and neither should you." Lex allowed the corner of his mouth to curl upward.

"Argh!" Brodie gave him a curdling look before sinking down on a stump. "Laddie, ye can try as ya like, but ye'll never convince me my bein' wed to an English lady…a *lady*, mind, not just an English lass, is not somethin' to give me more than a moment's pause. And then Harry arrives ta inform me my sister-in-law is none other than the infamous Lady Annabelle Spencer who near got both him and me killed back in the Old Country. How's that fer a kettle o' trouble?"

"Ya never saw Lady, not even when ya went to her home to steal the necklace?"

"Never clapped eyes on the lass. I stayed in the

barn with the horses, ready ta make a quick getaway. A stable hand was our cohort. He lives here in Riverhaven now. His name is Jonah Parsons, but he's been warned about talking of our past."

"Didn't ya know anything of yer wife's sister, of her family?" Lex sat down on the ground a few feet away, resting his forearms on his bent knees and clasping his hands.

"No." Brodie paused to take a swig from the whisky bottle he'd brought from the cabin, then handed it to Lex. "We agreed ta leave our pasts across the sea, never ta talk o' them. I knew only that Louisa was Louisa Abbot, widow of Dr. Neil Abbot, a Scotsman. Before that…well, I never asked and she never said. When she told me her sister was coming, she referred to her only as Anna. How was I ta know?"

"So now ye're goin' ta let Lady's arrival ruin yer marriage ta that beautiful woman?" Lex cast his companion a sideways glance. "Lady has told me her sister is by way of bein' quite a healer, as well, and a good one." He accepted the proffered bottle and took a swallow.

"Aye, that she is." Brodie rubbed calloused hands together. "She's saved more lives than I can count in this valley."

"And she keeps a right fine house, from what I've seen. That supper she was about to serve up looked tasty." Freed of the tossing of the ship, his appetite had returned, and days of keeping little inside had left him longing for that savory-smelling food.

"Aye, that she does. She conjures up a stew that would make the devil happy."

"Well, then…"

"It's not so simple, Lex. Trouble was brewin' before ye arrived. There's this doctor newly arrived in the valley. He's taken a land grant on the far side o' the river and begun ta build a homestead on it. Rumor has it he and his brother were privateers in the war and, as a result, became wealthy. I've seen both MacTavish men. They're not exactly ugly…and they're rich."

"I don't understand…"

"Listen and learn!" Brodie snatched the bottle back from Lex and took a swig before continuing. "Of late, Louisa has taken ta 'conferring' with Doctor William MacTavish. Oh, she claims it's purely professional, but still…"

"You don't suspect…?"

"Bugger all, I don't want ta, Lex." Brodie lowered his head and shook it. "But he's buildin' a fine house…a stone house…many times the size of our humble little cabin…and he goes about dressed like an English gentleman…suited ta an English lady. Now, if word leaks out that Louisa is one…newly rich men like him would be right pleased ta have such an acquisition to grace his halls. Her first husband was a doctor. She has a taste for educated men."

"Ye're daft, man!" Lex was quick to contradict him. "I've seen the way she looks at ya. And I doubt yer wife is so shallow as ta prefer wealth over love."

"That's as may be, but I need time to sort through this revelation. Come along." Brodie stood. "I'll show ya where ta stow yer gear in the men's barracks at the mill. There's a cookhouse beside it, where the men take their meals. Supper should be on the table about now, and I'm guessin' ye've got a fair-ta-middlin' appetite. The cook is a Frenchman and darned good at his trade."

He paused to look back at Lex. “I’ll be joinin’ ya and the boys there for a while. I need time to get my mind around what this day has revealed.”

Chapter 16

"Get your lazy arses out of bed!" Brodie's bellow woke Lex the following morning. "Who do ya think ya are, a bunch of bloody aristocrats?"

It took Lex a minute to orient himself, to realize he was no longer on a tossing ship, that his gut didn't roil, and that he was looking up to see the man he'd met only the previous day—Brodie MacMillan, striding up and down the barracks, fully dressed, yelling at his workers.

Coughs and mutters erupted as the men pulled themselves from their blankets and began to dress for the day. Lex followed suit, pulling on first his shirt and then his boots.

"Come on, come on!" Brodie strode toward the door. "Cook's got yer victuals ready. I'll not have ya upsettin' him by bein' late!"

"God almighty, he's in a foul state," one of the men Lex had learned the previous night was known as Mac muttered after Brodie had gone. "One night without his woman surely put his tail out of joint."

"You've seen his missus," another grunted as he pulled on work boots. "Doin' without her, if she were mine, would sure as hell annoy me."

"Aye, well, there's naught we can do about that. Sweet Jesus, I'm not lookin' forward to the day ahead. He'll have us workin' like mules."

****

"Louisa, I'm so very sorry about all the trouble I've caused." Anna sat at the table, teacup in hand. They were finishing their breakfast as she watched her sister working at the hearth. "We'll move on…to Upper Canada or to the American states. Once I'm out of sight…"

"Of course you won't." Louisa turned to face her indignantly. "You're my sister, my family. I want you here with me. Brodie will calm down, you'll see. And once the dust of the first shock has settled, you'll go to visit Margaret and explain everything to her. It will all work out. Furthermore, Brodie and I have made you that private room. We'd both be so disappointed if our efforts were in vain."

"Very well, if you're sure." Anna thought of the small, separate cabin that was accessed by walking the length of the veranda. With the security of being only a few feet from her sister's door, she never had to set foot in the yard to reach her accommodations. When Louisa had shown her inside, the previous day, she'd found a surprisingly cozy ambience. Enclosed by log walls, the little place had a comfortable-looking bed, with a colorful quilt and feather pillows, a tidy stone hearth at the rear, and a table and chair under a curtained window. There was a chest of drawers with a small mirror above it, and pegs along the walls for hanging clothing. A braided rug graced the plank floor in front of the bed.

"Certainly I am," Louisa continued the conversation. "Now, I must ride out to visit a few ailing people. Do you think you can manage on your own? I'll be back in time to prepare the evening meal. You won't have to worry about the noon repast. There is bread, butter, and cheese over there on the shelf. As for Brodie, he often eats with the men at the mill. Today I'm sure he will."

"Don't worry. I'll be fine. Anyway, what is there to do? Keep the fire burning, sweep the floor? I'm not totally inept, sister dear."

"You might also feed the chickens and throw some hay in to your horses. I've loosed Brodie's filly into the paddock behind the barn. You can take some out to her, if it's not too big a chore."

"Don't worry. I've watched the farm hands back home do such work. I can handle such simple chores."

****

Later, she stood on the veranda and watched as Louisa, dressed in trousers, shirt, and vest, swung onto her white mare, medical bag strapped to her saddle, the dog Jasper on a long lead by her side.

"Brodie insists I take Jasper with me when I ride alone," she explained as Anna glanced at the big white animal. "There was a kidnapping in the valley the other year. He's never felt I was safe on the trails since that time."

"Don't worry about anything here," Anna was quick to reassure her. "I'll manage very well."

Louisa glanced at her sister, and Anna saw apprehension in the look.

"What?" she asked sharply. "Don't you trust me?"

"Trust you, yes. Confident in your ability to run a farm, no. Just take care, sister. Only do what you feel capable of."

She clucked to her horse and sent it galloping off down the lane to the road.

"Only what I feel capable of!" Anna scoffed. "I'll show her!"

****

Anna hummed an old English ballad as she made her way down to the barn. In spite of the upset her arrival had caused, she found she was enjoying this new life with its freedoms and bucolic charms. She'd donned one of her sister's aprons over her muslin gown and put on half boots which she deemed suitable for the work she was about to undertake. She was proud of the fact that she'd remembered to place a pair of logs into the hearth before she left the house so the fire wouldn't languish in her absence.

In the barn, she looked up into the loft to see stacks of hay. A ladder led to it. She ascended, then began to bundle armfuls of fodder down into the horses' mangers through openings in the floor. When she was satisfied they'd received their share, she threw what she deemed a suitable portion for the filly down to the barn floor. When she'd descended the ladder, she gathered the hay into her arms and went out to the paddock where the filly was contained. At its gate, she dropped her burden and swung the gate open.

The young mare snorted, half reared, and bolted. Knocking Anna aside, the filly made good her bid for freedom.

"No, no!" Clutching at the fence to remain on her feet, she stared after the fleeing animal.

Vixen stopped a few yards off, in what appeared to be a sprouting vegetable garden, and began to graze.

Be calm, Anna. Take a deep breath. There has to be a way to get that wild creature back into the paddock. What do the stable boys do when a horse gets loose? Of course. They use a bucket of grain as a lure. Grain. Now where...?

Scurrying back into the barn, she looked around. A bin near the chicken coop in a far corner appeared the answer to her quest. She rushed to it and was relieved to discover it contained oats. As she was bending to dip into the grain with a tin pot she found on the bin's top, something scurried up her arm.

A *mouse, Good God, a mouse!*

Screaming, she brushed it off and toppled backward. As she fell, she caught her gown on the peg that held the chicken coop shut. The door swung open. In a twinkling, squawking fowl surrounded her in a cloud of dust, droppings, and feathers.

"Bloody hell!" Above the cacophony, she heard Lex's burst of expletive. "Whit aire ya doin', lass?"

"Can't you see?" she cried, scrambling to her feet. "I'm setting my sister's fowl free!" Shame at being caught in such a humiliating situation made her bitterly sarcastic.

"Sweet Jesus! Stand aside!" Muttering, Lex began to round up the flapping hens. Within minutes, he'd managed to herd most of them back into the coop. The few errant ones he gathered up one by one and carried them back to their enclosure under his arm. Once they were all contained, he turned to her.

"Whit in the name of time happened?"

"Louisa had...errands. I said I'd take care of the homestead." Planning to brazen it out, she put her hands on her hips, haughty and unrelenting, but a chuckle suddenly bubbled from her lips.

"Whit?"

"You've got feathers in your hair...and on your

shirt…and your breeches."

"Aye, well, you try catchin' a bunch of upset hens without them leavin' their presence on your person." He brushed at a smear down the side of his breeches. "Dirty bloody beasts!"

"Oh." She clapped a hand over her mouth to subdue her mirth as he whacked at feathers and excrement. "I am sorry."

"Where's the filly?" As he continued to try to free himself of fowl evidence, he looked around the barn.

"The filly? Oh, my God! The filly! She was in the paddock. She got away. That's what started this fiasco. I came in here to get grain to lure her back, and a mouse ran out of the bin and up my arm, and I screamed and backed into the chicken coop…"

"Bugger all! Again, a mouse?" In long strides, Lex was out of the barn.

"There she is!" Trotting after him, she pointed at Vixen standing in the middle of the vegetable garden. Her head had been down, but at the sound of Anna's voice, she raised it, carrot tops hanging from her mouth as she munched contentedly.

Lex ground out something in Gaelic Anna assumed was a curse worse than anything he could find in English.

"Stay here and don't move." He went back into the barn and came out with a length of rope, a loop in one end. Moving slowly, he headed toward the young mare. He spoke again in Gaelic, only this time in soft, soothing tones.

Continuing to munch, Vixen stared at him but didn't move. When he slipped the rope around her neck, a wave of relief swept over Anna.

"Thank you, Lex," she breathed as he led the filly past her and into the barn.

His reply was a grunt.

She waited outside. When he didn't come out within minutes, she ventured inside. Vixen was in her box stall, and Lex was shoveling manure out of Silverbell's enclosure.

"Aren't you going back to the mill?" she asked.

"I have work to do here. I've been given time for it." The words were gruff.

"Lex, I've said I'm sorry I made such a mess of things." She moved to where she could see his face. "I only meant to help. I told Louisa I'd look after the place. That's what I was trying to do."

"Ya had no business tryin' ta do something you know nothin' about." He kept his attention focused on the pitchfork as he lifted manure into a wheelbarrow. "If ya want ta help, ya might set about repairin' the mess the filly made in the garden."

"Very well." She drew herself up and headed for the door. "I'm not entirely without bucolic skills. I've watched the gardener back home. How difficult can it be?"

Something that sounded like a derisive snort followed her outside.

"I'll be gathering up Brodie's belongings after I'm done here," he called after her. "He's instructed me to fetch a list of things, including his fiddle."

****

"Give us a tune, Brodie." One of the men came out of the mill barracks at the back of the millyard and held out the fiddle Lex had brought down from the cabin that morning. The other men, lounging about on the veranda in the spring evening, joined in lively assent.

"Ah, lads, I don't feel much like playin'." Brodie sat on the railing, one booted foot pulled up beside him.

"She's up there, lookin' down at ya, laddie. Aire ya goin' ta let her see you're sad as a wet cat?"

Lex glanced in the direction the worker was pointing and saw Louisa and Anna seated on chairs on the veranda, teacups in hand. They looked content, unperturbed by recent events. The men knew, although they didn't know the details, that there had been some sort of rift between their millwright and his wife. Loyalty to this man they worked for and respected made them fall on his side of the trouble, even without knowing its nature.

Brodie looked up as well, then snatched the instrument from the man. "Give me that fiddle! And get ready fer a rip-roarin' good time!"

Within seconds music filled the air, a jig that set the Irish workers dancing and incited Lex to watch, grinning and clapping his hands. When several such tunes had ended, Brodie paused and turned to Lex.

"I'm reckonin' ya know how ta step dance, laddie. Come on, Lex. Are ya goin' ta let these Irish buggers think they can outdance a Highlander?" He pulled the bow across the strings and broke into a tune Lex had never previously heard but which had the power to set his toes tapping.

Lex hesitated and looked up at the two women on the cabin porch on the hill above him. Then he stepped up on the veranda and let his feet follow the music. Onlookers cheered and clapped as he demonstrated steps learned at his home years before and let the happiness they inspired ease up through his body. The interest he glimpsed on the face of Lady when he stole a quick glance up at her made it all the more pleasurable.

"Enough!" Brodie finally lowered his fiddle. "Lex and I won't have a tad of work in us tomorrow if we keep this up."

"Just one more, Brodie," one of the men pleaded. " 'The Banks of Loch Lomond' to finish off the night. We Irish lads can appreciate that song…we've all had family and friends that suffered at the hands of the English."

Brodie drew a deep breath and looked over at Lex.

"Go ahead." He nodded.

As Brodie drew his bow across the strings and the soft strains of the old ballad filled the darkening evening, Lex glanced again at the two women on the veranda. They were leaning back in their chairs, listening. Could these two English ladies ever truly understand what it meant to be a Highlander? What the words of the ballad really represented?

Music and memories moved him. He went to stand beside Brodie and began to sing, his voice ringing out true and clear in the soft spring gloaming. The workers stared at the two tall, ruggedly handsome men, their music so fine and pure it mesmerized them.

When the last notes drifted off into the shadows, there was for a few moments absolute silence. Then the men began to file quietly back into the barracks, more than a few sniffs and throat-clearings accompanying their leaving. Some moments were too powerful for words.

"That was fair fine playin'." Lex looked at Brodie. "You've got the gift."

"Aye, the gift." The reply came out in a tone of defeat. "Bloody hell." He looked at Lex, his face contorting into lines of regret. "I worked my men like slaves today, and they didn't warrant it. If Harry had been at the mill today instead of home tryin' to smooth troubled waters, he would have kicked my arse for such behavior. And well deserved it would have been."

"You made it up to them tonight with your playing. From what I've seen, they're pretty much a good lot. They understand you've got troubles at home."

"Aye, well, troubles at home shouldn't affect a man's work." He stood, tucked the fiddle under his arm, and strode into the barracks.

Lex took a last glance up at the log cabin before he followed Brodie. The women were standing, gazing down at them. Then, they, too, turned away and went inside.

Chapter 17

"I never knew Lex could sing." Anna took a seat at the table and watched her sister moving about, lighting candles. "He has a fine voice…strong and pure and…"

"He and Brodie certainly made amazing music together." Louisa finished her task and sat down opposite Anna. "They're a pair in many ways. I see them becoming fast friends. I just hope"—she sighed—"that Lex proves to have a cooler head and will be a restraint on some of my husband's more impulsive moves."

"Louisa, I'm in love with Lex." The words were out in a reflex. The moment after they'd broken free of her lips, Anna clapped a hand over her mouth. "I'm…sorry. I didn't mean… That came out…" She stumbled to retrieve her confession.

"No need to recant." In the shadowy candlelight, Louisa smiled across at her sister and reached out to take her hand where it rested on the plank table. "I've seen it in your eyes every time you look at him."

"Good God, do you think he's recognized it, too?" Aghast, Anna looked across at her sister.

"I'm not sure, but he most certainly carries a deep affection for you. Intimate glances go both ways, you know. What do you intend to do about it?"

"Nothing, of course. He's given me no reason to believe I'm any more than a great nuisance. And until tonight, I myself didn't recognize, or at least wasn't ready to acknowledge, how I felt about him. But when Brodie played and he sang…I knew. Oh, Louisa, what am I to do?"

"Give him time, my sweet. He's still stuck in the Old World conventions that tell him you're a lady and he's…he was our father's groom. He'll come around…just as Brodie will." She stood and headed for the hearth. "Now, I think we could do with another cup of tea."

****

"I have to ride to the village." Louisa came out of the bedroom dressed in breeches, shirt, boots, and vest. "One of the workers has informed me a ship has docked that will be carrying medical supplies I've ordered. Come with me. The homestead will be fine left to itself for a few hours. Lex, as he's told you, has been given time from the mill to tend the stock."

"Probably you don't trust me here alone, after the last fiasco." Anna looked up at her sister. "Louisa, I can't tell you how sorry I am about your garden."

"It's still early in the season." Louisa shrugged. "It will recover. You did a fine job of repairing it. I'm not asking you to accompany me for any other reason than that I'd enjoy your company."

"You're not expecting Brodie home any time soon?" Anna asked.

"Not in the middle of the day." She cast her sister a smug smirk. "He's more likely to arrive in the evening…or night…when he's missing me too much to bear."

"You're still confident he will forgive your family background?"

"He will. He loves me as I love him. Brodie MacMillan is a hothead, but when he loves, he loves entirely. Now go on. Get dressed in your riding clothes. It will be a joy to ride beside my sister once more."

****

"Louisa, do you really think you should be here?" Anna glanced around the rough village tavern. They were the only women, aside from the barmaid, in evidence. "I mean, I'm a stranger with no reputation to protect. But you…you're a respectable married woman…a doctor, for heaven's sake!"

"Not an actual doctor, sister dear, just a healer. As for being a respectable married woman, well, people around here have come to expect only the most unconventional behavior of any female who'd marry a rogue like Brodie MacMillan. Furthermore, Frank Miller, the proprietor, makes the best boiled dinner I've ever tasted."

"Boiled dinner?"

"Game meat boiled with carrots, turnip, and potatoes, and perfectly seasoned. Frank Miller could be a chef in a fine European dining establishment…if he were able to return across the Atlantic."

"Are you suggesting he's an outlaw of some sort?" Anna lowered her voice.

"No one is certain, but most suspect. Ah, here is the man himself now." Louisa smiled as a burly, barrel-chested man wearing an apron approached their table.

"Mrs. MacMillan." Standing well over six feet tall, he crossed muscular, hirsute arms revealed by rolled-up shirt sleeves, and grinned down at her. "Always a pleasure to see you. And you've brought a friend."

"This is my sister Anna, Frank. She's come to visit

and, I'm hoping, to stay."

"Delighted to meet you, ma'am. Now what can I get for you ladies?"

"Two servings of your excellent boiled dinner if it's on tap today, with some of your fresh biscuits and two pints of your best ale."

"Right away, Mrs. MacMillan. Glad to have met you, Miss Anna." He gave her a polite nod before heading back toward a door behind the bar.

"He seems a most affable gentleman." Anna relaxed to enjoy their unconventional setting. "But I shouldn't want to challenge him to a wrestling match…or fisticuffs."

"Frank's physical prowess is what keeps this tavern in tack. No one would dare start a kerfuffle in here. They know they'd land on their backside out in the road."

"Mrs. MacMillan, as I live and breathe! Who better to discover within hours of making landfall!"

The boisterous greeting startled Anna who, with her back to the door, hadn't been aware of anyone's entrance. Now she swung to face a tall, well-built man, a broad grin splitting his handsome face. He doffed his hat to reveal a tangle of dark curls as he came up to their table and bent to take her sister's hand and bow over it.

"As always, your servant, Mistress." Anna caught the roguish twinkle in his blue eyes. "Still married to that rogue Brodie MacMillan, I fear?"

"Definitely." Louisa met his bold greeting with unabashed poise. "Captain, allow me to present my sister, La…Miss Anna Spencer."

"Aw, a miss is it?" He swung to face her. "And a

right bonnie one at that." He released her sister's hand to favor her with a similar gesture. "Not betrothed or any like foolishness, now, are you, Miss Anna Spencer?"

"Definitely not, Captain…?" She looked the question.

"Captain James MacTavish, of the good ship *Highland Lass*, at your service, ma'am." He grinned. "And this"—he turned to indicate a man who'd arrived to stand quietly behind him—"is my brother, Dr. William MacTavish."

"Good day, Will." Her sister's familiar greeting told Anna this was far from their first meeting.

"Louisa." The doctor inclined his head in her sister's direction.

"Might we join you ladies?" James MacTavish was already pulling out one of the two remaining empty chairs at their table. "I'm fair starving for good food after weeks at sea, and if I remember rightly, Frank Miller is a decent cook."

"Don't you have to oversee the unloading of your ship?" the doctor said.

"My first mate is a fine lad. He'll do well without me meddling about. Sit, Will, and for God's sake, take that stern look off your face." He winked at Anna as he settled himself in the chair. "You'd never know it, but he was quite a lad during the war, when we were privateering together."

The doctor, after glancing at Louisa as she smiled in return, acquiesced.

"I'd have a care, Doctor." A lanky, raggedly bearded man who'd been leaning on the end of the bar turned to the quartette. His bloodshot eyes focused on

William MacTavish. His left arm hung limp at his side. "If that bastard Brodie MacMillan gets wind of the fact that you're cavortin' with his woman, all hell could break loose."

"Out of my way, Michael." Frank Miller pushed out of the kitchen, carrying a tray burdened with plates of food. "And out of my establishment. You've had enough, and it's just going on noon."

"Aw, Frank," the man whined, indicating his arm. "Just one more…for a poor cripple."

"I've seen you use that arm as good as the next man. You've been faking to get sympathy and handouts. Now get!"

Mumbling curses, the man headed for the door, dirty clothing and body sending off a rank odor as he passed their table.

"Pay Michael Kelly no mind, Doctor." Frank Miller distributed plates around the table. "He's a lazy tramp, nothing more. Molly"—he turned to call to the barmaid—"four ales here, if you please."

"Frank's right, Miss Anna," the captain was quick to agree. "Michael Kelly is just a foul-mouthed layabout. No one listens to him. Frank, my lad, two more dinners such as these." He indicated the steaming plates in front of the women. "You always were one of the world's best cooks."

"Go on with you, Captain. You could charm the birds out of trees and no mistake." Frank Miller winked at Anna. "Watch out for this one, Miss." He turned back toward the kitchen.

"Thank you, Mr. Miller, I will."

Anna had recognized James MacTavish's attempt to minimize the incident with the man Michael Kelly, but now that she knew Brodie MacMillan, fear that the tramp's assessment might be correct bothered her. She glanced from her sister to Doctor William MacTavish and caught them exchanging looks.

Is there something between them? Something beyond shared interest in medicine? Oh, God, I hope not!

Chapter 18

They ate their meal in a companionable atmosphere, largely due to the captain's affability and wit. James MacTavish fairly oozed charm even as she also guessed he'd be a formidable enemy. No shrinking violet under any conditions, that was Captain James MacTavish. Furthermore, both he and his brother were extremely handsome men.

"Louisa, are you planning to come down to Jamie's ship to claim your share of medical supplies?" The doctor addressed her sister as they finished eating. "I was thinking we might go over them together. There are a couple of new compounds I think you'll find useful. I've ordered enough that we might share."

"Thank you, Will." Anna saw her sister's face brighten at the idea as she stood. "I have sacks tied to my saddle to take my purchases home."

"I suppose that means we must accompany this pair." Captain James MacTavish cast Anna a mock-despairing look. "And just when I was enjoying this little party." He got to his feet and held out a hand to assist Anna. "But I'm hoping it won't be the last time we share each other's company, Miss Anna. I'll be in port for a few days." He turned to his brother. "You and Louisa go ahead. I'll pay for this fine repast and follow you shortly with this delightful creature as companion."

Her sister and the doctor left. Anna waited while

the captain paid for their meal. When he rejoined her, he crooked his arm to her, a roguish, difficult-to-resist grin on his handsome face.

"I'll be the envy of the village, with you beside me." He leaned close, speaking sotto voce. "The folks will see the MacTavish brothers at their best with two beauties in tow."

As she accepted his offer and they headed out of the tavern, trepidations fluttered inside her. The village's envy wasn't her concern. Brodie MacMillan's reaction, if he heard of this meeting, was.

****

"I can guess what you're thinking, Anna." Louisa addressed her as the pair rode slowly back toward the homestead. They had to keep their horses to a sedate pace to protect damaging the precious medical supplies tied to the saddles of both animals.

"And just what am I supposed to be thinking?" Anna focused on the trail ahead.

"That Will MacTavish and I are too friendly, too…companionable."

"Of course not. Louisa…"

"Anna, don't play false with me. I know you too well." Louisa drew her white mare to a stop. Anna paused Silverbell beside her. "I assure you, Will and I are simply friends who share a common passion for healing and innovations in the practice of medicine. Of late, however, our relationship has intensified."

"Oh, God, Louisa, you don't mean…"

"Not what you're thinking. I'm sharing my list of patients and the cures I've been using with Will. I'm going to be dropping back on my ministering to the sick and injured. Doctor MacTavish will be taking over. I have to be careful from now on. Anna, I'm pregnant…again."

"Louisa, that's wonderful! Brodie must be delighted. No wonder you expect him back at any moment."

"Brodie doesn't know…and he won't know until I'm well over the first few critical weeks. Last time I was pregnant I told him early on. His joy turned to such sadness when I lost the child that I won't risk putting him through that again. He blamed my work for causing the miscarriage, and I'm not sure it wasn't a contributing factor. So this time, I'll be cutting back and doing a lot less strenuous riding."

"You're content to let him be suspicious of you and the doctor?"

"For the time being. Promise me you'll keep my secret?"

"Of course. You know I will. But *promise* me you won't keep your husband uninformed any longer than necessary."

****

"MacMillan." The tall man in buckskins acknowledged Brodie with a curt nod when he and a neatly groomed and dressed friend joined Brodie and Lex as they waited at the bar for their ales in the village tavern. It had been two weeks since Lex and Anna had arrived in the community.

"MacPherson." Brodie's acceptance of the big man's greeting was equally abrupt.

"I see ye and yer man have brought in two wagonloads of decent-lookin' plank." The barmaid placed tankards before Brodie and Lex. "Two more of the same, lass," he ordered her.

"Aye, more than decent, MacPherson. Prime." Brodie quaffed a long drink of ale. "We've got fine logs and our noses to the grindstone. Hard work is the key."

"Maybe ya should lift yer nose and take stock of whit's goin' on around ya." Eyes narrowing with what Lex saw as malicious intent, Culloden MacPherson accepted his drink from the woman and looked over at Brodie. "Maybe it's time ya took stock of yer family affairs."

"And chust whit is that supposed ta mean?" Brodie's accent broke through as it always did when he was agitated.

"Yer wife's been seen in town with that doctor newly arrived in the valley. Rumor has it he's got rich privateerin' with his brother durin' the war, and now he's settlin' down across the river. At the moment he's livin' in a log cabin he's told people he plans ta use for his doctorin', while he builds a fine stone house on a hill above the river. Folks who've seen the foundation laid say it will be more than large enough ta satisfy the most elegant of ladies."

"Oh, aye?" Brodie turned to face the other man full on. Lex felt his gut tighten as his companion's hand went to the hilt of the sword he'd learned he always wore on trips to the village. Why had the man chosen to use the phrase 'most elegant of ladies'? Brodie MacMillan needed no further reminders of his wife's lineage.

"Aye." Culloden MacPherson paused to take a drink before continuing. "And chust now I saw her boardin' that new cable ferry with him, both of them with their horses. I reckon as how they're plannin' ta ride downriver from the ferry landin' ta his place…ta talk over medicine and cures and such…no doubt." The smirk he cast at Brodie brought Frank Miller the tavern owner into the situation.

"Hie, now, lads." The burly man placed large hirsute hands on the bar and leaned forward to look from one to the other. "I'll not have the pair of you comin' to fisticuffs in my tavern. I'll be thankin' you to take your quarrel outside."

"Cully, don't go promoting a confrontation." His friend, who Lex saw had the cut of a gentleman, tried to intervene.

"And don't ya go interferin', Fletch."

"Let's go." Lex touched Brodie's arm, feeling the muscles tensed into rock-hard readiness. When Brodie looked at him, Lex jerked his head toward the door. "Our loads will be shipboard by now," he said, watching Culloden MacPherson and his companion warily out of the tail of his eye. "We'd best be having a talk with the captain."

"A good idea." Culloden MacPherson voiced the snide remark. "It never hurts to make certain of what exactly is going on."

"That does it!" Brodie pulled his sword belt over his head and handed it to Lex. "Outside, MacPherson!"

"It will be my pleasure, MacMillan."

The man Culloden MacPherson had referred to as Fletch looked over at Lex, gave a rueful shrug, and followed the pair out of the tavern. Lex, after a slight pause, did likewise.

Chapter 19

Lex sat in the jail cell and rubbed a hand over the left side of his face. It had to be a lovely shade of black-and-blue, he reckoned. Beside him, Brodie MacMillan sported a black eye and cut lip. Across from them, in similar confinement, were Culloden MacPherson and his once neatly groomed friend looking equally abused.

What had started as a fist fight between MacPherson and Brodie had rapidly become a general donnybrook, with local men quickly taking sides with either of the pair. Lex had found himself in the heart of it, at first avoiding punches as best he could but finally giving in and planting as many as he could himself. Only the arrival of the local magistrate and his deputy riding into the center of the melee and firing off their pistols had brought the battle to a close.

Now here he sat, in prison again, battered and sore, in this new country where he'd hoped for peace and freedom. He glanced over at Brodie, hoping his disgust and annoyance was mirrored in his expression.

"I'm right sorry, laddie," Brodie said softly. "I'm a hothead, and that's fer certain sure. But"—his tone rose so the men in the opposite cell might hear—"I'll not let any man cast aspersions on my wife."

"Aire ya such a dour Scot ya cannae bear a bit of teasin'?" Culloden MacPherson rose and came to stand at the bars of his cell.

"And have ya forgotten how my men and me joined forces with yers to rescue yer friend's future wife not so long ago?" Brodie was on his feet, blue eyes flashing.

"No, no, I've not forgotten." The man's tone moderated. "Ah, come along, MacMillan. Ya know we were both fair spoilin' for a bit of a scrap. Life's been gettin' way too dull of late." He chuckled.

"Aye, well, maybe yer right." Lex was surprised to hear Brodie's next words come out in a heaved sigh. "Maybe we were both ripe for it. But"—his words took up the pace—"no more tauntin' about my wife. Next time yer on for a scrap, just punch me in the jaw."

"Brodie MacMillan, you and your man are free to go." The magistrate, Captain Caleb Cameron, and his deputy stepped into the cell block. "But you'll be making a hefty contribution to the new fever isolation hospital being built on the island downstream and then immediately collecting your wagons and getting out of the village."

"Oh…of course, aye." Brodie drew himself up and smirked across at his nemesis. "A hefty contribution, and no mistake."

"You, Culloden MacPherson, and you, Fletcher Atkin, will be free to go an hour later under the same conditions. Mr. MacDougal, release Mr. MacMillan and his companion."

"Aye." The tall, broad-shouldered deputy stepped forward to produce a ring of keys and open the cell door.

"Thank you, Cal." Brodie paused beside the magistrate and, to Lex's surprise, spoke to him in a friendly manner. "I've spent a deal too much time in these stinkin' cells."

Too much time in the cells? Bollocks, what has this man done? Lex glanced at his friend.

"Just keep your nose clean and you won't have to come back," the magistrate advised.

As they walked up the street to reclaim their wagons, Lex could not contain the question.

"Why were you in those cells?"

"Ah, nothin' much…and wrongly accused, mind." Brodie's reply was casual. "Seduction, bastardry." He chuckled. "It amuses me to think that the one mischief I did commit in this country I was never jailed for."

"Which was?"

"Raidin' Joe Carmody's estate on the night I first arrived in Riverhaven. The old bastard had it comin'. He had his men frighten Harry's wife and her youngest daughter near out of their wits and set his mill afire."

God Almighty! Brodie MacMillan is a rogue of the first order, and no mistake. I'll have to watch my step around him, or I'll be back in those cells with him again.

****

"Louisa, I'm going for a walk." Anna put on a straw hat with a broad brim as she called into the bedroom where her sister, resting after a bout of nausea, was lying down. "Do you mind? I'll stay if you feel…"

"I'm perfectly well," Louisa replied. "Go. It's a lovely summer's day. We don't get many that are this agreeable. There's a nice breeze to keep flies at bay, and it's not overly warm."

"Very well. I'll be back shortly."

She set off out of the cabin and along the top of the hill to where the lane to her sister's homestead joined the main wagon road to the mill. Pausing, she looked down at the activity in the valley. A melee of men and horses worked steadily about the mill and its yard. She saw Lex among them, dark red curls making him distinguishable from the others. Much as she willed herself to ignore the fact, she had to admit he was a fine figure of a man.

Well, enough. She squared her shoulders and started down into the valley. She'd made her resolve as she lay in her bed the previous night. It was time she made peace—or at least tried to make peace—with Margaret Wallace. She might not be able to bring her sister and Brodie back together, but she could at least do her best to fix the other marriage her arrival had mangled.

She clutched at her hat as a sudden gust threatened to pull it from her head. With determined strides, she ignored the glances of the working men as she passed their place of employment, even that of Lex who'd paused to stare at her. Holding her head high, she marched across the bridge over the millpond and up the hill to the rambling log house that was the home of Highland Harry, his wife, and…was it nine?…children.

As she entered the deserted dooryard, her resolve began to melt. Margaret Wallace had demonstrated she was a woman of spirit, not, Anna suspected, above becoming physically violent to protect her family.

Nothing ventured, nothing gained.

Choosing the back door, she went up on the step and knocked. It was opened by a pretty, sandy-haired girl in her teens.

"Yes?" The coldness in the word indicated she knew who Anna was.

"Good morning." Anna smiled. "Will you tell Mrs. Wallace that Anna Spencer would like to see her?"

"I..." the girl began, but suddenly Margaret Wallace was behind her, her expression hard and cold.

"It's all right, Bella," she said. "You finish tending to your chores. This woman and I will take a walk down to the stream."

Closing the door behind her, Margaret Wallace stepped outside. "This way," she said, leading the way around the big log barn. "I do not want the children overhearing anything you might have to say."

Shortly they were on a trail leading through trees down a slope to where the brook babbled free after serving its purpose at the dam. She paused beside a rough bench and indicated Anna was to sit.

"Well, what is it?" Margaret Wallace's tone was anything but cordial as she seated herself beside her.

"Mrs. Wallace, I've come to explain." Anna untied her hat, removed it, and placed it in her lap. "Your husband and I were never lovers. We were both playing a particularly dangerous game...myself to capture the famous Highland Harry, and Harry to get his hands on an elegant necklace I had in my possession. I'm assuming he planned to sell it to further the Highlanders' cause. We were each foolishly bold."

"That seems a most unlikely thing for a *lady* to do." Sarcasm reeked in Margaret Wallace's tone as she turned narrowed green eyes on her companion.

"I agree, but you see, I'm not a typical lady." She toyed with her hat's ribbons. "You know my sister Louisa. By now, you've no doubt come to realize she's her own woman, not averse to a bit of adventure."

"She is that." Margaret Wallace said, and Anna

was relieved to hear a bit of the enmity go out of her tone.

"I believe her often unorthodox behavior has been instrumental in helping a number of injured and ailing people in this area?"

"That it has."

"My attempt to capture the outlaw Highland Harry came from a bit of the same desire to help, to rid our region of a sly, bold rogue…and have a bit of adventure along the way." She cast Margaret a sideways, speculative glance. *Is the woman softening, becoming willing to listen?*

"You say you were never his lover?" The words sounded speculative, definitely opening up to what Anna had to say.

"Definitely not." Anna turned fully to face her. "I may be a bit of an adventuress, Mrs. Wallace, but I'm not a whore. I will give my love to one man and one man only…when I find the right one."

"What about the man Lex? You traveled with him unchaperoned."

"Lex was a groom on my father's estate. I brought a pair of horses with me. He came to care for them." She avoided her companion's eyes. She wasn't lying, just not going into complete details.

"Very well." Margaret Wallace stood and held out her right hand. "I will believe you."

"Thank you." Anna accepted the offer.

They started back up the trail together, but as they emerged from the trees Margaret stopped and turned to her.

"But let me tell you, Anna Spencer, if I catch any woman trying to steal Harry, she'll be in for the fight of her life. Do you understand?" Green eyes flashed emerald fire.

"I do. And I do not blame you. A good man is definitely worth fighting for."

"Very well. I'll no doubt be seeing you at the tea at the manse this afternoon. Good morning to you." Margaret walked to the house and went inside, closing the door behind her.

No invitation to come in for refreshment…not even the offer of a glass of water on this warm day. Well, I've done my part. I've given her the truth. With a resigned sigh, Anna started back down the hill. She recalled Margaret Wallace's parting words…something about tea at the manse that afternoon.

At the log cabin, she found Louisa pouring hot water into a teapot on the table.

"You're feeling better?" Anna asked.

"Much. Tea?"

"Please, but you sit down and enjoy yours. I'll fetch a cup for myself."

"Very well." With a smile, Louisa took a chair. "I'm not above a little cosseting."

"I went to see Margaret Wallace," Anna said, once she'd poured herself a cup and seated herself across from her sister.

"Oh. And how did that go?"

"As well as can be expected, I suppose." Anna shrugged. "We're not blood enemies any more, but we're a long way from becoming fast friends."

"Margaret can be a stubborn woman, but it's well worth the effort to win her over." Louisa paused to sip her tea. "She can be a valuable ally. Give her time. It will work out."

"She mentioned seeing me at the manse for tea this afternoon. Do you know what she meant?"

"Good heavens, yes. I forgot about it in all that's been happening around here. Mary Morgan, Reverend Morgan's wife, always holds an afternoon tea to introduce women new to the Riverhaven area to ladies of the community. This gathering will be to welcome you. We must choose suitable dresses."

"We can't ride?" Anna called after her sister as Louisa bustled into the bedroom.

"Hardly." Sounds told Anna her sister was shuffling around among her belongings. "We must give the *appearance* of being ladies. I'm sure I have a gown that will fit you."

Her sister's emphasis on the word "appearance" made Anna smile. The Spencer sisters, while having the ability to behave as ladies, definitely weren't the demure, retiring creatures the word suggested.

Later, when they set out for the manse, Louisa driving her white mare Snow harnessed to the farm wagon, they wore white muslin dresses decorated with dainty flowers, lace gloves and shawls, and sunbonnets. Anna hadn't been able to bring a variety of clothing with her, but as she and her sister were the same size, she fitted well into borrowed garments suitable for a ladies' afternoon tea.

"I'm glad you'll be getting to meet the women of the community," Louisa said as they drove along the sun-dappled path toward the manse. "I'll give you a bit of their background so that you may be prepared to make their acquaintance. They're a varied lot…from former Highland outlaw to privateer to tavern worker to English lady. Then, of course, there will be Hazel

Green and Lillian Gardiner, wives of local farmers. You must watch out for that pair. They're extremely straight-laced and judgmental, not like most of the other citizens who make up the community of Riverhaven."

"It should be an intriguing afternoon." Anna cast her sister a grin. "They sound like a most eclectic group."

"They are." Louisa held Snow to a walk. It was a lovely spring day, and both women were enjoying the drive through the burgeoning forest. "First, of course, there's Margaret Wallace, whom you know. She arrived in this country alone and nearly penniless and was forced to find employment in the village tavern to support herself. Shortly afterward, William Fowler, a widower with seven children, asked her to marry him and help raise his children. Good-hearted Margaret, known as Maggie at the time, couldn't bear to see those little ones motherless, so she agreed. From what Margaret has told me, it was a marriage of convenience, for the sake of the children."

"It wasn't…a love match?" Anna asked cautiously.

"If you're asking if it was consummated, no, it wasn't." Louisa drew a deep breath. "Margaret is a fine woman with a kind heart. It was her concern for those seven youngsters that caused her to agree to a marriage to a man she'd known only a week. Sadly, they were together but a short time when William was killed—murdered, it's a widely held belief, by Joseph Carmody, a businessman who wanted to take over William's mills."

"Good God! Was the perpetrator apprehended?"

"No, nor was his culpability ever proven. However, he was later killed. That's another story. Margaret was left alone with seven children to raise, and with Joseph Carmody still alive at that point and determined to take over her industries. When a ship arrived from the Old Country with Harry aboard and she heard tales of his prowess as a warrior, she decided he was just what she needed to help her and her family. She asked him to marry her, and he agreed."

"What an amazing woman! Again, a marriage of convenience?" Anna shook her head ruefully, amazed at Margaret Wallace's tenacity.

"At first, but not any more, definitely not any more." Louisa looked over at her sister with a sly smile. "You saw how she reacted at the possibility of you and Harry having had an affair, how he rushed after her to make amends. It may have started out as a marriage of convenience, but it's evolved into one of passionate love."

"How fortunate. Tell me about the other women."

"Well, Anna Cameron and Ginny MacDougal will be there, I've no doubt. They're an interesting pair. They both served as privateers beside their husbands in the recent war. Anna is the wife of Captain Caleb Cameron, our local magistrate. Ginny is married to Duncan MacDougal, who is now the magistrate's deputy. Captain Cameron was master of the famous privateering ship *Lady Ghost*. Duncan MacDougal served as his first mate. Their wives sailed with them."

"How exciting! Lady privateers! I look forward to meeting this pair. Who else will be making up this amazing gathering?"

"Isabella Atkin will most likely be there, with her former lady's maid, Lucinda MacPherson. Isabella, although not a titled lady, is of gentle birth but is adapting well to our society. You'll like them."

"The only lady you haven't mentioned is the minister's wife, Mary Morgan. Is she the only woman among this diversified group without a past?"

"Definitely not. Mary Morgan once rode with her husband, then known as Lachlan Cameron, as a rebel in the Highlands. Her name, then, was Iona. When she became pregnant, they gave up the outlaw way of life, moved to Riverhaven, changed their names to Mary and Edward Morgan, and took over the church. Amazingly, it turns out Lachlan—Edward—actually is an ordained clergyman who adopted the rebel way of life when his congregation was attacked by redcoats."

"I can see I'll be entering an interesting community…if I decide to stay," Anna said softly, ignoring her sister's glance.

Chapter 20

"A word." Brodie stopped in front of Lex where he sat on the barracks veranda, talking with other workers in the sunset. Tired after a hard day's work, the men were leaning against the log walls and sitting on the steps enjoying a few moments of respite in the cooling air before heading inside the stuffy, hot cabin for the night.

The bright, triumphant expression in his friend's face and eyes brought a sense of unease washing over Lex. What had the man been up to?

Better to know than to be ignorant and vulnerable. He pulled himself to his feet and followed Brodie down a trail that led into the trees beyond the millyard.

"I got it!" As soon as they were well out of the hearing of the men, pulling a piece of paper from inside his shirt, Brodie turned on Lex.

"Got what?" Lex stared at it. Surely not the map. The paper was much too new.

"The directions ta the location o' the treasure, you great daft oaf! Look!"

Lex took the paper and, in the fading light, saw that it was a drawing…a copy of the treasure map, if his memory held true.

"How did you manage this?" He looked up at his companion.

"While the ladies were at tea at the Reverend

Morgan's manse this afternoon, I sneaked into the cabin and made this copy. I wouldn't be so daft as ta take the original. Louisa would be right quick ta suspect me of the theft. She knows I'm good at thievin' when the need arises."

"And chust how do ya propose ta get away ta go treasure hunting? The mill is busy right now, and yer the millwright. Yer needed on the job."

"In a week or so, we'll have fulfilled all our pressin' orders. Harry always allows his men a few days' leisure at such a time. I'll tell him I need ta go ta Richibucto…that's a village about fifty miles to the south…to get parts for the mill. I'll be takin' ya along to help with loadin' the wagon and share the drivin'."

"I cannae go dashin' off! Who will do the barn work at your homestead? That filly of yours needs a strong hand."

"Sam, Harry's youngest stepson, will see to it. He's a dab hand with livestock, a farmer if ever there was one. He'll enjoy doin' it after workin' in the mill."

"I…" Lex tried to find another objection but failed.

"Stop mumbling, lad, and pull yerself up by the bootstraps. With the wealth that treasure will produce, ya can stand up to the Lady Anna, make her an offer she won't refuse. I see how ya look at her, hungry and longin', and I've caught her castin' ya a not ugly glance."

Impossible as it appeared, Lex realized he would like to be in a position to think of Lady as more than someone to protect, more than someone who came to him only at night in erotic dreams. And then there was Marie. The dear old Frenchwoman longed for proof that her uncle hadn't simply been an addled drunkard spinning tales in taverns of a treasure that was pure fantasy. He owed Marie his life.

"Verrae well." He squared his shoulders and drew a deep breath. "I'll do it."

"That's a good lad!" Brodie slapped him on the back. "We'll show our lasses what we're made of, sure and certain."

****

"Ye've not gone ta church?" Lex sat down on the log beside Brodie.

On seeing the millwright head away from the barracks, Lex had followed him. The man had paused at a point where the stream, freed from the restraints of dam and mill, bubbled happily toward the river and bay. The summer Sunday was sultry, gray and heavy with the threat of a thunderstorm.

"I'm not a church-goin' man these days." Brodie pulled a flask from inside his vest and took a swig.

"An atheist, then?"

"I said not church-goin' *these* days," he snapped. "That doesn't mean I'm not God-fearin'."

"Isn't it a bit early for that?" Lex jerked a thumb to indicate the flask. "Sun isn't yet over the foreyard."

"Did ye come here to devil me?" Scowling, Brodie swung on him. "If so, ya can chust be takin' yerself off to hell."

"Nay, nay." Lex leaned forward, rubbing his hands together between his spread knees. "I thought ye might be in need of company."

Silence fell. Lex noted that even the birds were quiet. *Storm coming, definitely a storm coming.*

"Here." Brodie extended the flask to him.

Lex hesitated, then accepted.

"Sun must be over the foreyard somewhere," he said. He quaffed a swallow.

"Good lad." Looking over at him, Brodie relaxed into a semblance of a grin, lines of humor crinkling around his mouth and blue eyes. "Now, I haven't been idlin' my brain of late. I've been formin' a plan…a plan that can benefit both of us."

"Oh, aye." Lex wiped his mouth with the forearm of his shirt sleeve and handed the flask back to his companion. Suspicion niggled in his gut. Knowledge of his companion's wild deeds and the witnessing of Brodie MacMillan's quick temper had made him apprehensive. He wasn't sure he wanted to be a part of any of the man's schemes that might land him, Lex, back in trouble with the law.

"Can ya swim, laddie?"

"Aye."

"Can ya dive and hold yer breath fer a wee time underwater?"

"Aye." With each question, Lex's apprehension mounted.

"Figured as much." He narrowed his eyes as he looked speculatively over at his companion. "Probably had to use those skills on more than one occasion when the redcoats were hot on yer tail, no? Well, then, it's decided. Next week, work will be easin' off at the mill and we'll be able to start lookin' for that treasure. Once we find it, I can build Louisa a house that will make that shack MacTavish is constructin' look like a hovel."

Lex wet his lips and looked off into the trees.

"Ah, well, not yet ready to trust me." Brodie turned his attention to the copy of the map. "Ya will…in time. Now, let us get to plannin' how we'll find this treasure."

"I'm not about ta go stealin' from Lady." He stood to glare down at the other man. "That treasure is rightly hers."

"Take it easy, laddie, take it easy." Brodie reached up to restrain him by grasping his wrist. "We won't be stealin', just protectin', and then seein' all involved get their fair share."

"And chust how are you figurin' that?"

"Well, I reckon as how ya know yer lady as well as I know mine. They're more than sisters. They're birds of a feather, as brave as they are beautiful. Yers, however, I'm thinkin', might be just a tad more rash. I'm believin' yer lady will shortly want to set out, possibly with only ye in tow, to find that treasure. That wouldn't be safe. Now, if ye an' I were to find it for her…"

"What's ta insure ya'd give it up…even a portion of it…ta her…ta us?"

"I dunnae fleece my friends." Brodie was on his feet, facing Lex, expression taut and bellicose. "I am a man of honor."

"A confessed highwayman, a man most likely with a price on his head in Scotland?"

"A rebel. The highwayman bit was simply a necessary offshoot. Now, what do ya say? Are ya with me…to protect our ladies?" He held out his hand.

"Let me sleep on it." Lex turned to go back up the trail. "I need ta think."

Brodie's snort of derision followed him.

****

Anna watched as Louisa answered the knock at the door, Jasper protectively at her side. A young lad not more than twelve years of age stood on the veranda. At the sight of the dog, he paled and moved back a step.

"It's all right," Louisa reassured him with a smile. "Jasper won't hurt you. What can I do for you?"

"I…I've come from the village with a message for Mistress Anna Spencer," he stammered, still eyeing the animal apprehensively. "I'm to wait for a answer." He held out a folded paper sealed with wax.

"Come in." Louisa held the door wider. "I've just brought up milk from our ice house, and there's fresh bread. "I'm sure you must be hungry after your ride."

"Yes, do come in." Anna stood from where she'd been sitting by the hearth and held out her hand. "I'm Anna Spencer."

"Well…" The boy, his nose moving slightly at the scent of the baking, moved cautiously inside and gave her the paper.

"Sit." Louisa indicated a place at the table while Anna remained staring down at the message in her hand. As Louisa bustled about, getting the boy milk, bread, maple syrup, and butter, Anna eased her finger beneath the wax seal and opened the paper.

She suppressed a small gasp of surprise. It was an invitation from Captain James MacTavish to go riding with him. Louisa must have caught her surprised reaction. She left the lad engrossed in his lunch and came to stand beside her sister.

"Anna, what is it?"

She handed the paper to her.

"Oh, my, an invitation from Jamie."

"Yes."

"And what will be your reply?"

"I shall accept." She gave a defiant toss of her

head. “Lex has made it clear he doesn’t welcome becoming involved with ladies he considers born above his station. Therefore”—she winked and gave her sister a mischievous grin—“I believe it’s time to show him I’m not above finding a man who will.” She went to the cupboard and took down ink and quill.

“Oh, Anna, tread carefully.” Louisa cautioned as her sister seated herself at the table to fashion her reply. “I suspect Lex is not a man to be trifled with. Pricking him with jealousy might be a dangerous thing to do.”

“Never fear, sister dear. I know Lex. A sharp prick of what you term jealousy may be just what he needs.”

Chapter 21

"Well, will ya look at that!" Brodie MacMillan stopped outside the mill and glared up the hill toward his homestead. "Bloody bastard! What right does he think he has to come ridin' onto my property?"

Lex came to stand beside him and squinted in the same direction.

"You know that man?" he asked. The new arrival swung down from a fine-looking bay and strode toward the house He tossed the horse's reins about the veranda railing as he made his way up the steps to the door. His clothes marked him as a gentleman and a dashing one at that.

"Jamie MacTavish...Captain James MacTavish." The name came out as a wheezed curse. "Brother to Doctor William MacTavish, the two bastards Culloden MacPherson made remarks about when we were in the tavern. The pair o' them got rich during the war. Privateering, they called it. I call it piracy."

"Ah." Lex pursed his lips in acknowledgement.

"He's no doubt come on his brother's behalf. The guid doctor knows better than to show his miserable face around here." Eyes narrowing, jaw tensing, Brodie brushed sawdust from his pants and reached for the shirt he'd thrown over a pile of lumber earlier in the morning. "I'll chust be helpin' him on his way."

"Perhaps you'd best hold off a bit." Lex sought to

be the voice of reason. "I don't think coming to fisticuffs in your dooryard will endear you to your wife."

"Aye, well, we'll see about that." Brodie jerked his arms into the shirt and was about to start up the hill when Anna emerged from the house. Dressed in a green riding habit, she paused to greet the man. Something in Lex's gut jerked as Sam, Harry and Margaret's youngest stepson, led a saddled Silverbell out of the stable.

"An assignation!" Brodie paused, blue eyes snapping with anger. "Lady Anna was ready and waitin' for him. He must've sent her word of his comin'."

"I saw a young lad on a mule come to your house earlier," Lex recalled.

"Ah." Beside him, Lex heard Brodie's voice slide into an ominous mutter. "So that's the lay of the land. The bugger has come courtin' Miss Anna, and probably with words from his brother for my wife as well. Lex, I'm thinkin' it's time the pair of us should be gettin' involved. I don't trust either of those MacTavish brothers."

Brodie's suggestion that they investigate the relationship between Anna and the well-dressed man appealed to Lex. Although he had no claim on her, he considered himself her protector and, as such, he had an obligation to keep her out of harm's way. Brodie had described the man as a former privateer…a pirate…definitely not someone with whom Lady should get involved.

Then reason overtook him. She was a free woman, and he, Lex, had no claim over her. And she'd proven herself on more than one occasion to be capable of dealing with the unwelcome advances of men.

"We'd best be getting back to work." He tried to dissuade both himself and Brodie even as he longed to keep Lady away from this well-turned-out man. Jerking his head in the direction of the mill, he started to head back toward it.

"Wait a bit, wait a bit." Brodie placed his hands on his hips. "Let us chust see what transpires."

With a guffaw, Lex acquiesced. Curiosity, and not a small roil of jealousy which he consciously denied, held him in place.

"I cannot countenance that bastard ridin' off with my sister-in-law. Captain MacTavish," he yelled, striding up the hill. "Takin' Miss Anna ridin', aire ye?" His Highland accent was thick, his words ice cold with threat. Lex wasted no time following him.

"Aye, Mr. MacMillan." Jamie MacTavish, appearing unabashed by the other man's appearance, cast him an affable grin. "A right fine day for it, dunnae ya think?" He, too, let the Scottish brogue color his speech.

"I don't think any day is a guid one for a MacTavish to come sniffin' around my women." Reflexively, Brodie's hand went to his side, where his sword would have hung had he not come from working in the mill.

"Ya seem ta be bereft of yer famous weapon." The captain continued in the same friendly tone and manner. "Well, niver fear. You'll discover you'll have no need of it. I assure you my intentions are strictly honorable."

"Honorable! A pirate's idea of honorable!" Brodie spat out the words.

"Mr. MacMillan, enough!" Anna stepped between the two men. "I'm a grown woman, perfectly capable of deciding with whom I'll keep company and perfectly capable of taking care of myself." She indicated a knife in a scabbard on her belt. "Now, I'll be obliged if you'll move aside and let us get on with our ride. Captain, if you'll be so good as to give me a leg up?" She turned to cast a bright smile on Jamie MacTavish.

"Allow me." Lex stepped to the forefront and cupped his hands into a stirrup. A whiff of that mesmerizing scent she'd worn back in the Old Country assailed him.

God Almighty!

She hesitated, looking at him with demure, coquettish eyes.

"Very well." She slipped her booted foot into his palms and allowed him to propel her onto Silverbell's back, landing astride in the saddle she'd brought from England.

Swinging onto his mount, Captain MacTavish touched his hat brim to the two men before nudging his horse into a trot to keep pace with Anna, who was already moving out of the dooryard.

As Brodie watched them go, Lex noticed Louisa had come out onto the veranda and was gazing after them, hands on her hips. When her husband turned in her direction, she threw an annoyed glance in his direction before whirling and striding back into the house. The door banged shut after her.

"Bloody hell!" Brodie slammed the fist of his right hand into the palm of his left. "Bastard!" He stared after the pair trotting off down the lane before swinging on Lex. "And there ya stood, mute as a stump! Have ya no balls, lad? The man is ridin' off with yer lady."

"She's hardly my lady." Lex's shoulders rose in a huge sigh. "No matter what my position now, I was her servant, and she remains an aristocrat. And did ya not take a decent gander at the man? Dressed in the finest, barbered ta perfection. And here I stand." He spread his arms to indicate his bare chest, glistening with sweat, his dirty work pants, aware of his hair tied untidily back into a queue, a day's stubble on his face.

"Ah, laddie, don't put yerself down." Brodie came back to a bit of his natural good nature. "Ye're not exactly ugly. And I've learned that women…at least the few I've had the honor to know well…are not always averse to a man without a shirt and wet with the results of hard labor. In fact"—he looked up with what Lex could only describe as longing at the closed door of his house—"I recall some verrae fine times when I came up from the mill in such a condition." He drew a deep breath as he started back toward the mill. "Of course, I paused at the washstand on the porch to make certain sure I didn't stink."

In spite of the events of the morning, Lex felt a grin pulling at the corners of his mouth. He liked Brodie MacMillan, no doubt about it. They were fast on the way to becoming boon companions. Then he remembered that soft, erotic fragrance Lady had been wearing, and all semblance of humor vanished.

"Lady was right." Lex fought to be the voice of reason, although in his chest something was pounding hard. "She's free ta do as she pleases. That's why she came ta this country."

"Aye, and ye're tellin' me it didn't make your hackles rise just a wee bit to see that sea tramp ride off with her?" Brodie put emphasis on the last word.

"No more than yer wife's slamming the door on ya made yers."

"Argh!" Brodie took off in long, angry strides down the hill toward the mill.

After a final glance down the lane, where the mounted couple was turning onto the road to the village, Lex followed his companion back down the hill to the mill. Work. Hard, back-breaking work. That's what he needed to force what he was loath to acknowledge as jealous rage out of his system. He had no claim on Anna Spencer and never would have. Still…

****

Lex couldn't sleep. It wasn't because of the conditions in the mill workers' barracks. He'd spent many nights confined with other men and was accustomed to their snoring, mumbling, and breaking wind. No, it was thoughts and visions of Lady Anna Spencer, of the swashbuckling sea captain, well dressed and swaggering…thoughts and visions of what could have or might have transpired during the course of their outing, of what acts that sensuous scent might have encouraged the bounder to attempt, of what possible effect it could have had on the captain.

"Argh!" He rolled from his bunk, pulled on his shirt, picked up his boots, and moved silent as a shadow out the door. It came naturally. He'd had years of practice sneaking away into the night. Once outside, he sat down on a bench to pull on his scuffed footwear. He walked a few paces, then paused.

Drawing a deep breath of cool night air into his lungs, he stood and stared up at the quarter moon rising above the trees beyond the MacMillan homestead on the hill. From down by the pond, frogs raised a chorus. Peace reigned in the small valley…everywhere but in at least one Highlander's heart.

"Couldn't sleep, laddie?" Brodie's voice so close behind him made him start. His hand flying to where a sword had once hung on his hip, he swung to face the man.

"So ye've still got the skills." Brodie's response was a chuckle. "Silent as a shadow, quick as a ferret. All in keepin' with yer former days…except for the fact ya forgot ya weren't armed. Whit brings ye out here at this time o' night, man? Haven't I been workin' ya hard enough to make ya need yer rest?"

"You've been working me hard enough."

"Then it must be somethin' else that's makin' ya restless. Not thinkin' about yer lady ridin' out with that bastard MacTavish, is it? If so, believe me, I understand."

"I've no claim on Lady. She's free to do as she pleases."

"Free, aye, but I believe ye've an obligation to see to her safety. And I can tell ya certain sure she's no' safe with either of those MacTavishes."

"Lady's a self-reliant woman. She carries a dagger. Captain MacTavish would find he's taken on no helpless damsel."

"Damsel? Whit have you been readin', laddie? Somethin' out o' *The Legends of King Arthur*?"

"No, it's just a word." He remembered Anna calling him her liege man. Inwardly he scoffed. *Stop being a fool, Lex. You're not living in some romantic fantasy.*

"I miss my wife like hell, Lex." Brodie looked up at the cabin on the hill, narrowing his eyes. "But a man has his pride. She deceived me, married me as an ordinary woman…married a Highland rebel without revealin' what she truly is. I cannae accept the fact."

"Pride goeth before destruction." Lex spoke softly.

"Aye, 'and a haughty spirit before a fall, Proverbs 16:18,' no?" In the darkness, Lex could not clearly see his companion's expression in shadow, but he caught a return to affability in the tone. "I'm no' such a great heathen…nor, apparently, are ye. Now…" He slapped a hand onto Lex's shoulder. "Let us hie ourselves back to bed. Worryin' about women isn't doin' us any good, and we have a full day's work ahead of us tomorrow."

Brodie turned back toward the barracks, but Lex's next words stopped him.

"I'm in."

"Whit?" Brodie swung back to face him. "In whit?"

"The treasure search. I'm in it with you."

"Aye, now ye're talkin'!" Brodie came back to throw an arm about Lex's shoulders. "Good lad. Come on now. Back ta bed. We've plottin' ta do on that, an' we'll need our brains in rested order. Maybe the bastard MacTavish's visit had one good result," he continued as they walked back to their sleeping quarters.

"Whit do you mean?"

"Made ya realize how ya felt about Miss Anna…made ya realize ya want ta be a man o' means ta start courtin' her."

"Man of means…courting her? Man, you're daft." He scoffed.

Brodie's response was a chuckle as Lex followed

him across the millyard, hating to admit his friend was right.

****

Lex sat beside Brodie on the high seat of the wagon loaded with sawn lumber. They were headed for the wharf in Riverhaven. A ship captained by a man Brodie had told him was named Duffy was waiting to upload their produce.

"Captain Duffy is a good man," Brodie explained as they drove along. "Harry came out ta this country on his ship and got ta know the man. The captain took on our first load of lumber, when Harry and I first started working with the Fowler family, when no other ship masters would."

"Why was that?"

"Long story. That local bastard, Joe Carmody I mentioned ta ye before, was dead set on ruinin' us. I'll tell ya the whole tale sometime over a bunch of ales. The only other ship in port right now belongs ta Jamie MacTavish, and ya understand why I won't be doin' business with him. I wouldn't put a single stick on a MacTavish vessel if it were the only one leavin' Riverhaven this year and I had ta leave our lumber to rot."

They came out of the tree-lined trail and were heading down into the cleared area around the village. Brodie slowed the wagon on the slight incline to allow the horses better footing with the weight behind them. Prince, the gelding of the team of Clydesdales, obeyed, lowering his head and plodding carefully. Bonnie, the mare, always on the fractious side, shook her head, rattling her harness and bridle in protest.

"Whoa, you great pain in the arse!" Brodie

ordered. The mare snorted.

"Disrespectful bitch," the driver muttered, and Lex grinned.

As they drove into the east end of the village, Brodie drew rein sharply, his gaze on the riverbank. Lex followed his companion's line of interest and saw them…the MacTavish brothers, Louisa, and Anna boarding the cable ferry with their horses.

"Sons of whores!" Brodie's words were a snarl. He threw the lines to Lex and stood, ready to jump to the ground.

"Hold, there, laddie." Lex managed to contain the reins in one hand and grasp Brodie by a shirtsleeve with the other. "They're casting off. You won't reach them in time."

Chest heaving, Brodie broke into what Lex recognized as a vicious Gaelic curse.

"Aye, now that ya've got that all out of yer system, will ya sit and take over these lines?" Lex spoke when Brodie fell silent, his eyes burning with anger. "If this mare keeps on cavortin', she'll throw ya clean off this contraption. I've no' got yer way with her."

"Argh!" After casting one more hateful look in the direction of the retreating ferry, Brodie did as bidden. Taking the reins, he flapped them over the team's back and sent them lurching forward.

"Hold there, lad," Lex cautioned. "No need ta go spillin' our load, no matter how pissed ya aire."

"My team, my lumber. I'll be thankin' ya ta keep yer great trap shut, Lex…or whoever ya might be."

****

"I'm thinkin' an ale might be in order before we head back to the mill." Lex put his hands on his hips and thrust out his chest in a stretch. They'd finished off-loading their lumber onto Captain Duffy's ship with the help of shoremen. Lex thought to cool his companion's anger before they headed back to the mill by giving him time to unwind.

"It's more than ale I'm needin'." Brodie was yanking at Bonnie's harness.

"Whit do ya think yer doin'?" Lex stared at him.

"I'm goin' ta do something to stop this foolishness once an' fer all." He wrenched the leather straps from the mare's back and threw them into the empty wagon. Gathering up her reins, he used a wagon wheel as a mounting block to vault onto her bare back. She pranced and cavorted at the unaccustomed weight.

"Man, have ya gone daft?" Lex's words held all the astonishment he felt.

"If it's fancy clothes that impresses Lady Louisa, it's fancy clothes she'll get. And Culloden MacPherson's dandy o' a foreman Fletcher Atkin will have chust what I need."

"And chust whit am I supposed to do with a single horse and a wagon fitted for a team?"

"Get one from the stables at the end o' the village. The blacksmith knows me and Harry. He'll be more than willin' ta rent one out ta ya."

He kicked out with a booted foot. A moment later, he was galloping off down the dusty street.

****

Lex was unharnessing his mismatched team in the barnyard beyond the mill when he saw Brodie appear over the rise at the top of the valley. The rest of the mill workers were at supper in the barracks. Lex knew he was late at his work, but driving the pair of horses from the village had been a chore. Prince hadn't taken to his new team mate and had exploited every opportunity to express his dislike.

He paused to stare as Brodie rode down the hill and reined to a stop a few feet away. He didn't believe he'd ever seen such a rare sight. Brodie MacMillan wore the fine coat, vest, neckcloth, and breeches of a gentleman. All appeared to be several sizes too small, as the garments strained over his muscular form. His wrists showed high below sleeves that were far too short. A tall hat had been jammed over his unruly thatch of sandy curls. His feet, incongruous with the rest of his attire, were still encased in the working boots he wore in the mill. Both he and his mount were drenched with wet mud. Riding bareback on the big Clydesdale, Brodie MacMillan looked like a creation out of a book Lex had once read, *Don Quixote*.

"Well, don't chust stand there with yer mouth gapin' open catchin' flies," Brodie snapped, throwing his leg over the horse's neck and dropping with a grunt to the ground. "Ye're late with yer chores. I thought ya knew yer way around horses. How long did it take you to drive back here?"

"Prince didn't like his new mate." Stifling a chuckle, Lex went back to his task of freeing the horses from the wagon. "We had a wee battle of wills."

Leaving the rented horse in the traces, he started to lead the gelding into the barn. Bonnie whinnied shrilly, and Prince stopped dead in his tracks to look back at her.

"Ah, verrae well." Scowling, Brodie took the mare's bridle and led the way. "Ye're worse than an old married woman," he muttered to the mare as he passed her. "Always makin' men do yer biddin'."

As they passed Lex, he noticed the shoulder seams of his friend's coat had split. Brodie MacMillan was apparently broader of beam than Fletcher Atkin. As the men put the team in side-by-side stalls, Lex glanced over at Brodie, curious to know what had transpired, but his friend's bellicose expression warned him from inquiring.

"Well, go ahead, ask!" Brodie came out of Bonnie's stall and glared at Lex as he finished securing Prince in his.

"Ask whit?" Lex reverted to his Highland brogue.

"Ask me how I impressed the Lady Louisa. Ask me if she couldn't resist me in these fancy rags." Sarcasm reeked from each word.

"Verrae well. How did you impress her?"

"Not at all." Like a balloon suddenly punctured, Brodie's anger left him, and he slumped with one arm against Prince's rump. "I took the ferry across the river and followed them down to that house the doctor is buildin'. Laddie, it's a stone mansion three floors high, with the roof and half the walls already done."

He paused and stared down at his worn boots. Lex waited.

"I should have stood down right there, when I came in sight of the place, but when I saw the four of them walkin' around it, admirin' it, I couldn't help myself. I kicked Bonnie into a flat-out run and rode as hard as I could toward them. I reined to a stop a few feet from them, fair scarin' the daylights out of them and raisin' a great cloud of dust and gravel. 'If this is what ya want, Lady Louisa, then ye're welcome to it!' I yelled. Then I circled them at a full gallop, makin' them dance away from Bonnie's great hooves. After that, I rode full speed back to the ferry."

"And did that fine conveyance sink?" Lex couldn't resist asking as he looked at Brodie's wet, dirty clothing.

"Whit? Oh, no…no." Suddenly aware of his appearance, Brodie looked down at his outfit. "The ferry was on the far side when I arrived at its dock. I was hot to get away from the MacTavishes, so I rode Bonnie into the river and swam her back."

"That's a mighty distance. The river is wide in front of Riverhaven. You took a great risk for both yourself and the mare."

"Bonnie is a good swimmer. She's been tested on other occasions. By all that's holy, Lex, I had ta put distance between me and Will MacTavish or I wouldn't be able to control myself."

"A wise move, then." Lex went back outside to fetch the rented horse. When he came back into the barn leading it, Brodie had begun rubbing the mud and dirt from Bonnie's coat.

"I'll do that." Lex advised. "You'd best get out of those wet clothes and put them to dry. I reckon Mr. Fletcher Atkin will be wanting them back at least half decent."

"Oh, aye." Brodie relinquished to Lex the rag he'd been using. "I suppose I'll have ta take them to Harry's wife and daughters fer a bit of repair. I think I may have split a few seams. Atkin is a tad smaller than me." He picked up the coat he'd slung over the side of the stall and started away but paused to turn back. "I think it's nigh on time we took a look fer that treasure."

"Maybe."

"Argh! Pull your guts together, laddie. We make our move now."

As Brodie strode out of the barn, in spite of the man's bellicose words, Lex had to suppress a chuckle. His friend had indeed split a seam. The back of his breeches was rent from waist to crotch. He could only speculate about the damage done to that fine coat.

Chapter 22

"I think we could do with what Brodie would call a wee dram." Louisa took the flask from the top shelf in the kitchen of the log cabin and reached for a pair of mugs. She and Anna had returned to the log house.

"I agree." Anna sank into a chair at the table. "It's been an…amusing day."

"Amusing? I'd call it exasperating." Her sister poured generous amounts into the cups, shoved one across to her sister, and took a seat opposite her. "I'm glad to be home." The last came out as a weary sigh, and Anna looked anxiously at her.

"Are you feeling unwell, Louisa?"

"No, no, not physically." She drew a deep breath. "Just a tad weary of my husband's antics."

"Perhaps it's time you tried to talk to him, to reassure him your having been a lady is in the past."

"That wouldn't work, Anna." Louisa shook her head ruefully. "Brodie is much like a wild animal in some ways. You can't capture him or force him to do anything that's not to his inclination. You have to wait until he comes to you."

"And you think that's possible, that he'll eventually calm down and return to you?"

"I believe in love, Anna, our love. It's strong and abiding."

"Still, I wish he knew about the child. It is his

right, as the father, Louisa."

"Agreed, but I don't want him back simply out of a sense of duty or obligation. I want him to come back to me, to our marriage."

"Can no one talk sense to him, tell him there is no reason for his jealousy of Doctor MacTavish?"

"The only one who has ever been able to talk sense to Brodie is Harry Wallace." Louisa paused to take a sip of her whisky. "At the moment, he's got all he can handle, trying to put his own marriage back together."

"That's my fault as well." Taking her mug in her hands, Anna stood and began to pace. "I've made a mess of so many lives by coming here." She paused beside her sister's chair and placed a hand on her shoulder.

"You had no way of knowing what would happen." Louisa put her hand over her sister's. "You had no way of knowing how Brodie would react when he learned who I was…had been…or that Harry Wallace would be our neighbor. Don't distress yourself, Anna. We're Spencer women. We've been bred strong since before the time of old Will Shakespeare. I see no reason why that trend should change." Suddenly she chuckled.

"What is it?" Anna went to take her seat facing her sister. "You're finding humor in this mess?"

"I was remembering how Brodie looked mounted bareback on that Clydesdale, wearing dress clothing several sizes too small. And that hat! It was never intended for a rogue such as him."

"He did look a tad unusual." Anna grinned. "Still, it was a gesture of how much he cares for you, to what lengths he's prepared to go to win you back. He must believe you want and deserve a gentleman, and he was trying to be one."

"I'm not sure about the winning back part, but most definitely it does show our estrangement hasn't lessened his bravado." Louisa leaned across the table to pour more whisky into Anna's cup. Then she stood and carried the flask back to the cupboard.

"You won't be joining me in a second?" Anna asked.

"No. I will be modest in my alcohol consumption from now on. I don't want our child born with a taste for it. Now, tell me, sister dear, what happened during your ride with that rascal Captain Jamie MacTavish? You've avoided the subject quite skillfully ever since. I'll brook no further off-putting."

"He was a perfect gentleman." Anna heaved a sigh.

"You sound disappointed."

"Definitely not. He treated me as a lady." She settled into her chair and remembered. "I believe the good captain has sufficient experience to know the difference between a lady and a trollop and will treat each as is expected."

"I think you're correct. Go on." Louisa took a sip of her drink.

"We rode for a while, then stopped. Captain MacTavish helped me dismount, and we walked for a short distance. He told me a bit about his love of life at sea. It's been a rollicking one, I can tell you. It was enough for me to learn it isn't for me, that I want to spend my life on dry land in"—she paused to look at her sister—"a cozy cottage like this with…"

"With Lex." Louisa filled in the words.

"Yes." Anna spoke softly, lowering her gaze to the cup in her hands.

"Well, then, why not?" Louisa's response was spritely. "There is a great deal of land on this grant. I'm sure Harry and Margaret can find a suitable site for you to build upon…"

"Louisa, you don't understand." Anna looked up at her sister. "Lex sees me as somehow above him and insists on calling me 'Lady.' He's not about to see me as a marriage prospect"—she stood and walked to the hearth to stand staring down into the embers—"or even a lover."

"What makes you think such a thing?" Louisa got up and went to stand beside her. "You're clever, you're beautiful, you're courageous…"

"He kissed me passionately on two separate occasions—and each time, he refused to continue!" Anna failed to keep the cry out of her response. "He's found me lacking…in some way. I'm not wise in ways that can truly please a man. I'm not a…trollop, and I feel Lex has had his fair share of them."

"Anna, Anna." Louisa faced her, her tone placating. "No decent man expects the woman he wishes to marry to display the skills of a trollop. In fact"—she turned away with a sly smile and a swish of her skirts—"I believe most men enjoy teaching their brides what pleases them. I know Brodie did."

"But you were married before…"

"Ah, yes, but to a very different type of man. Neil and I loved and respected each other. Brodie and I are in love. There's a difference…which I've no doubt you'll come to understand."

"Are you saying Lex's turning away from me wasn't repulsion because of my lack of carnal knowledge?"

"I am. Lex strikes me as a man of honor. I think his failing to proceed with lovemaking came out of respect for you…possibly from seeing a more serious relationship ahead."

Could it be true? Her sister's words of wisdom had set a flush of hope flooding through her.

****

"A word." Brodie drew Lex away from the group of mill workers lounging on the veranda of the barracks at the end of a long day's work. His tone became confidential. "I've something I would tell ya."

"Oh, aye." Lex stood and followed Brodie across the yard to a spot outside the silent grist mill.

"It's time ta find that treasure."

"I thought you'd forgotten about it. Any road, I've given more thought and decided it most likely is only a fable."

"Fable, is it?" Eyes narrowing, Brodie strode around to once more stand before him. "I don't fer a minute think you believe that. I'll prove it exists. Before the week is out, I'll be able ta show ya where we'll locate the trollop's treasure."

Brodie winked, gave him a pat on the shoulder, and strode off, leaving Lex with an unpleasant sense of trouble to come.

****

"Dusted and done." Brodie put his hands on his belt buckle and stood, feet planted shoulder-width apart, as he watched the last of the load of lumber he and Lex had brought to the Riverhaven dock put aboard a ship. "Now, laddie, I'd say it's off ta the tavern fer a couple of ales. The sun's been over the foreyard a few hours now. We have some plannin' ta do."

Lex heaved a resigned sigh as Brodie took the team by their bridles and led them toward the drinking establishment. Feeling as if he were definitely heading into trouble, he followed as his companion led the horses to a hitching rail in front of Frank Miller's business and tied them securely.

"Well, come along, lad. Look smart." Brodie was headed for the door. "I don't want ta leave these beasts tied here until nightfall."

Inside, with ales in hand, Brodie led the way to a table in the back with no other patrons nearby.

"Now," he said, leaning toward Lex and speaking softly, "we've got ta get a plan in place. I'm gettin' right eager ta fix things up with Louisa…but not so much that I will do it on any other terms than my own. Now, here's my idea…"

"Brodie MacMillan, a word." The tall, ruggedly built man Lex recognized as the village magistrate's deputy had entered the tavern and was striding toward them.

"Dunc…Duncan MacDougal!" Brodie greeted the newcomer warmly. "Come and take a seat. Molly"—he hailed the barmaid—"an ale fer my friend." He turned to his companion. "Lex, this is Duncan MacDougal, a boon friend even if he can't sit a horse ta save his soul. I didn't get a chance ta introduce ya when last we met after the scuffle with that bastard MacPherson and he helped throw us into jail. Dunc, meet Lex. He accompanied my sister-in-law ta this country."

"Lex." Duncan MacDougal acknowledged the introduction seriously. "I'm afraid I already know about the gentleman."

"Gentleman? Already know? Whit is it, Dunc?

You're gettin' right formal." Brodie's grin began to fade. "The last time you spoke ta me in that manner I was in deep trouble."

"And you might well be again, Brodie. Captain Cameron has sent me to fetch you. He's received a…document that will be of interest to you both."

"I do not like the sound o' that, Dunc." Shoving his chair back noisily, Brodie stood. "But no point in puttin' it off. Come along, Lex. Let's face whatever music Riverhaven's magistrate has ta play fer us."

****

"Gentlemen." Captain Caleb Cameron got up from behind the scarred desk in his small office that served as an antechamber to the jail behind a door at his back.

"Good mornin', Cal." Lex recognized Brodie coming to his most affable self after scowling all the way from the tavern down the dusty street to the office. "You wanted ta see me and my friend Lex here?" He indicated his companion.

Going to try to charm the magistrate. I don't think it will work. This man looks sober and no-nonsense to the core. Sweet Jesus, I wonder what kind of trouble he's—we're—in?

"I do. Gentlemen, take seats." Without offering Lex a hand at the introduction, Captain Cameron indicated a pair of much-abused chairs in front of his desk.

Out of the corner of his eye, Lex saw Duncan MacDougal take up a guard's position in front of the door, arms crossed on his muscular chest. *Not good, definitely not good.*

"I received documents from a ship newly docked." Captain Cameron resumed his seat. He paused, looking down at the papers on his desk.

"Oh, aye? And how would they be concernin' us?" Brodie's eyes narrowed.

"They are warrants…warrants for the arrest of two Scotsmen…Brodie MacMillan and another for the man known simply as Lex."

"Warrants!" Brodie jumped to his feet. "On what charge, may I ask? I've done nothin'…recently."

Recently? Bloody hell, I was right. Lex felt his gut knot. *I've thrown in my lot with a rogue of the first water.*

"Abduction…the abduction of Lord Dunstan's daughters, namely Lady Louisa Spencer and her sister Lady Annabelle Spencer."

"Abduction!" Brodie placed his hands on the front of the magistrate's desk and leaned across toward the official. "Sweet Jesus, Cal, the woman is my wife…has been fer months now. And before that, she was married ta Dr. Neil Abbot. He's the one she ran off ta marry, years ago. If this arse of an aristocrat wants ta charge anyone with abduction, let it be the deceased Dr. Abbot. He's well beyond the reach of earthly law. As fer my friend, Lex"—he swung a hand to indicate him—"he's innocent as a newborn babe. The Lady Annabelle came with him of her own free will—more than free will! Willin'ly, eagerly. She enlisted him as her protector."

"That will be for a court to decide." Unruffled by Brodie's outburst, Captain Cameron remained calmly seated behind his desk. "Copies of these warrants are now on their way to the provincial capital with a request that a detachment of soldiers be sent to take you to confinement there while you await trial later in the summer. I've orders to detain you both until they arrive."

"Bloody hell, Cal." Brodie straightened up to glare at the magistrate. "Ya know what will occur if that happens. With my past…and maybe with Lex's…we won't stand a chance. We'll be sentenced ta rot in prison…or sent back ta England ta hang."

"I'm well aware of your record, Mr. MacMillan." Captain Caleb Cameron's grim countenance made the knot in Lex's gut further tighten. "I'm also aware that underneath all that devil-may-care brashness there lies a good man. Therefore"—he stood—"I'm going to give you a day to disappear from my jurisdiction. At the moment, only Mr. MacDougal and I know of these warrants. I'll keep it that way for as long as I can, but I've no way of estimating that length of time."

"Rotten bloody hell!" Brodie aimed a kick at the chair from which he'd gotten up and sent it skittering across the room. "On the run again! I'm gettin' too damned old fer this, Cal!"

"Perhaps if you avoided trouble, if you stuck to being a millwright and farmer…"

"Aye, and if ya'd stuck to bein' a merchant seaman, ya wouldn't ha' become rich as a pirate or gotten into this almighty position."

"Privateer, Mr. MacMillan, privateer." The magistrate's expression told Lex his companion hadn't furthered their hopes of freedom with the remark.

Shut your great trap, Brodie. Just shut up!

"I've given you a window of escape." Captain Cameron crossed his arms. "It's the best I can do. Go into hiding somewhere…don't tell me the location. That way I won't be forced into too many lies when that contingent of soldiers arrives. Now, go."

Lex watched as Duncan MacDougal moved aside to give them access to the door.

Brodie hesitated a moment longer, then with a muttered curse in Gaelic, he strode out of the office. Lex followed.

Chapter 23

At the tavern, Brodie, still muttering obscenities in his native tongue, untied the team and jumped aboard the wagon.

"Get aboard, ya great fool!" he yelled as Lex paused to adjust a bit of harness. "We've got twenty-four hours ta get the hell out of this place!"

Lex jumped up beside him as Brodie turned the startled horses about with such violence the wagon careened dangerously to the left.

"Hold there, laddie." Lex tried to caution him. "No need to get our necks broken."

****

"Sweet Jesus, I never thought I'd end up like this again." Brodie swatted at mosquitoes and blackflies as he guided Silverbell along the woods road.

The night had been blessed—or cursed, Lex hadn't decided which—with a full moon. It was allowing them light to pick their way over the ruts and roots of the trail, but it had also proven a detriment when he and Brodie had stolen into the barn on his homestead to purloin Silverbell and Storm and saddle them. Later, the two men had slunk, silent as shadows, into Brodie's ice house and root cellar to gather what provisions they could to take with them on their escape. Earlier they'd taken the team and wagon back to the mill stables as if nothing untoward had happened. They'd waited until night to gather provisions and make their escape.

"Do you think hiding out at the winter logging camp owned by Harry Wallace is a good idea? Will those redcoats not think to look there?" Lex held a light rein on Storm, letting the sure-footed gelding pick his way.

"Not fer a while. The officers are generally dumb as posts, sons of rich or powerful families who've proven themselves either so useless or such an embarrassment their fathers saw buying them a commission in the army the only way to get rid of them. As fer the ordinary soldiers"—Brodie scoffed—"they've mostly been pulled from prisons or from among general troublemakers the British establishment wishes ta be shucked of. They're never in a hurry ta obey orders, especially here in the colonies, where army justice is generally haphazard. My only concern…"

His words trailed off.

"Aye, your only concern?" Lex was quick to take him up on the comment.

"My only concern is that big mouth Michael Kelly. He knows about these camps and might just clear a spot in his whisky-befuddled brain long enough ta remember them. He'd take great delight in givin' out information that could land me in prison…or worse."

"Why would he do that?"

"He bears a grudge." In the moonlight, Lex saw his companion shrug. "He believes I shot him some time back…in a gun battle over the mill."

"And did you?"

"I could have. There were a lot of musketballs and pistol shot flyin' around. Who knows who hit what? But it doesn't matter. Kelly believes it was me and is always out fer revenge."

"How long do you think we'll be safe at the camp?"

"Bloody hell, man, how can I know? Michael Kelly might not sober up enough ta help the soldiers fer days. Then again, he might just have a clear spot in his brain long enough ta do it within hours. I'm thinkin' we'd best not stay over a day or two…and keep these horses saddled and ready at all times."

****

"My husband and I are estranged. I have no idea where he is. Nor do I care." Louisa stood on the cabin veranda and glanced at her sister as the last sentence came out with haughty vehemence. Anna was impressed. She'd had no idea Louisa could lie so convincingly. Beside them, Jasper stood, muttering his discontent with the situation.

"Estranged, ma'am?" The young officer heading his contingent of four soldiers eyed her warily. "When did this happen?"

"Does it matter, Lieutenant? He's gone, and that's all I care about." The arrogance in Louisa MacMillan's tone evidenced disgust.

"Mr. Levitt." Lieutenant Garfield turned to one of his men. "Check the stable."

"You mistrust me, sir?" Louisa glared up at him as he sat mounted on his horse by her veranda. "I am the daughter of Lord Dunstan." She drew herself up in apparent self-righteous anger. "I am Lady Louisa Spencer. Back in England, you'd face a severe reprimand for treating my sister and me in such a disrespectful fashion."

"Ah, yes, ma'am, but we're not back in England

now, are we, and you've been declared abducted and compromised by the outlaw Brodie MacMillan. Therefore, I feel comfortable treating both you and your sibling as the circumstance warrants."

"Evidence of four horses having been stabled." Private Levitt returned from the barn. "But only two in residence."

"Where are the other two animals, Mrs. MacMillan?" The young lieutenant narrowed his eyes as he looked down at Louisa. "Perhaps used to aid your husband and this man Lex in their flight from justice?"

"I have only the white mare and an unbroken filly. The evidence of other horses your man found is that of a pair of mill drays sometimes stabled here."

"Huh." Lieutenant Garfield pursed his lips thoughtfully. "Well, there's apparently nothing more to be gleaned here." He started to swing his horse away but paused to once again address Louisa. "I will expect you to report any appearance of your husband and his companion to the magistrate immediately."

"I shall be only too happy to do so." Louisa put her hands on her hips and cocked her head to one side, green eyes gleaming. "My sister and I will be delighted to see those two rogues behind bars."

"Good day to you, ladies." The officer touched his hat brim, then turned away to lead his men down the lane to the trail that led to the village.

"Louisa, you were magnificent!" Anna turned to her sister, feeling like dancing in delight at her performance before the soldiers.

"When you're associated with a man like Brodie MacMillan, you become adept at lying, deceiving, and all other necessary nefarious arts." She heaved a deep breath. “Now, I desperately need a cup of hot, sweet tea. In keeping with your learning the ways of a farming household, I’ll let you do the honors.”

Wondering if this would be *her* way of life in the future, Anna followed Louisa into the house.

****

“Look.” Brodie’s instruction was a hiss.

Lex tensed. When he saw where his companion was pointing, he relaxed. Brodie indicated a caribou casually munching lichen a few feet from where they were attempting to net trout in a stream near the winter lumbering camp.

“A right magnificent lad, wouldn’t ye agree?” Brodie whispered. “Almost as fine as a Highland stag. If this was November instead of midsummer, he’d make prime eatin’. This time of year, this far from an ice house, it would be a sinful waste to kill such a beast only ta let his flesh rot in the heat.”

The animal raised its head, heavy with antlers, glanced briefly in their direction, then ambled away.

“Not the smartest o’ creatures.” Brodie returned his attention to the net. “Makes ’em easy prey. I fear for their future, what with some careless bastards killin’ them just fer their rack. We lumbermen aren’t helpin’ their future either, cuttin’ down the old trees with all the lichen, the caribou’s main source o’ food— Blasted flies!” Brodie whacked at the buzzing insects. “Between them and this God-awful heat, I’m gettin’ fair short-tempered. On top o’ that, my gut’s rumblin’ something fierce. Time for a meal, no doubt about it.”

“Hie, there!” Lex yanked at the net and brought it up to reveal a large trout twisting inside. “Here’s a fine supper.”

"Good lad! Let's get ourselves up ta the camp. We'll risk a small fire ta cook this creature and roast a few o' those potatoes we brought from my root cellar."

****

Later, as they sat beside the small fire in the clearing before the woods camp, Brodie wiped his mouth with the back of his hand and heaved a contented sigh.

"That was more than a decent repast, laddie," he said, looking over at Lex. "And with the smoke from the fire keepin' those bloody bugs at bay, I'm feelin' a sight better. Not that I'm happy ta be on the run again, you understand"—he changed his tone—"but I'm as best I can be under the circumstance." His eyes narrowed. "Unless I'm no judge of men at all, I'd say you've done your share of runnin' as well…back in the Old Country, no?"

"A bit." Lex shoved another small stick into the fire and watched it flame.

"Someday, maybe you'll see fit ta tell me about it…as I'll tell you a bit about myself."

"Aye, someday." Lex wet his lips.

"I still cannot understand why the old man…Sir Maxwell…waited until now ta come after me." Brodie put his arms around his bent knees and clasped his hands. "Louisa wrote ta tell him and Anna of our marriage last summer. Of course she didn't tell me her father was a lord or herself a lady…or him that I was a suspected former Highland rebel. He knew of her marriage ta Dr. Neil Abbot but chose not ta chase him down as an abductor. Louisa said her mother had approved of her marrying the doctor and had actually given her a right fine green cloak lined with ermine fur as a wedding gift. She wore it when she married me. Maybe the old man didn't have the heart…or balls…ta go against a marriage that had his wife's approval. But now Louisa's married ta me, and I'm a horse of a different color. Not a man of education, and our union unable to obtain the blessing of his wife, who departed this life a year or so ago. The old man wouldn't care that I'm a millwright by trade and a right fine one, if I do say so myself. No, in Sir Maxwell's eyes I'll always be a Highlander, branded an outlaw and a traitor."

"Was Louisa's first husband a Scot?"

"Aye, Dr. Neil Abbot was a Lowlander, though, and as I've said, a man of education. Not near as objectionable as me. Still I'm not understandin'…why did the old bastard choose to come after me…us, now?"

"I do." Lex stretched out on the ground and leaned back to support himself on his forearms. "You and I are birds of a feather in Lord Dunstan's eyes. I think he let Louisa's marriage to you slide at the time because he felt she was lost to him and she'd never be an asset to his family if she returned to England. All in all, a decent solution. But then Lady ran off with me. She was his hope for an aristocratic marriage, one that would compensate for his son having to marry a merchant's daughter to shore up the family fortunes. In his eyes, I ruined that possibility even if Lady did declare she'd never marry the man her father had chosen. Losing two daughters to Highland rebels was more than his lordship could stomach. So, in for a penny, in for a pound. He decided to take revenge on both of us."

"Well, then, damn you, Lex." Brodie pulled a flask from one of their traveling sacks. There was no real vehemence in the accusation as he yanked out the cork. "Good thing I had a wee stash of good whisky hidden away in the ice house." He raised the container and took a long swig before handing it on to his companion. "It appears we're in this together for the long run."

"It appears so." Lex accepted the flask and drank.

"And I've been thinkin'." Brodie settled his back against a tree trunk, his expression pensive.

"Aye?" Apprehension rose in Lex's belly.

"If we've got to be from home, we may as well make the most of it. We can't stay here much longer. I'm thinkin' we should head down river, out ta the bay, and make a play fer that treasure."

Lex pulled himself into a sitting position to rest his elbows on his bent knees, his hands holding the flask between them. *Maybe...*

"Think, laddie, think." Brodie leaned toward him. "If we find it, we can take our lasses and head fer Upper Canada...or, better still, the United States. The redcoats won't pursue us south o' the border, in fear o' startin' another war. We can make new lives fer ourselves."

"I'll sleep on the idea." Lex took another drink before handing the flask back to Brodie. "Let me sleep on it."

****

"I hope ye're done pukin', because by my calculation, this is the spot." Brodie shaded his eyes and took bearings from the point of land extending out into the water about a quarter mile away. "And this net we've been draggin' appears ta have snagged somethin' big. We'd best get to it at once. It's not often the bay entrance is as still as it is now. I trust you can swim and dive better than you can sail."

The two men stood in a boat they'd managed to borrow from fisherman Nate Bendel and now floated off the small peninsula known as Escuminac Point.

"I don't choose to throw up all that's in my gut." Lex wiped his mouth with the back of his hand and glowered at his companion. The two men had stripped down to their breeches in readiness to explore the waters beneath the small fishing boat they'd rented.

"No, no, I doubt you do. Still, we must get on with it. Off you go!" He slapped Lex between the bare shoulders with such a mighty blow he was knocked over the side of the boat. Lex catapulted headfirst into the water.

"Bastard!" Lex came to the surface, sputtering.

"Ah, laddie, ye've got first crack, the easy part." Brodie grinned. "Just see what our net has snagged on. I'll take next jump and investigate. You said you can dive. Get to it."

His head full of curses aimed at his companion, Lex sucked in a deep breath and dove beneath the surface.

****

"It's down there, laddie, you're right!" Brodie's confirmation was a gasp as he surfaced. "The *Belle Michelle*…name on her bow."

"It's still there…her name?"

"Aye." Brodie grunted as Lex helped him back aboard the small fishing vessel. "A lot of her still intact. We'll have ta take turns hacking inta the deck beneath the captain's table to find the treasure where your friend the French lady said it was located."

Lex squinted toward the horizon. Dark clouds were

gathering, intimidating in their intensity.

"I'll make another dive, but then we'd best get the hell out of here," he said. "There's bad weather coming. We can return later."

"Ah, where's yer nerve, laddie? The sea is flat as a pancake."

"Did you never hear of the calm before the storm?" Lex eased himself over the back of the boat and down into the water. He thought of his promise to retrieve the C-shaped pendant for Marie. He dove.

****

The rotting boards gave beneath the hammering of his ax. With his lungs bursting for air, Lex ripped up the floorboards and saw the cask beneath. The treasure! But he couldn't linger. His chest on fire, he kicked himself toward the surface, suffused with a sense of victory he hadn't experienced since his first successful skirmish with redcoats.

"It's there!" he gasped as he surfaced and grasped the gunwale of the boat. "Brodie, it's there! I've seen it!"

"Good lad!" His companion wasted no time in wrenching him out of the water with arms beneath his. "Bugger all, good lad!"

As Lex slid back over the side like an exhausted seal, Brodie dropped to his knees in front of the man fallen exhausted on the deck and hugged him.

"Sweet Jesus, laddie, this is a gift from heaven, sure and simple!" Brodie untied the rope from about Lex's waist and began to fasten it about his own. "You rest while I fetch it."

"Wait." Dragging himself to a sitting position, Lex held up a restraining hand. "You'll need another rope, as well…to tie about the cask."

"Oh, aye, aye. I'm not thinkin' clear, what with the joy of it." Brodie caught up another length of rope and threw it to Lex. "When I have it secured, I'll give a yank, and you pull it up."

Again he started for the edge of the boat, but again Lex stopped him. "Hold there. You'd be well advised to put a loop in the end before you go below…save time when you're securing the chest."

"Aye, aye, you're a wise one, my lad." Brodie set about doing as Lex suggested, his expression bright with victory. "I knew I chose well when I included you in this venture."

****

They sat in the boat and stared at the gems glittering before them. Securely wrapped in oiled cloth inside the container, the cask itself tightly sealed, the treasure had suffered little in the twenty-five years since it had disappeared.

"Sweet Jesus, will you look at that!" Brodie ran a trembling hand through their booty. "Can you chust imagine, laddie, what kind o' house I can build fer Louisa with the profit from these? And you, my friend, can feel worthy o' makin' a proposal ta your lady." He let out a war whoop that echoed out across the still waters.

"Aye, well, I'll take that under consideration." Lex reached into the cask and drew out a pendant, the diamonds, rubies, and emeralds descended from it forming a large letter C. "At the moment, this trinket is my main interest." He clutched it in his hand and shoved it deep into an inner pocket of the vest he'd donned. "Now we'd best be heading back. Those clouds are threatening a right downpour, and this small skiff won't be much in a storm."

He'd barely finished speaking when a bolt of lightning rent the black clouds, a blast of wind cannoned in off the gulf, and the little boat was thrown into a maelstrom that sent it bucking like a mad horse.

"Jesus!" Brodie yelled.

Chapter 24

Lex lay gasping on the boulder-strewn shore. He'd survived…somehow he'd survived the violence of the storm, to be washed, like a beached whale, onto this rocky shingle. Spitting salt water, he pulled himself up on an elbow.

Brodie. Where was his friend?

The rain was still coming down in torrents, but the wind had abated, and the sea, from what he could observe before him, had quieted.

"Brodie!" He drew air into his weary lungs and forced a cry.

"Over here, ya great fool." With a huge sense of relief, he saw his friend staggering from behind a boulder. A bruise was purpling his left eye, but aside from that injury, he appeared unscathed. He cast Lex a crooked grin. "We survived, laddie." He grinned as he walked crookedly toward him. "And even the treasure cask." He pointed back in the direction from which he'd come. "It was washed up right close to me. Maybe"—good humor continued to brighten his face—"partly because I clung to it like grim death as long as I could."

"You were a fool." Lex struggled to his feet, relieved that his arms and legs appeared intact. "No treasure is worth a man's life."

"Ah, this one is, my fine Highland laddie. It will bring my Louisa back ta me and show her I'm chust as fine a man as the fancy doctor."

"You're daft." Lex looked around the desolate shore. Beyond the beach, it appeared there were only miles of barren peat bog. "We'd best be putting our minds to how we're going to get out of here. The boat"—he indicated its wreckage washed up several yards down shore—"is a loss."

"Not to worry." Brodie drew himself up and puffed out his chest. "With this booty, we can buy Nate Bendel a much finer one. Now, come along. Take that length of rope from the boat…it's about all that's left of value from the poor wee vessel. We'll tie it about the cask and drag it along with us."

"Drag it along with us where?" Lex looked out over the peat bog plains. "There's no way we can cross that morass, never mind dragging a burden."

"Of course not, you daft beast! We're goin' ta pull it along the shore. There're French fishermen and their families livin' a few miles away. We'll convince them to lend us a boat ta get back to Riverhaven."

****

By the time they reached the tree line, the sun blazed down from directly overhead, informing Lex it must be noon or thereabouts. Glancing at his companion resolutely taking his turn at dragging the chest, he saw sweat running down his face and felt it on his own.

"Time we took a wee rest." Brodie spoke the words Lex had been thinking. "That mighty pine hangin' out over the shore is chust the place."

With a final grunt, he pulled his burden into the shade and dropped down on the gravel of the shore. Lex joined him.

"You don't look half as spent as I feel, laddie." Brodie squinted over at Lex as he used his forearm to wipe sweat from his face. "Highland hill runnin' been keepin' you in shape, I'll venture?"

"I did my share." Lex let a corner of his mouth curl at the memory.

"And I reckon ya were right good at it?"

"A lad gets proficient when his horse has been shot out from under him and the only alternative to running up into the hills is a noose."

"Aye." Brodie leaned back on his elbows and closed his eyes. "The specter of a rope hangin' from a gallows can put wings on a man's heels, and no doubt about it. Now I suggest we both take a nap before headin' out again. It could be a few more miles before we find transport."

****

Lex awoke to find himself staring down a pistol barrel.

"Good day to you, Sir Head Groom." Harvey Brant stood over him, holding a gun aimed into his face. "We meet again. No, no, sir, don't trouble yourself to get up. I much prefer to look down upon you."

"Whit…!" Brodie's choke of surprise brought Lex fully awake. No, this wasn't some mad dream. Harvey Brant, former head groom at Sir Maxwell's estate, was standing over him, wielding a pistol. Glancing in his friend's direction, Lex saw another man, a younger man, holding a weapon pointed at his friend.

"It was kind of you to find the treasure and rescue it for us," Brant continued. He tucked the fingers of his free hand into the front of the waistcoat straining across his paunch, a smug smirk on his reddened countenance.

Lex squinted and saw another person standing behind Harvey Brant. As he focused more clearly, he recognized, even with her hair tucked under a cap, Lady's former maid, Rose.

"If ya think ye'll be takin' what rightly belongs to us, think again, ya bastards!" Brodie yelled.

"Confiscating the treasure is only a part of my revenge." Harvey Brant leered down at Lex. "You took my dignity, my standing in the community, when you stole my position on the estate…you and that bitch, the so-called Lady Anna. Now Rose, Mitchell here, and I will see to it you and your aristocratic whore will pay. You won't see her nor her witch of a sister any time soon. They're on their way right back to where they belong!"

"Sons o' whores!" As Brodie lunged at Harvey Brant's knees, the pistol fired into the air. Lex made a leap to help his friend, but a hard blow to the head collapsed him, unconscious, onto the pebbly beach.

****

Lex grunted as he came back to the moment to find himself bound to a boulder at the waterline. Waves lapped at his boots.

"Awake at last, aire ye?" His companion's disgruntled words came to him. "Well, this is a fine pickle. I thought ya were a fighter, but ya let a bit o' trash knock ya cold without gettin' in so much as a blow. Now look where we aire, about to be drowned by the risin' tide. And what of Louisa and Anna? What have those bastards done with them?"

"Shut yer great trap!" Head pounding, Lex's anger brimmed. Brodie was tied to the opposite side of the boulder, or so he surmised from the direction of his voice. “You couldn’t have done much better or we wouldn’t be here now.”

“Argh!” Silence except for the lapping of waves followed.

“Can ya move at all?” Brodie’s calmer tone told Lex he was ready to become rational and work on their predicament.

“Not much, not enough to make a difference.”

“Bollocks.”

Suddenly Lex became aware of being watched. Looking up into the trees behind them, he saw two children in shabby clothing staring wide-eyed at them.

“Hello.” He forced a smile that made his head pound even harder.

They drew back and moved closer together, the girl putting an arm about the smaller child, a boy.

An idea occurred to him.

“*Bonne journée*.” He tried to speak as pleasantly as if he were meeting them in a social setting. “Are your mama and papa nearby?” he continued in French. “Will you fetch them?”

For a few moments they continued to stare, then the girl turned and, taking the boy by the hand, scampered back into the woods.

“Ya speak French?” Brodie’s words mirrored his surprise.

“*Oui*. I spent a few years in France as a youth.”

“Huh! Maybe such learnin’ will finally come in handy this day.”

“We can but hope. The tide is rising right fast.”

“Ya know, laddie, of all the ways I pictured myself meetin’ my Maker durin’ my outlaw days, this isn’t one of them.” Lex heard Brodie shifting about on his side of the rock, his tone becoming contemplative. "I fancied I'd be taken down by a musketball, run through with a sword or bayonet, hung from a gallows, or thrown from a horse ta break my damn fool neck. Drownin' tied to a rock never once crossed my mind. Bloody hell, isn't fate grand!"

Lex couldn't help smirking at his friend's ability to take the situation in stride. An affable rogue, indeed, and not a bad companion if he had to meet death with anyone.

"I wouldn't give up on us chust yet." Lex drew a deep breath. "I've set a score of hope on those two children."

****

"Row, you daft bastard, row!" Pulling on his oar, Brodie yelled at Lex manning the other. "God only knows what those bastards have done with Louisa and Anna. We have ta get ta Riverhaven fast! *Monsieur*!" He turned his urging to the French fisherman working the sail on the small craft. "More sail…more canvas!"

"He doesn't understand you, so shut the hell up." Lex, putting all his strength into rowing, was losing patience with his companion. "He's doing the best he can."

"Look, laddie, I've promised him a wagonload of our best sawn lumber and another filled with flour, oatmeal, tea, and sugar. That's right fine pay fer a sail of a few miles upriver."

"And what would we have done if he'd refused? We had no other options."

"Aye, aye." The words were a mutter as Brodie bent his strength to the oar. "You're right. But, sweet Jesus, Lex, our women could be dead!"

"I don't think so. If they'd killed them, they wouldn't have stopped at murdering us. I believe murder is a step beyond what they were prepared to do. They were willing to let us perish at the hands of the elements, but they lacked the guts to outright kill us. Any road, they may have been bluffing, torturing us as much as they could with dire thoughts of the women."

"I hope ye're right, laddie. I hope ye're right."

"And leave off ordering Marcel about. It took my best effort at Acadian French to convince him we're Scots, not English. I have a feeling he wouldn't have helped two Englishmen, not for all the supplies in the world. You know his people were unjustly expelled from this area sixty years ago by the English on the mere suspicion that they might help the French if war between the two nations spilled over into this area. Families were separated, homes lost forever…"

"I am no' in the mood for a history lesson. So chust shut yer trap and row!"

****

"The *Linnet* sailed south bound on the evening tide." Captain Jamie MacTavish told the two sweating, bedraggled men who confronted him on the Riverhaven dock in the late summer gloaming. "The ones you've described were aboard."

"Bollocks!" Brodie slammed the fist of his left hand into the palm of his right. "Did ya see what they took with them?"

"Each of them carried bags, the big one who seemed to be in charge had two, and the one slung over his shoulder he had a right tight grip on."

"But nothing else? No trunks, nothing overlarge?" Lex had to clear one idea from his mind.

“Nothing of that description. What is going on, lads? You both look as if you’ve been through a war.”

“You ha’ no idea.” Brodie’s chest was heaving. “Christ, but I need a drink!” He turned and strode off toward the tavern, where lights beamed from windows. “As soon as I’ve wet my whistle,” he yelled back over his shoulder to Lex, “we’ll be off. We’ve a deal of searchin’ to do.”

“Searching?” The captain looked at Lex, a question in his expression.

Lex explained.

Chapter 25

The village of Riverhaven was alive with torches. Mounted searchers and those on foot filled the single trail that residents had named Water Street. In the midst of it, mounted on a big bay horse, Captain Caleb Cameron was seeking to bring order to the chaos. Finally, unable to do so, he nodded to his deputy, Duncan MacDougal. Catching the meaning, he nodded back, pulled his pistol from his belt, checked its prime, then fired it into the air. Silence followed.

"Thank you, ladies and gentlemen," Duncan MacDougal shouted. "Now, if you'll be so kind as to listen to your magistrate, Captain Cameron, he'll tell you how we're to go about this search with method and order."

****

Without a single complaint, they'd spread out, torches at the ready, through the sultry night thick with buzzing, biting insects. Although his mind was flooded with worry about Lady and her sister, Lex had to marvel at the way this community of reputed rogues had come together in the face of adversity. There appeared to be no dissenters for the search. He'd even recognized Brodie's nemesis, Culloden MacPherson, riding off into the night in the quest for the women. Riverhaven was a good place, a strong place, a place where he would like to put down roots and call it home.

But there was no time for speculation. He straightened from where he'd been slouched against a pile of lumber on the dock and drew a deep breath. Captain Cameron had ordered Brodie and him to take a rest and nourishment before joining the search.

Seeing the wisdom in the captain's words, Lex had acquiesced. At the tavern, he'd stuffed food that tasted like sawdust into his gut and washed it down with a tankard of ale in an effort to shore up his strength.

Brodie, of course, hadn't obeyed. He'd snatched a horse's reins from a bystander, vaulted onto its back, and ridden off. He'd yelled to Lex that he was going to his homestead to search for indications of what had become of Lady and Louisa, that if he didn't find them, he'd bring horses that they might continue to search more effectively.

As food and a modicum of rest flushed into his body, Lex found rationality returning to his thoughts. Harvey Brant and his friends hadn't killed the women, of that he felt fairly confident. He mulled over Brant's last words…something to the effect that they'd be going back to where they belonged.

Where they belonged. Where they belonged. England?

He looked up at Captain James MacTavish's ship resting against the dock. Denuded of its sailors, who'd been pressed into duty in the search, it appeared deserted save for one man left on watch.

England! Was the Highland Lass *headed in that direction when she weighed anchor?*

Long strides took him across the wharf and up the gangplank. The dozing sailor on guard snapped alert and jumped to his feet, belaying pin in his hand.

"Hold there!" He confronted Lex. "This ship's loaded. No one is allowed aboard save captain and crew…and I don't recognize you as one of them."

Lex's foot shot out, knocking away the sailor's weapon. Grabbing a lantern that had been hanging nearby, he strode to the storage hatch and yanked it open. Followed by the sailor's cries to stop, nimble as a cat, he leaped down into the hold and began his desperate search.

Holding the lantern aloft, he located them in a far corner, all but crushed by planks and deal. Gagged and bound, they sat propped against the ship's side. Hands shaking, he set his light on the lumber and began to untie them.

"Lex." Lady spoke once he'd freed her mouth. "Oh, God, Lex, I was beginning to fear you'd never find us. I just saw a mouse!"

"Niver fear, lass." His Highland accent thick, he struggled with the knots that bound her hands. "I'd find ye if I had ta go ta the moon."

"Lex…" Her tone trembled. "Never mind me. See to Louisa. I fear she's in a sad state. Lex"—she looked at him, eyes wide—"we've been down here for hours…and she's pregnant."

Chapter 26

Brodie paced the deck of the *Highland Lass*, his face so taut the skin seemed stretched directly over its bones. Once in a while, he paused at the rail to grip it with white-knuckled hands before once again setting back to his desperate strides.

Lex, sitting on the deck, and Anna, wrapped in a blanket and huddled against him, knew words of encouragement would be pointless. All they could do now was wait and rely on the skills of Dr. William MacTavish, who was in Captain Jamie MacTavish's cabin with Louisa, fighting to save the woman and her unborn child.

Beside him he felt Anna move and burrow deeper against him. As she did, the pendant pressed against his side. *Bloody hell.* In his concern for the safety of the women, he'd forgotten its presence secreted in his pocket. He adjusted the blanket more snugly about Anna, kissed the top of her head, and stood.

"Lex?" She looked up at him.

"I have to speak to Captain MacTavish. I have something I must ask him to deliver back to England for me."

****

Dr. MacTavish emerged from the hatch onto the deck. In the first rays of dawn, he placed his hands on his hips and drew a deep breath of fresh morning air that shoved his shoulders back.

"Well?" Brodie confronted the doctor. He looked like a man who'd been desperately ill, Lex thought. Or suffering the tortures of the damned.

"She and her child are doing well…as well as can be expected after what they've been through," William MacTavish replied.

"Then both will be…all right?" Lex had to look away from his friend's face, its expression eager and begging at the same time.

"It's too soon to be overly optimistic, but, yes, if her condition continues to improve as it has overnight, I'd say there's a good chance you'll have a healthy child in December. Nevertheless, I want her to stay where she is for a few more hours. Jamie"—he turned to his brother, who'd been waiting with the others for news—"you'll have to delay sailing until this evening. Louisa…Mrs. MacMillan cannot be moved before then."

"Oh, aye, for certain sure." The captain was quick to fall into agreement. "I'll hold off for as long as you see fit, brother."

"Now…" The doctor turned back to Brodie. "Go to her…and stay. She's asking for you. She needs you. I must leave. I have another patient who needs my attention."

"Aye, aye." Brodie headed toward the hatch, but at the entrance stopped short. He paused, then strode back to William MacTavish.

"I owe ya a great debt, Doctor," he said. "And I'm thinkin' I've misjudged ya…and my wife. I'm right sorry." He held out a hand.

Lex stared. He could scarcely believe his eyes.

Brodie MacMillan, who only days before had been suffused with jealousy of the doctor, was attempting to make amends.

"If you believed there was anything of an improper nature between your wife and me, you did indeed misjudge us." He looked at Brodie with an unwavering stare before accepting his hand.

"And chust to further reassure you, MacMillan," Jamie MacTavish cut in, "my brother is betrothed to the vicar's daughter and head over heels in love with the lass."

"Vicar's daughter?" Brodie turned to stare at the captain. "But Reverend Morgan's child is but three years old."

"Not that clergyman, you great fool," the captain scoffed. "Reverend Scott's daughter, vicar of a church across the river. She's a right bonnie lass of twenty years, perhaps a bit more. Now get to your wife. She's needin' you, although what she'd want with such a lout as yourself is more than I can fathom." The last was uttered with a chuckle.

"Aye, aye." Brodie turned once more to the hatch but came back to the doctor once more, again holding out his hand. "Congratulations, sir. I wish you and your intended all the happiness Louisa and I share."

****

"Hie, there, laddie." Brodie's voice roused Lex from where he'd been sleeping propped up against a mast on the deserted deck of the *Highland Lass*.

Blinking into the bright sunlight, he looked up at his friend.

"How is your wife?" he asked over a tongue dry as sawdust.

“Fine, doin’ chust fine.” His friend dropped down to sit beside him. “Anna is with her now. They’re both sleepin’, beautiful as something out of a perfect dream.” He pulled a flask from inside his vest and squinted up at the sun riding high in the sky.

“Reckon as how it’s over the foreyard?” he asked.

“High enough.” Lex snatched it from him, pulled the cork free, and took a swallow.

“Looks like a fine day.” Brodie retrieved his container and took a drink before continuing, “And all would be well with the world…even if we lost the treasure…except…”

“Except you and I still have serious charges hanging over us.” Lex drew a deep breath. “I’m reckoning Captain Caleb Cameron and his deputy will be along any minute to arrest us and herd us off to jail.”

“Aye, aye.” Brodie looked down at the flask in his hand and shook his head. “If I wasn’t so damned knackered, I’d say we take another run fer it and leave it ta Harry and the rest of our friends ta sort out the mess. As it is…”

“Gentlemen.” Brodie and Lex turned together to see the magistrate and his deputy coming up the gangplank toward them. The former carried a paper in his hand.

“Speak o’ the bloody devil,” Brodie muttered.

“I’ve come with news.” The magistrate stopped in front of them and looked down. “I’ve received another notice from England.”

“Oh, aye?” Brodie squinted up at him. “Execution orders? That’s all that’s left.”

“Hardly. Sadly, Sir Maxwell Spencer has died. His son Archibald is now lord and master of his father’s estate. As such, he's had the warrants against you two rescinded. You're both free men."

He took up the paper and read, " 'In view of services rendered, I, Archibald Spencer, revoke all charges previously preferred by my father, Sir Maxwell Spencer, against the man known as Lex and my sister's husband Brodie MacMillan.' It goes on, but there's no need to read the rest of it." Captain Cameron lowered the paper and handed it down to Brodie. "Guard this with your life, my man. It's your freedom."

"Sweet Jesus!" Brodie glanced over it, then handed it to Lex. "Ya mean we're free men again?" He narrowed his eyes as he looked up at the magistrate.

"In this country, at least, but I'd advise you both not to venture back to England any time soon."

Chapter 27

Lex wet his lips, straightened the neckcloth he'd purchased in Portsmouth, and hoped the shirt he'd scrubbed in the mill pond the previous night appeared clean and presentable. He rubbed the toe of his left boot against his right calf, then repeated the process with the other foot. His boots were clean of mill dust and barn leavings, but still they were shabby and worn. Thinking of Captain Jamie MacTavish, Lex felt he cut a poor second.

The barracks behind him was empty. It was Sunday, and the Irish workers had been granted a team and wagon to take them to the small Catholic church in the village. Father Flynn was visiting the valley and would be performing mass there. Harry and his family had gone to church with Brodie and Louisa. The couple had left Anna alone in the cabin on the excuse that someone must tend the roast cooking slowly over the low hearth fire.

Ah, well, nothing ventured, nothing gained. He squared his shoulders and strode up the hill toward Brodie's log cabin. He'd never proposed to a woman, and the thought of it was fair making his stomach reel.

"Go fer it, my lad." Brodie had slapped him on the back earlier that morning. "I have a feelin' she's expectin' it."

The door of the cabin stood open, letting in the

sunlight and letting out the heat from the small fire on the hearth. Anna had been bending over the large roast, but his booted footsteps on the veranda made her turn.

"Lex." She turned to him, smiling. "What a lovely surprise."

She was wearing a low-cut white muslin gown sprinkled with dainty green leaves. Her hair was done up in a coiffure that left a few errant curls tickling her soft pink cheeks.

Now, why do I get the idea my arrival isn't that, not at all, at all? She's hardly dressed for cooking. Good God, could the woman look any more lovely!

"Come in." She crossed the room to take his arm, and he caught a whiff of that scent, that exotic scent that had taunted his senses on more than one occasion.

"Would you care for a cup of tea?" She was smiling up at him. "Or perhaps a wee dram? You're looking a tad pale."

"No…no tea…nor whisky. Lady…" His words were stumbling, his tongue suddenly thick. "Lady…"

"Yes?" She was gazing up at him, green eyes so beautiful they took away all the words he'd planned.

He wet his lips and tried to begin again. "Lady…"

"Oh, Lex"—she gave his arm a shake—"do just get on with it. Ask me to marry you, so that I may say yes."

"You know what I'm trying to say? You know…?" He stared down at her, astonished.

"Of course. Don't you think my sister's husband has alerted me to your plan? He's a right crafty bugger." She was grinning up at him. "But you must agree to one condition."

"Which is?" Still in shock from her taking the situation in hand, the question came out automatically.

"That you must cease to call me 'Lady.' I shall be your wife, Anna, no more, no less. I shall be Mrs....?" She gave him a quizzical look. "Good God, I'm marrying a man whose last name I still don't know!"

"It's Wallace, Lady. Alexander Kenneth Wallace."

"I like it." Further words were cut off as he kissed her, kissed with a passion he'd been holding in check far too long, and allowed himself to be immersed in the wonderful scent that would forever enslave his body and soul.

"We've the cabin to ourselves for some time." When he finally allowed her to breathe again, she cast him a coquettish look. "My room is just outside."

"Nay, nay." He moved her out to arm's length and looked down into her beautiful face. Was ever a man so tempted? "We'll wait until we're well and truly wed."

"Lex, sometimes your sense of honor can be extreme." She ran a hand along his jaw. "But if this is what you wish, so shall it be...under one condition."

"Whit?"

"When we're well and truly wed, when we're alone and about to make love, I want you to speak as a Highlander. If my perfume inflames your passions, your soft brogue has an equal effect upon me."

"An easy request ta honor, lassie." Blue eyes twinkling wickedly, he immediately slipped into the tones she'd requested. "I shall be as Highland as ye wish. Perhaps ye would be further inspired by a bit o' the Gaelic?"

She didn't answer. She was kissing him again.

"Lass, lass." Finally he drew her away from him again. "I think it's time I tell ye exactly who I am. Maybe, then, ye'll wish ta withdraw your pledge ta marry me."

"But you've already told me your name is Alexander Kenneth Wallace."

"There's more…a deal more."

"Oh, very well, Lex." She heaved a sigh and went to sit at the table. "Regale me with your life story. But be forewarned. Nothing you can say will extract you from your offer to marry me."

****

"Mr. Wallace, sir, a word." Lex stood to address the mill owner from where he'd been sitting on a pile of sawn lumber. He'd been waiting until the mill had shut down for the night and Brodie and the other workers had gone.

"Aye?" Harry paused at the bottom of the ramp that led up to the saws. His shirt, like Lex's, was stained with sweat. He took a rag from the back pocket of his breeches to wipe his face. "A complaint about the work? I admit it can try a man's muscles."

"Not a complaint, sir. Just an honest introduction."

"Aye?" By now Harry was facing him squarely, a questioning expression on his countenance.

"Your father was Brian Wallace, was he not?" Lex found himself struggling not to hold his breath as he headed into the revelation.

"Aye." Suspicion colored the response. "But how would you be knowing…?"

"Because your father and mine were brothers. My father was Kenneth Wallace. We're cousins."

"Whit?" The word came out in a gush of incredibility.

"I'm Alexander Kenneth Wallace." Lex held out a hand.

"Sweet Jesus!" For a few moments Harry stared at his companion. Then, as realization dawned, he grasped Lex's hand, a delighted grin widening his mouth and crinkling the corners of his eyes. "Uncle Kenny's boy! Well, I never! Welcome, welcome!" He hesitated only a moment longer before gathering Lex into a bear hug. "It's good to see you, laddie," he muttered against his shoulder.

Regaining control, he stepped back to hold Lex out at arm's length to peruse him.

"You've grown since I last saw you as a young lad," he said. "Grown well, too. And"—he slowed his words—"moved into some dangerous escapades, if news from the Highlands is true. Known as the Highland Fox, if I'm not mistaken?"

"That moniker is best left behind in the Old Country…much as yours, Highland Harry." Humor curled lines in Lex's face. "I received the title simply because I was the last of my bunch to evade capture."

"Aye, aye. Well, it is a treat to discover you here." Harry paused a moment and stepped off from Lex. "But how in hell did you end up coming here with her…Lady Annabelle Spencer…the woman who all but got me captured and hung, back in England?"

"I was captured and put in prison, with the prospect of being hung not out of the question. Then a British officer came to recruit men to replace those killed in the fighting in France. I was chosen to go. The long and short of it is that I ended up rescuing Archie Spencer, the son of Lord Dunstan, after he was wounded. Although we were both actually deserters, Sir Maxwell was so grateful to have his son home, he allowed me to remain on his estate as a groom."

"But that doesn't explain how you came here with *her*. Running off with Sir Maxwell's daughter hardly qualifies to keep you in good standing with his lordship."

"Nay." Lex looked down at his boots, shaking his head. "I never planned to do any such thing. But then the redcoats arrived, looking for me. I was starting out on the run when she forced her companionship on me."

"Forced? Alexander, she's but a bit of a girl." Harry stared at him.

"Well, perhaps forced is too strong a word. She insisted on accompanying me. Her father was pushing her into a marriage with a stick of a duke, something she didn't want…and I can tell you, after meeting the man, I understood. So…"

"So she ran away with you."

"Aye, and though I'm loath to admit it, she had the wealth to finance our escape."

"Didn't the prospect of freedom in a new country beckon just a wee bit? Weren't you tempted by the thought of a fresh start where the Highland Fox is but a legend? Where the law is stretched too thin to be concerned with a Scottish outlaw? Come, come, lad, I hardly see you in the role of anyone's fancy man."

Seeing the humor in Harry's face, Lex relaxed and nodded, returning his cousin's amusement.

"Aye, that it did. I was getting right tired of running and fighting."

"And what is it you hope to do in this country?"

"For now, I'm happy working in your mill, not having to bow and scrap to any whims of milord or milady, not having to be watching over my shoulder at every minute. A warm bed and good food are real pleasures. And now, the prospect of a wife, a home…a family."

"Aye, understood. My wife and bairns mean the world to me. And running this business and the farm, seeing to the needs of nine children and a high-spirited wife—" He waved his free hand to indicate the mills behind them. "Well, on some days, it's nigh on as big a challenge as keeping ahead of the redcoats. Now, have you told her your father is laird of Loch Glen and that you're next in line for the title?"

"Aye, and I've also told her I'll be rejecting the title in favor of my younger brother. I've no desire to become aristocracy, and neither has she. We'll be quite happy as Anna and Lex Wallace, living on our bit of land here and, God willing, raising a batch of bairns."

"Well, then, guid, verrae guid!" Harry's Highland accent burst into fullness as he was overcome by emotion. "Come along up to the house. I must introduce you right and proper to my wife."

Together they started up the hill to the log house, Harry's arm about Lex's shoulders. Lex noticed, as he had over the time he'd known his cousin, that he was limping, favoring his left leg. The mill accident of the previous summer had left Harry Wallace with a noticeable and probably painful reminder that his family and friends had dangerous enemies.

****

Bare chest glistening with sweat, Lex rolled his shoulders, then raised the tin mug to his mouth to take a long drink. The cold water freshly drawn from the well near the workmen's barracks trickled down his dry throat, welcomed as the finest ale or brandy might be. It was an abnormally hot day for mid-September, and the mill was in full swing, the grist section inundated with grain to grind, the lumber part still rushing to finish up the processing of the previous winter's cuttings.

Not for the first time that morning, he looked up the hill to the place across the road from Brodie and Louisa's homestead to the piece of land Harry Wallace had given him to build his own log house. How long would it be before that could happen? Although Anna had vowed to marry him, and he didn't doubt her word, he'd also vowed he wouldn't marry her until he had a home for her. With the wage he was making at the mill that would take time…too much time. Fortunately, he was possessed of more patience than his friend Brodie. He smirked. In a similar circumstance, he guessed his companion from the treasure adventure might find more creative if not entirely legal ways to speed up the process.

He drew a deep breath as he headed back into the grist mill with its deafening grinding and flying chaff. He wasn't Brodie, he thought as he looked at his friend whitened with the cloud that infested the building. He could wait. And hadn't he fulfilled the major part of his quest? By now, Captain James MacTavish would be handing that pendant to Marie Roi. He could envision the old woman's joy as she accepted the trinket that would absolve her beloved uncle of being a drunken liar.

He'd completed that quest. Now all he had to do was get the fair lady.

Chapter 28

"Mr. Wallace." Mounted on Silverbell, Anna had been waiting at the end of the lane that led to her sister's house when Harry rode up out of the valley on his way to the village. "A word, please."

"Mistress Anna." He paused to give her one of those roguish smiles she believed many women had found irresistible. "What can I do for you this fine autumn day?"

"May I ride with you for a distance? There is something I wish to discuss with you in private."

"And our bustling little community offers scant opportunity for such intimacy?"

"Yes."

"Very well." He urged his charcoal mare ahead, and she moved Silverbell to fall into step with her.

"Mr. Wallace…"

"Harry, please. Lady Anna, we've known each other too long to stand on formalities." A sly sideways glance.

"Very well, Harry. And I am Anna. Harry, as you know, Lex and I plan to marry."

"Aye, and with my blessing."

"Then you also know Lex refuses to do so until we have a house." She reined Silverbell to a halt. He also paused his mount. "I do not plan to wait for months, maybe years. I have the means to expedite the process."

From an inner pocket of the vest she wore, she pulled the remains of the necklace that had first brought her and Harry together. Many of the stones were missing, sold over the past months to facilitate her and Lex's escape, but there remained several diamonds and one large emerald.

"I wish to purchase lumber and hire some of your workers." She dangled it before Harry's rounded eyes. "I want a log house and stable on our land by December. I plan to marry Lex on Christmas Eve."

"Sweet Jesus! That necklace. You still have it!" He stared.

"Parts of it. Now what do you say, Highland Harry? Can we make a deal?"

"Normally, I wouldn't consider accepting jewels in payment." Harry put out a hand to examine the piece hanging from her fingers. "But this…with that excellent emerald…I can have it reset with the diamonds around it and make it the perfect Yuletide gift for Margaret." He closed his fingers over the necklace. "You have a deal, Miss Anna Spencer. I'm glad this bauble will finally do some good."

A broad smile brightening her face, she let him have it. Then, slapping her heels to her mare's sides, she took off at a full gallop, giving a whoop that echoed back along the trail.

****

"Hold up a minute," Lex said. "All that ale you fed me is fair overflowing."

"Ya got ta take another piss?" Brodie eased the team to a stop. "Man, ya lack capacity."

"Hardly. You could have floated a small ship in what we drank." Lex jumped to the ground and turned away.

"Well, ya can't say ya didn't enjoy it." Brodie leaned back on the seat as he waited. "And I needed a respite. Sawin' may be done for the year, but the grist mill is goin' full capacity now, what with wheat and oats comin' in daily. I'm right glad young Geordie has seen fit to learn the trade. Otherwise I'd never get a second ta myself. And I do want ta spend time with my beautiful wife…now that's she's stayin' at home and not racin' off ta care for the sick and injured."

"And about to present you with your first bairn." Lex adjusted his clothing and pulled himself back up onto the seat. "You're a lucky man, Brodie MacMillan."

"Aye, that I am." Flapping the reins over the team's broad backs, he urged them back into a walk. "And so will ye be, Lex, now that my sister-in-law has agreed to accept such as yerself." He cast Lex a taunting grin.

"Weeks, months, maybe even a year down the road." Lex couldn't keep weariness out of his tone.

"That's yer own damned fault…makin' her wait until ya can build her a house." Brodie frowned over at him. "Ya know ye're welcome ta live in that room I built for Anna at the end of our veranda, and share our kitchen fer the time bein'."

"Brodie, I thank you for your offer, but I won't rest until I have a house of some sort ready for Anna. I'm thinking that after I spend the winter in the woods working with your cutting crew, I'll have earned enough to at least make the beginnings of a cabin."

"Well, then, ya great proud fool, if that's what ya want…"

They were nearing the place where the trail emerged into the cleared land above the mill valley. Lex became aware of noise—men's voices yelling orders and laughing, work in progress. But it was too near to be coming from the mill yard. Perplexed, Lex sat up straight as they emerged from the trees.

Astonishment gushed through him as he looked for the source of the sounds coming from his and Anna's plot of land.

Men were hard at work putting the finishing touches on the sides of a cabin and, farther back, the walls of what appeared to be a stable. In the foreground, tables had been set up with food and drink. Presiding over them were Anna, Louisa, Margaret, and Margaret's eldest stepdaughter, Bella.

"Whit…?" Lex remained on the wagon seat, dumbfounded, as Brodie pulled into what would be the dooryard of his new home.

"Welcome to our home!" Anna turned to him, face glowing. She spread her arms to indicate the beehive work area. "What do you think?"

The men, becoming aware of Lex and Brodie's arrival, stopped work and turned to grin at the pair. "Hie, the lord and master arrives!" one of them yelled, gesturing toward Lex.

"We built you a wee bit of a homestead," another teased. "Now you must marry this lovely lass."

****

Captain James MacTavish rode into the dooryard of the homestead Lex and Anna would soon be calling home. He dismounted and, leading his horse, headed toward Lex, who had paused in chopping firewood upon his arrival.

"Lex." Affable grin in place, he held out a hand. "I hear congratulations are in order."

"Aye." Lex eyed him suspiciously. He still wasn't ready to trust this charming rogue. The captain had made his interest in Anna all too clear.

"Aye, well, I'd like to say the best man won, but that would be demeaning myself more than I'd care." The good humor continued. Lex put down the ax and accepted the captain's hand.

"I assume you have a reason for riding all the way out here…aside from what I'm telling you will have to be your *former* interest in my intended." Lex straightened to his full height and put his hands on his hips.

"That I do." The captain pulled a flask from an inner pocket of his vest and removed the stopper. "Fancy a wee dram? Splitting wood is right thirst-provoking work."

"Thank you." Lex accepted the offer and took a swig. "Now, Captain, the reason for your visit?"

Jamie MacTavish raised the flask, took a swallow, then thumped the cork back into place with the heel of his hand. "There's been news of the *Linnet*," he said, replacing the container inside his coat.

"Oh, aye?"

"Aye. She went down in a great storm off Bermuda. The captain was a fool, risking a voyage into those waters in hurricane season. I can only assume those three bastards who robbed you and Brodie MacMillan must have offered him a sizeable reward for taking on such a risk."

"So the trollop's treasure is well and truly lost." Glad he'd saved the most important item, Lex squinted into the sun and thought of Marie Roi and the pendant. "Perhaps it's as well."

****

"Lex! Anna! Wake up!"

"Jesus!" Lex looked down at Anna lying in his arms and cursed. He'd waited so long for this time and now, here at the crack of dawn on the morning after his wedding, was that great fool Brodie MacMillan pounding on his door.

"Anna, Lex, open up!" The hammering continued.

"You'd better see what he wants." Smiling, Anna put up a hand to touch the stubble beginning to form on her husband's cheek. "We both know better than to think he'll go away."

"Aye, aye." With a deep sigh, Lex pulled himself out of bed and into his trousers. "Bloody, thoughtless bastard."

"Lex!" Brodie, wearing boots, shirt, and breeches, burst inside when Lex unbarred the door.

"I…we have a son!" He clasped Lex in his arms in an embrace that all but crushed the air out of his lungs. "Can ya believe it? A healthy boy with a voice and appetite ta match the best o' his kind! Anna…" He turned to her, as she emerged from the bedroom wrapped in a robe, and strode to gather her into a huge hug and swing her off her feet. "Ye're an aunt, and this"—he swung on Lex, his grin so broad it seemed to split his face—"this daft bastard is an uncle!"

"Brodie, how wonderful!" Anna gasped as he replaced her on the floor. "Louisa…is she well?"

"As fine and happy as an angel in heaven." Brodie put his hands on his hips and puffed out his chest. "Now, I'd best be gettin' back." He turned toward the door. "But we'll be expectin' ya in no less than an hour, to view our excellent prodigy, newlyweds or no'."

"Wait, wait!" Anna hastened into the bedroom and came out carrying a quilt. "Wrap this about yourself. We can't have the new father catching his death of cold."

"Aye, aye." Grinning sheepishly, he let her place it about his shoulders. "I was so full o' the joy of it I fair forgot my coat." He pulled open the door, letting in a flood of sunlight and the view of a sparkling blanket of fresh snow. "Come as soon as ye're both decent. Our son is a delight ta behold."

****

Lex dismounted from Storm in his dooryard and paused to suck in a deep breath of fine spring air. Around his house, grass was greening, deciduous trees were leafing out, and Anna's gardening was sprouting in a fenced enclosure beyond the barn. In the paddock, Silverbell cavorted and snorted as she recognized her stable mate had returned.

"Verrae well, lass." He grinned and led the gelding to the fence. "Ye'll have yer friend back as soon as I can rub him down and set him free.

He admitted he was eager to finish the task. In his vest pocket, he carried a letter bearing the Haven Hall crest.

As soon as he'd finished caring for his horse and turned him loose into the pasture with Silverbell, he headed for the small log house with long, hasty strides.

"Lex, you're home earlier than I expected." Anna looked up from the task of mending his shirts as he entered. "I didn't hear you ride up."

"There's a strong, warm breeze blowing. It

probably covered the sound." He pulled the paper from his pocket. "And I'm home earlier because this arrived on a ship newly docked at Riverhaven."

He handed it to her. Giving him a questioning look, she took it. Slowly, almost apprehensively, she slid her finger under the sealing wax, spread the paper, and began to read. He sat down in a chair by the hearth to observe her reaction.

Likely afeard it's news of another warrant for my arrest, he surmised.

He watched as her expression turned from misgiving to utter delight.

"It's from Marie," she began. Then her face brightened with one of the widest smiles he'd ever seen her exhibit. "Oh, Lex, she has the pendant! Somehow you managed to save it and send it off to her!" Jumping to her feet, she rounded the table to sit on his lap and hug him. "When? How?"

"The night I discovered you and Louisa prisoners on Jamie MacTavish's ship, I gave it to the captain and asked him to deliver it to her."

"You are a kind, caring man." She planted a kiss on his cheek. "Small wonder I love you so."

"Read on." He indicated the letter. "Is there more news?"

"Yes, there is. Good news. Marie reports that Gallant is doing well, that he has become the pet of Haven Hall and Archie personally sees to his care. Oh, Lex, this is indeed the best of news!"

"Now I have a small favor to ask of you." He pulled a small bottle from inside another pocket of his vest and handed it to her.

"Perfume…my special perfume!" Amazement

colored her soft words as she stared down at the crystal container. "Lex, how…?"

"Along with requesting the captain to take the pendant to Mademoiselle Marie, I asked that he appeal to her to purchase this and send it along at the first opportunity."

"Alexander Kenneth Wallace, you are the most thoughtful of men." She removed the stopper and, closing her eyes, inhaled, an ecstatic smile curling her lips. "Oh, this is such a delightful extravagance! How can I ever repay you?"

"Perhaps ye might oblige me by dabbin' on a wee drop?"

"Of course." She put her fingers to the top, tipped to let a bit of the contents escape onto them, and placed the scent behind her ears. Then, meeting his gaze with a coy expression, she slowly, sensuously touched her fingers to her cleavage.

"Enough!" He gathered her into his arms and stood to head into the bedroom behind a curtained doorway at the back of the cabin.

"Whit do ya think yer doin', my fine Highland lad?" she chuckled. "Aire ya no' expected at the mill?"

"Brodie will understand." He shouldered the curtain aside and headed for the bed. "He'll understand I've been tempted beyond denyin' by a Spencer lady."

A word about the author…

Gail is the award-winning author of thirty-six published books. She is delighted to be an author with The Wild Rose Press, "where writers are encouraged, tutored and mentored in the best of ways," she says.

Contact her at:

macgail@nbnet.nb.ca
Twitter: tollerbeagle44
Facebook: Gail MacMillan

Thank you for purchasing
this publication of The Wild Rose Press, Inc.

If you enjoyed the story, we would appreciate your letting others know by leaving a review.

For other wonderful stories,
please visit our on-line bookstore at
www.thewildrosepress.com.

For questions or more information
contact us at
info@thewildrosepress.com.

The Wild Rose Press, Inc.
www.thewildrosepress.com

Stay current with The Wild Rose Press, Inc.

Like us on Facebook

https://www.facebook.com/TheWildRosePress

And Follow us on Twitter
https://twitter.com/WildRosePress

www.ingramcontent.com/pod-product-compliance
Lightning Source LLC
Chambersburg PA
CBHW060529260626
47161CB00003B/829

9781509223084